The Mountain

Ray Knight

AN M-Y BOOKS PAPERBACK

A CIP catalogue record for this title isavailable from the British Library

ISBN–978-1-909908-26-0

A word from the author…

'The Mountain' started life as a subplot in a manuscript about a pending oil crisis. It took on a life of its own and became more significant than the original story line. The deeper I researched into Native American culture, the more its philosophy and spirituality fascinated me.

Day by day, the story evolved and I learned from the experience. Each time I planned an outline, the characters took me in a different direction. I learned to go with the flow much as Peter, the protagonist, does in the novel.

It was rewarding, enjoyable and fun to write this novel and I hope it's equally fulfilling to read.

Ray Knight
May 2014
Spanish Wells
Bahamas

When the blood in your veins returns to the sea
and the earth in your bones returns to the ground,
perhaps then, you will remember that this land does not
belong to you,
it is you who belongs to this land.

Native American Wisdom

Prologue

The Predators Motorcycle Club rode to the Sturgis Rally in a convoy of two hundred motorcycles drawn from twenty chapters nationwide. Ten days later, only three machines and five members survived.

They'd abandoned two other Harley Lowriders after raiding a pharmacy three days previously. They rode in procession with Mitch riding point, Jeb and Billy-Bob following with Cydney and Spice riding pillion. They kept a steady but sedate pace designed to eat up miles not gas. The three male members of the club were all big, bearded and dirty after days on the road. The girls were not much better.

Mitch's bike slowed and he pulled to the side of the empty road, stopped, knocked the kickstand down with his booted foot and dismounted. The others stopped but stayed astride their machines. Mitch unstrapped the gas can attached to his bike's backrest, gave it a shake and shook his head. He spat onto the road and looked at the others.

'Damn thing's almost empty. You guys got any left?' They shook their heads. They were subdued and grim. The further north they'd traveled, the fewer gas stations they'd found. They sat and watched as Mitch drained the last half-gallon of fuel into his Harley's tank and carelessly threw the empty can into the roadside brush. He replaced the gas cap, pulled a battered map from his vest pocket, squatted down and unfolded the map on the black tarmac. He ran his oil-stained finger along a spidery line that marked their route on the map. His hand stopped, he looked up and stared down the road into the distance.

'There's a small town about ten miles from here. It'll be our last stop. We'll get our supplies there. You all strapped and loaded?'

They nodded as Mitch stood and folded the map. He pulled a pistol from the back of his waistband, checked the clip and tucked it back in his pants. He lifted his leg over the bike, settled himself into the seat and pressed the electric starter, which turned the big motor with a slow rumble. It caught, sputtered then caught again. Mitch twisted the throttle until he was satisfied the machine wouldn't stall and eased off to conserve gas. He put the Hog in gear, dropped the clutch and took off with a growl from the exhaust. The others fell in line and followed.

The bikes thundered along in procession, consuming the road with an insatiable appetite. The road twisted and turned as each ascending mile took them further into mountain country. The trees lining the road grew taller and closer together as the altitude increased. They were over two days ride from the nearest city and snowy peaks loomed ever closer.

They passed a Ranger Station and found the town less than a minute later – a scant collection of buildings scattered along one side of the road made up the entire community. It would have been easy to blink and miss it. The settlement had grown up around the gas station and truck stop that serviced the old logging companies. The companies had long since closed following years of bitter litigation with conservation groups. The town struggled on long after it should have died.

A passing glance at the derelict gas station confirmed their worst fears. Neglected hoses dangled from pumps that hadn't seen gas for some time. They slowed, pulled to the side of the road and parked their bikes alongside each other in precise formation. The maneuver demonstrated the familiarity they had with each other. It wasn't all they had in common; each one held a weapon as they marched in silence to a general convenience and supply store only yards from their bikes.

Cydney reached the shop's door first, turned the handle, pushed the door open and walked right in. The others followed. A bell attached to the doorframe signaled their arrival with a hollow ring. They stood inside the doorway and surveyed the shelves. It wasn't Wal-Mart, but it would do.

A woman entered the shop through a door behind the counter and approached them with an uncertain smile on her lips and a wary look in her eyes. It had been a long time since anyone had greeted the Predators with anything but fear and caution. The shopkeeper's eyes dropped to the gun in Mitch's hand and she drew in a sharp breath. She glanced over her shoulder but no one was there to support her. Stone-faced, she tried to ignore the weapons.

'Good day, folks. What can I get you?' Her voice was surprisingly deep. She attempted a smile but it froze on her face like a clown's mask.

Cydney shot her in the middle of her face; the back of the woman's head blew across the counter and blood splattered the wall. The blast reverberated in the small store and rattled the windows. She stayed on her feet for a few seconds, as if suspended by invisible puppeteer strings, and then just crumpled into an untidy heap on the floor.

'I didn't like her attitude,' Cydney said. There was no emotion in the brunette's voice.

No one replied. Jeb moved to the window anticipating a response to the gunshot. The rest inspected the merchandize in a familiar scenario that had played out in many establishments in many towns.

'Grab a backpack each, and load up with basics for a camping trip. Billy-Bob – you're in charge of weapons and ammunition so make sure we're "loaded for bear".' The authority in Mitch's voice hinted at military discipline. The others worked quickly and efficiently to strip the store. It had been a while since they had paid for anything.

'Someone's coming,' Jeb sounded the warning from the window. He'd watched the Ranger emerge from his station, climb into his vehicle and start for the store only to pull up after a few yards. He now walked towards the store casually holding a shotgun.

'It's a cop of some sort. But, he don't look too dangerous. He's holding a shotgun in one hand, sort of relaxed. He's got a pistol in a holster but the flap's shut. The moron's just strolling down the middle of the road like he's out for a breath of air. Stupid bastard.'

Mitch looked up from behind the counter where he'd found a brand-new hunting rifle.

'Take care of him. Go with him, Billy-Bob.'

'Hey, don't kill him. We could use him to carry some of this stuff,' Spice said. There was silence as they stared at her. Spice held her breath, waiting for the inevitable backlash from Mitch at her suggestion. He surprised her.

'Ha! Junior's had a good idea, at last. We can use the pig as a mule.' The gang laughed at the clumsy metaphor and the two bikers left the store, to apprehend the Ranger, suppressing grins behind their beards.

The door behind the counter slammed open and a young boy burst into the store. He held a shotgun and struggled to lift it above the counter to point at Mitch who now stood in the middle of the shop cradling the hunting rifle like a newborn. The Remington was too heavy for the boy and the barrel wavered with his effort. Tears streaked his reddened cheeks.

'Leave my mom alone!' he shouted. With a young child's naivety, he ignored the fact that his mother lay dead on the floor. With an almighty effort, the youngster finally got a bead on Mitch and pulled the trigger. A hollow click signified the gun was empty. The boy howled in frustration. Mitch took two huge strides, leant over the counter and snatched the gun from the boy's grasp just as a bespectacled man lurched through the doorway and grabbed the boy in an enveloping hug.

'Please don't hurt my son. He's just a kid. He don't know any better,' he pleaded, crouching on his knees as if using his son as a shield. The fact was not lost on Mitch.

'I'm not gonna hurt him. He has more guts than you have. Take him over in the corner and keep him quiet until we leave. You let him loose and I'll kill you both.'

The man scrambled to obey before the biker changed his mind. He squatted down in the corner clutching his son with trembling arms.

The storekeeper watched in horror as the door opened and Ranger Martin stumbled through followed by the two bikers who had captured him. Tim Martin's holster was as empty as his hands. The storekeeper's last hope for rescue evaporated as the bikers forced Tim into the same corner he occupied with his son. The Ranger sat down on the floor alongside the cowering man and his weeping son.

The gang systematically stripped the shelves of basic supplies, clothes and weapons. They filled five large backpacks with anything they felt would help them survive in the wilderness. Billy-Bob filled one extra pack with all the ammunition he could carry and found a canvas holster for the hunting rifle. They littered the floor with the items they didn't want.

The storekeeper held his son close and shielded his eyes from the grisly sight of his mother's corpse. He looked on in helpless frustration as the gang pillaged his store. The Ranger reached out to reassure him that everything would be fine, but the storekeeper pulled away and turned his back on the wretched official.

'Hey you! Lawman. What are you anyway? A sheriff?'

Ranger Martin looked up into the cold, dark eyes of the brunette, Cydney.

'No... I'm a Forest Ranger.'

'What do you do? Arrest trees for littering when they drop leaves?'

The bikers thought this was hilarious and laughed loud and long. Martin sat on the floor in silence and endured their ridicule. The laughter left Cydney's eyes as quickly as it came.

'Get up, Ranger. Make yourself useful. Carry this bag.'

The humbled lawman clambered to his feet, picked up the heavy rucksack containing the ammunition and struggled into its harness. The girl looked at him with cold eyes.

'Go wait outside, boy.' Her dominance was total and he obeyed, walking out the door with his head bowed.

She hovered over the shopkeeper. 'You're lucky to be alive, mister. I'm only leaving you alive to take care of your boy. He showed some balls. I respect that.' He didn't respond or even look at the girl. She shrugged, kicked him viciously in the ribs, turned and left the store. As the other bikers followed her outside, the storekeeper sat in the corner with his devastated son and watched in horrified fascination, as flies began to congregate on the congealing pool of his wife's blood.

Chapter One

Peter lay back in the wooden chair and rested his feet on the rail surrounding his porch. He took a deep breath of crisp mountain air and let out a contented sigh. He could hear Mishka thrashing about behind the tree line thirty yards away. She disturbed a flock of birds, and they took to the sky with a flurry of wings. Seconds later, the big dog burst into the clearing and, tongue lolling, ran to the porch as if seeking approval from her master. Peter ruffled the animal's furry neck until it settled.

'Good girl,' he said, his only words for the day.

He stood, stretched, let out a yawn and ducked through the door into the cabin. The dog followed. Peter took a pot from the stove, retrieved a bone with some flesh still attached and tossed it to Mishka who caught it expertly and swallowed it without seeming to chew. Peter chuckled and shook his head. *Damn dog's gonna choke one day,* he thought.

He rekindled the pot-bellied stove and waited for the remains of the stew to heat. *Might as well finish it tonight, otherwise it'll go bad.* Peter dipped in a spoon and sampled the brown liquid. He grimaced at the lack of salt, but he would have to get used to that. His supply had dwindled, and he didn't plan on going into town any time soon. He ate the stew straight from the pot, savoring the hot liquid and relishing each morsel of meat. He salvaged another small bone, which disappeared down Mishka's eager throat with little fuss.

Peter took his utensils outside and washed them in rainwater from a storage barrel tucked away at one end of the porch. He'd designed the system himself and was proud of his ingenuity. His only regret was the use of plastic piping, which he had hauled up the mountain against his better judgment. Still, the rain that came off the roof kept the barrel full most of the year. He rarely had to supplement his supply from the nearby creek.

He felt a tingling sensation and his scalp crawled. He'd had these feelings before when danger threatened and had learned to listen to them as the years progressed. He dropped his utensils, grabbed his shotgun, which was never far from his side and listened intently. He scanned the tree line, using all his senses to find the danger. A strange silence settled over the forest as nature held its breath in anticipation. Seconds passed and nothing happened.

The dog bristled and its ears pricked. Peter heard the noise a few seconds later. His eyes widened and he froze where he stood. The noise was familiar but out of place. He had heard it constantly during his tour of duty in Afghanistan over a decade earlier. It was the background to his world in those days. His stomach lurched now. That was a different time and a different life. He had sought refuge in the wilderness to escape sounds like this. It was the unmistakable growl of a military jet fighter. It was low, close and getting closer. The noise turned into a wail, then a scream, as the plane shot across the clearing just feet above the cabin. Leaves flew across his yard and trees bent as the plane passed. Mishka jumped and barked but Peter heard nothing. Years of quiet solitude had sensitized his hearing and he was momentarily deafened.

Peter lost sight of the F22 Raptor as it passed the tree line. Recovering from his shock, he propped his shotgun on the porch, ran around the back of his cabin where the ground was higher, and scrambled onto the roof. The plane disappeared quickly, getting smaller by the second. Without warning, it rose into the evening sky, flew straight up for a few seconds, and stalled. There was silence as the plane fought gravity. It was a fight with only one outcome. A blinding flash, followed by the deep rumbling of an explosion signaled the destruction of the expensive machine. Peter fancied that he felt a tremor beneath his feet. *What the hell?*

He retrieved a pair of binoculars from his sleeping area and clambered back onto the roof. He tried to get a fix on the plane's position before the light faded for the evening. Black smoke rose into the evening sky, marking the crash site. It was roughly fifteen miles away. Peter's mind raced as he tried to process what he had seen. Maybe the pilot ejected - that would explain the sudden upturn in the plane's trajectory as the aviator sought height for a more controlled parachute descent. He didn't fancy the man's chances. The forest was dense in that area, and he was bound to end up tangled in a tree.

Peter squatted on the roof and gathered his thoughts. The plane had crashed over a dozen miles to the east. That was in Ben's territory, and that irascible old fool would hardly welcome the intrusion. If Hollywood needed a bitter version of Grizzly Adams, Ben Atwood would be ideal. He was almost a caricature of a mad mountain man. Peter chuckled to himself; helicopters would soon be criss-crossing the wilderness in search of the downed plane, and Ben would wave his bow and arrows at them in impotent rage.

Three men shared his wilderness, and they each kept to their own loose territory. Ben was his closest neighbor, and he hadn't seen him in over two years. Peter stood and walked to the far end of the roof. He knelt and examined a small solar panel that was one of his concessions to the modern world. It was free of debris and seemed intact. He would soon find out if it was functional. The battery it charged serviced a basic shortwave radio stored next to his bunk. He made a courtesy call to the Forest Ranger every six months to stop the man from climbing the mountain to check on him. Apart from that, it was for emergencies only. This was an emergency.

Peter jumped nimbly from the roof and entered the cabin. He turned the radio on and was relieved to see a green light. It was pre-set to the Ranger's wavelength so Peter just picked up the handset, pressed a button, and spoke.

'Mayday, mayday. Peter Friel calling Ranger Martin. Repeat, Mayday, mayday. Peter Friel calling Ranger Martin.'

He released the send button and waited for a response but only received hissing static. Repeated attempts produced the same frustrating results. Peter changed wavelengths and sent out a general Mayday call but continued to receive nothing but static. He went up and down the channels with no success. What was happening? *All those damn tablets and smartphones! No one bothers with shortwave radios anymore!*

He turned off the obsolete gadget and lay down in his bunk. Mishka took up her customary position on the floor alongside the bed, and Peter absently stroked the dog's head while he thought.

There was little point in setting off for the crash site. The terrain was difficult and it would take at least three days to get to the area. The Air Force would launch a search-and-rescue mission at first light in any case. Besides, he didn't feel like encroaching on Ben's territory and risking an arrow for his troubles. He would let the military take care of it.

Dusk gave way to darkness; Peter yawned and stretched his lean frame. He turned on his side, slipped an arm under his pillow and drifted into a deep dreamless sleep.

He woke as the first rays of sunlight penetrated his window and warmed his face. It was late August and winter approached but the weather was still good. The summer's temperate climate allowed him to perform his morning ablutions in the nearby creek. At this altitude, the water ran clear and cold. The melted snow hadn't yet gathered the sediment that would turn the stream a murky brown lower down the mountain. He sat on the porch, in his shorts, and let the morning air dry his body. Mishka had escaped the cabin at first light and gone hunting for breakfast. Peter followed his morning ritual of fixing herbal tea while chewing on a strip of pemmican.

He sipped his tea from an enamel mug and searched the skies for signs of a rescue. Peter's refuge was in the northernmost part of the United States, and he was used to seeing passenger aircraft in the distance as they navigated the great circle route that linked Europe to the Pacific. He couldn't recall seeing a plane for a long time. He tried to organize his thoughts. Had he seen one of the huge passenger planes to the north recently? Was he so inured to their unobtrusive passing that he had ignored them? Had they changed their route? That wasn't likely. He periodically checked the sky as he went about his morning chores.

He used an axe to split logs, which would fuel his fire during the winter months and collected smaller kindling for his stove. The morning wore on and no helicopters appeared. There were plenty of birds but no aircraft of any kind, not even distant passenger planes. He worked in an old pair of army boots and khaki shorts. He had built his cabin just at the edge of the tree line where mosquitoes didn't flourish.

The sun climbed the azure sky and Peter's skin glistened with sweat. Still no helicopters appeared. He downed his axe and drank deeply from a small barrel of boiled water he kept in a shaded area of the porch. The water escaped from the side of his mouth and trickled down his bare chest causing him to shudder. The water was still cold from the night air and he liked the sensation. Thirst satisfied, Peter rested from his chores and once again checked the empty skies. There was no sign of a search unless the Air Force employed feathered search and rescue personnel. Peter frowned in exasperation.

He entered the cool interior of the cabin and switched on the short wave radio. He repeated the exercise of the previous night with the same fruitless results. The receiver only picked up static. *What the hell is going on down there in the 'real' world?*

He sat on his bunk to gather his thoughts. He hadn't been into town for almost a year. The memory of that trip was fresh in his mind. A mini recession, due to rising oil prices, had caused an unemployment crisis and a sharp spike in food costs. These things went in cycles and the locals tightened their belts to ride it out. They blamed OPEC and greedy oil magnates for their problems. Peter had been grimly pleased that he had made the decision to opt out of society. Had things worsened?

He sighed. Somewhere in the back of his mind he knew what he must do. He tried to bury the thought but it came unbidden to the forefront. He had to go into town. It was the only logical thing to do. He thought of a dozen reasons why he shouldn't. He kept on returning to the same inescapable fact; he had to find out what was happening and how it would affect his sanctuary. Besides, there could be an injured man needing medical attention somewhere in Ben's territory and he needed to report that.

He yearned to discuss his options with someone, but he only had Mishka. For the first time in years, he felt lonely. *Damn that plane! Damn those stupid people down there! Why can't they just leave me be?*

He could just ignore the downed plane and the empty airwaves. He could stay on his mountain and overlook the problems of the rest of the world, but there was one thing that no years of solitude could overcome. The natural curiosity of his species tormented him. *Besides, I need salt!* he reasoned.

Two basic routes led to the nearest town. The safest choice would take at least three days. It was the long way down with the gentlest slope, and he used it when he had to haul stuff up the mountain. The shortest route involved steep inclines and some climbing skills. He had ropes hidden at strategic points to assist in the descent. It would only take a day and a half. He would take the short route in the morning.

Peter rummaged around the cabin and found his razor and scissors. He used a small mirror propped on the porch rail and spent thirty minutes removing his beard and trimming his long hair. He examined the results and smiled into the mirror. He wouldn't win any beauty pageants but at least he wouldn't frighten the children in town.

He packed a small rucksack with essentials for the trip, loaded his shotgun and ensured the safety was on. He would take enough water to last the short trip, as he didn't want to waste time boiling the water he would find en route. He tried the shortwave radio several times during the course of the afternoon but with no success.

No helicopters or passenger planes disturbed the quiet tranquility of the wilderness. Around three in the afternoon he heard the distant report of a shotgun, Mishka responded with a cacophony of barking. It was hard to tell how far away the shot came from and it never reoccurred. Peter worried. Only rarely over the years had anyone ventured close to his sanctuary, and no one had found him yet.

The afternoon passed slowly for Peter. He toured the traps close to his cabin and came across a rabbit trapped in one. He spent the hours until darkness making a stew and went to bed at dusk with a full stomach.

* * * *

Peter fought the heaviness in his tired legs. He'd spent the previous afternoon descending steep terrain. He was on the lower slopes now and had heard an unusual amount of human activity. Many people had ventured into the foothills of the mountainous forest, and he had skirted a couple of camps. He didn't want any contact with people just yet. Why were they here? Most of them had little or no experience of the wild, and he had smelt cooking and seen the discarded garbage they created. If he could smell it, so could the bears. One bear every square mile in the area made contact with humans inevitable and potentially deadly.

He heard sporadic gunfire, mostly shotguns and hunting rifles. He had never seen so many humans in the woods. He diverted around another group and broke free onto a tarmac road. He was two miles from town. For some reason Peter took the shotgun from over his shoulder, released the safety and carried it military style, pointing at the ground with one finger on the trigger. There were many gun-happy people around, and he needed to be alert. He glanced from side to side as he went and frequently scanned the horizon. He patrolled as if he were in enemy territory. He never questioned his actions, just followed his instincts. The hairs on his neck bristled; he wished Mishka accompanied him but the route he had taken was too difficult for his four-legged companion to follow.

He relaxed a little as he approached the Ranger Station just outside of town. No vehicles cluttered the small car park. Peter climbed the steps and turned the door handle – he found it locked. He peered in through the window and saw the office in disarray. The desk drawers gaped open, papers covered the floor and spilt coffee stained the desk. He rapped on the door.

'Hey, is anybody here?' His words echoed eerily in the silence. Once again, the hairs on his neck bristled and his grip tightened on the gun. *Where is everybody? There's always somebody manning the station. What the hell is going on?*

He scanned the area and found himself alone. He left the station and continued towards town. His pace quickened, but he remained alert. His next destination was the supply store. He passed the Ranger's SUV a few minutes later. It straddled two lanes with the door open and the seat-belt signal beeping away as if abandoned in a rush. Peter looked into the open cabin and saw the fuel gauge read 'empty'. He turned off the ignition and gently closed the door. He needed to come across someone soon and find out what was going on. The morning's events left him confused and scared. *Hold it together, Peter,* he told himself and pushed on.

He jumped at the sound of gunfire. The sound reverberated off the mountains. It proved impossible to identify where it came from. Main Street stretched out before him without a soul in sight. He passed three tricked-out Harley Lowriders parked neatly next to the curb with swastikas decorating their tanks. He made it to the supply store with no further incident and found it locked. He banged on the door, more in frustration than hope. He slumped to the ground and sat with his back against the door with his shotgun across his knees. He recoiled as he heard the door unlock behind him. He scrambled to his feet and brought the gun up level with the door.

'Whoa, Peter. Put the gun down it's me.' The closed door muffled the man's voice. The door swung open and Peter recognized a friendly face at last.

'God, John. It's good to see you,' Peter said.

Before he could say anymore, the storekeeper grabbed him roughly, pulled him into the shop, slammed the door shut and locked it.

'What's going on, man? Where is everybody? Why are all the doors locked?' Peter looked around the store. 'John, your shelves are empty; where are your supplies?'

'They took it all.'

'Who did?'

'They had guns...One of those biker gangs...They cleaned me out.' His voice cracked and he trembled. 'They killed the missus.'

Peter's jaw dropped. He stared long and hard at John. The poor man stumbled to a chair and sat down.

'Someone killed your wife?'

John nodded and said nothing. He just stared at the floor. Peter looked around, found another chair, pulled it next to his friend and sat down.

'Did you call the State Troopers? What did they do? Did they catch them?'

John stared at Peter as if he didn't know him. His eyes slowly came into focus and a spark came into his eyes. He grabbed Peter's arm and held it tight.

'Man, you gotta take my boy. Yes, it's the only way. Peter, you gotta take my boy back up the mountain!'

'You're making no sense, man. Calm down and tell me what's going on.'

'Promise me you'll take my boy!' He squeezed Peter's arm until the mountain man could take it no longer. He yanked his arm from the storekeeper's grasp and stood back.

'Calm down and tell me what's going on? Did the police catch your wife's killer? What about the Ranger?'

'Ha, fuck the Ranger. The whole world's gone to shit. It's the law of the gun, man. The strongest survive. My boy's got no chance.'

'How did all this happen, John?'

'It was the oil. The damned oil. The oil ran out. Can you believe that shit? All the time I thought those doomsayers were talking bullcrap. All those tree-huggers and their green energy, and all along they were right!'

'Good God!'

'First the gas stations ran out, and food prices shot up. Then the power went off. The stores ran out of food 'cos deliveries stopped. Then we ran out of drinking water. People will shoot you for that water you're carrying man. The whole world's fucked. You had it right all along, my friend. You turned your back on the whole sorry mess years ago. I thought you were nuts, but you were smarter than all of us.'

Peter walked to the front of the store and looked out the

window, but the street was still deserted. Another shot rang out, this time it seemed closer. Peter's stomach churned and he shuddered - he hadn't had this scared feeling since Afghanistan. John grabbed his arm from behind and Peter jumped like a startled rabbit; instinct and training kicked in, he turned and in the same motion hit John with the shotgun. He was unnerved and reacted as if attacked.

'God, I'm sorry man. It was automatic. I didn't mean it.' Peter rested his gun on the floor and bent to the stricken man. Blood trickled from John's scalp. John looked at him beseechingly. He grabbed both of Peter's outstretched arms with a firm but trembling grip.

'Take my boy, man. Take him up the mountain. He'll die if he stays here. There's no food and I can't protect him. His mother's dead and I don't know what to do.'

'I'm sorry, John. I can't. I barely survive myself, and I wouldn't know what to do with a boy. It's impossible.'

'Please, man. I'm begging you!'

'Look, John. People go hide up the mountains 'cos there's something wrong with them or they're running from something. We aren't the most sociable people. I'm sorry, John. I can't take him.'

'Man, he's only ten, and he won't see eleven unless you take him. You're sentencing him to death if you leave him here.'

'Don't lay that guilt trip on me.' Peter extricated himself from John's grasp, picked up his gun, unlocked the door and looked up and down the street. He turned back to the kneeling man.

'Good luck with your boy. He's your responsibility so man up and take care of him.' He closed the door and strode briskly up the street in the direction of the mountain. The door opened behind him and he turned at the sound.

'What you running from, man?' John shouted at him. Peter opened his mouth to respond but no words came.

'Fuck you, you crazy mountain motherfucker.' The door slammed and silence descended on Main Street. *That's it, man. Stay angry. Your son might have a chance if you stay angry.* The thought swirled in Peter's head.

Peter now understood why people filled the forest. The stores were out of food and everyone wanted to live off the land. Trigger-happy greenhorns had invaded his sanctuary. Bears would eat them all if they didn't shoot each other first. He imagined Ben Atwood laying in wait for the invaders with his trusty bow and arrow. Peter almost chuckled at the thought, but he had a problem. He needed salt and he had to avoid the crazies on his way home.

Peter retraced his steps back to the forest. On impulse, he stopped at the Ranger's SUV, removed the emergency medical kit and stuffed it in his backpack. There were no weapons or ammunition left in the vehicle. That was the least of his problems as his cabin was a veritable munitions store.

His mind raced as he walked. It all made sense to him now. The Air Force hadn't mounted a rescue because of the fuel shortage. They wouldn't waste precious reserves on a wrecked plane and a dead pilot. He hadn't seen any passenger aircraft for the same reason. No jet fuel would be available outside the military, as they would commandeer all reserves. He knew how they worked. He realized that most shortwave radios within range were down because of the lack of electricity. It was ironic that his was the only one working in the vicinity and he never had power to begin with.

Boy, you people really messed up big time! Playing your damned politics and screwing over the people. What on earth did you do?

Peter weighed up his options. He craved the safety of his cabin but it would be foolish to rush. The short, steep route would leave him vulnerable to attack every time he climbed a rock face. Anyone with a steady aim could pick him off as he hung exposed against the rock. He'd heard many shots fired in the last few hours. In the hands of the inexperienced and scared, guns became extremely hazardous to anyone in the vicinity. Whether by accident or design he could easily fall prey to a bullet. He decided to take the circuitous route. It would take twice as long but would afford him plenty of cover and would be safer.

He took a deep breath, adjusted his backpack, left the road and struck off into the forest. His peaceful life was shattered. What should have been a pleasant hike, with just a hint of danger from errant bears, was now a patrol in enemy territory. He was familiar with the threat from the bears. He'd learnt to read their tracks and smell their scent. He'd learnt to move unobtrusively through their territory. He was never complacent about how dangerous they were, but it was a danger he'd lived with for many years. It was familiar to him. This new scenario was altogether more frightening. It was unpredictable and scary. His military background and training took over. He was back on patrol in enemy territory where every tree could shelter a sniper or conceal an ambush. He walked carefully with his senses attuned to every sight and sound. He was so in harmony with the forest that anything out of the ordinary would easily alert him to hidden dangers.

The light faded as evening struck. The temperature dropped a few degrees but Peter perspired more than usual because of the tense situation. *Boy, this is gonna be a long hike home,* he thought. *I wonder what I'm gonna run into on the way?...* He would soon find out.

Chapter Two

Death in the animal kingdom has a certain symmetry and beauty. It is a matter of survival. There are foragers, scavengers and predators. There are hunters and the hunted. There are survivors and victims. It is a simple matter of energy. Conserving, hoarding, using and obtaining this precious force are matters of life and death. Killing and eating is just a means of obtaining that life-sustaining energy. Generally, animals do not kill for pleasure, greed, revenge or satisfaction. They do not waste precious reserves on such human emotions. They kill to eat. Animals are amoral creatures with no sense of guilt; only an instinct for survival. This is the way it was on the mountain. Peter accepted the routine deaths he saw as natural selection and the survival of the fittest. He could accept the simple logic of the food chain especially as he was at the top.

'Civilized' man had changed all that. He did kill for pleasure, greed, revenge or satisfaction. He killed in anger and with blatant disregard for his moral code. He could kill and feel no remorse, not because he was amoral but because he could be immoral. Modern man had removed himself from the food chain and the majority hunted their meat in the supermarkets. Peter had re-entered the food chain the moment he elected to live in the wilderness. He knew the risks and how to minimize them, but most of the newbies running around in the forest were oblivious to the dangers.

Stumbling across the dead body was a stark reminder of why Peter had opted out of 'civilized society' in the first place. He crouched over the fallen man. An arrow protruded from his neck and his eyes were wide and sightless. It wasn't the first corpse that the ex-soldier had seen but it shook him nonetheless. The death seemed cold, senseless and callous. He bent and examined the arrow closely. He drew in a sharp breath. *It's one of Ben's arrows! What does that old fool think he's doing?*

A twig snapped with a loud crack that jolted Peter from his thoughts. Behind him, someone cocked a shotgun and Peter froze when he heard the distinctive sound. *Damn.* He had focused so much on the body that he had let down his guard. Someone had the drop on him now.

He was twenty-four hours from town, on his way back to his cabin, when he had found the body. He'd avoided the few humans he had seen but now found himself in deep trouble. He should have skirted the body and kept moving. *Damn me for being nosey,* he thought.

'Raise your hands, mister. Nice and slow, no sudden movements.'

Peter strained to hear every nuance in the voice. He searched for any hint of weakness or fear in the tone.

'Don't play with me, mister. Leave your gun on the ground and raise your hands. *Now.*'

There was plenty of fear in the voice but no weakness. Determination dominated the young woman's voice. A frightened, determined girl was a dangerous combination. Peter raised his arms above his head.

'I didn't kill this man. I don't have a bow,' he said.

The young woman did not respond.

'You should be concerned that whoever killed him's still around.' Peter kept his tone calm and measured. Still the woman did not respond.

'I'm going to turn around so that I can see you, miss.'

'Keep your hands high and do it slowly.' Her voice cracked.

Peter turned and caught sight of the girl for the first time. She was short and stocky with jet-black, shoulder length hair. Her eyes and cheekbones gave away her Native American roots. She held the gun like an expert with the butt tucked tightly into her shoulder. She stared at Peter through eyes that had recently cried. She was a strange combination of danger and vulnerability.

The gun was a black Winchester, twelve gauge; a heavy weapon for the girl to hold in that position for long. He was relieved that she pointed the gun at his face. At this range, the recoil would send the pellets a couple of feet over his head. He held the woman's gaze as he spoke.

'My name is Peter. I mean you no harm.'

'How do I know that? What are you doing here?'

'I live here.'

'In the forest?'

'On the mountain. I have a cabin just above the tree line about two days' hike from here. I was on my way home when I came across the body.'

'The body?' her voice rose, 'That *body* is my brother. He's called Raphael. His tribal name is Little Bear, and he is a chief among my people. He's also the greatest brother anyone could have. He's not just "the body". You got that, mister?'

'I'm truly sorry about your brother, miss. But, you have to

be concerned about your safety now. What are you doing out here?'

The young girl stared at Peter. He realized that she didn't trust him and could hardly blame her under the circumstances. He saw movement in the trees behind her and caught a pungent and familiar scent. His pulse quickened as his body reacted to the danger.

'Miss, please don't move. There's a bear behind you somewhere in the trees. I'm gonna reach for my gun, OK?'

'Don't move! You can't fool me, mister. I'm not that stupid.'

'Can't you smell it? You have your back to it. Let me get my shotgun. When I pick it up, I want you to slowly lie down on the ground and play dead. It won't see you as a threat and I'll have a clear shot. It's the only way.'

'Leave the gun where it is mister. I won't tell you again.'

The end of her weapon dropped a few inches as her arms weakened and she arched her back to compensate.

Peter stood on the balls of his feet, like a boxer, ready to move at the first opportunity. He saw movement in the trees behind the girl and caught a glimpse of a large creature. Something puzzled him. It may have been a trick of light but the color seemed wrong. The sharp crack of a breaking twig made the girl jump and Peter flinched, half expecting a shot.

Sudden fear invaded the girl's dark features; she turned on her heel and took a step backward in panic. The maneuver, together with the weight of the gun, threw her off balance, and she fell heavily. Peter saw the huge bear rise from all fours as he dove for his shotgun. The animal stood on its hind legs with its forepaws raised over its head. Its fur was almost white, but it was neither an albino nor a Polar Bear. Peter had never seen one like it before. He hoisted the gun and released the safety, ready to fire. The bear raised its head and sniffed the air. Peter planted his feet ready to shoot.

'No,' the girl shouted and sprang to her feet. She turned her back to the bear and faced Peter, 'don't shoot!'

Peter froze. He couldn't get a shot at the bear without hitting the girl.

'Get out of the way!'

She spoke softly, 'He won't hurt me. Put your gun down.'

Peter remained in position ready to shoot. The girl turned away from him and faced the bear. She raised her arms in imitation of the great beast and stared up at it. The bear stared back. Peter tried to control his breathing. The girl did everything wrong and he cursed under his breath. The bear would attack but Peter could only wait. At this distance, half the pellets from his shell would hit the girl and not the bear. He could only wait and look for a way out of the quandary.

A sudden grey flash and a cacophony of barking signaled the arrival of a fourth participant in the strange scenario. Mishka came running into the clearing with hackles raised and tail aloft ready to defend her master. Peter was still miles from his cabin but didn't stop to think how the dog had found him.

'Mishka, no!' he shouted.

The dog stopped but not at Peter's command. Mishka planted her feet and cocked her head as if listening to some sound only she could hear. She stared at the strange scene of the girl facing off with the bear. Her tail wagged slowly as a strange silence descended over the clearing.

Peter felt a tingling all over his body and fought an irrational urge to drop the shotgun. The bear moved its head from side to side, as it stared at the immobile girl. Without warning, the beast turned, dropped to all fours and calmly ambled away.

The man, the dog and the girl didn't move for some time. A spell rooted them to the spot. They were stuck in time and place. Mishka broke the enchantment by jumping up at Peter and licking his face.

'Get down, Mishka. What are you doing here, girl?'

Peter made a fuss of the dog for a few seconds. He looked up at the girl and found her staring at him with a ghost of a smile playing on her lips although it didn't reach her eyes.

'I guess your dog can vouch for you, mister. She seems to think you're OK, so I'll go along with that for now.'

'You trust animals more than humans.' It was a statement and not a question. The girl shrugged. Peter engaged the safety on his shotgun and shouldered the weapon.

'That was a crazy stunt you pulled with that bear. He was huge; he could have killed you with one swipe. I've never seen a bear that big or with that color fur. You're lucky to be alive, miss.'

'My people call them Spirit Bears. Very few white people have seen one. They have a special place in our culture. He would never harm me.'

'I'm not sure that bear knows anything about your culture, miss. I just think we got lucky. You'd better get out of here before he comes back.'

'I have to bury my brother. I can't leave him like that.'

'Miss, you're in danger. Even if you're not afraid of the bear, the man who killed your brother may still be around.'

'My brother's body may return to nature, but I can't leave him where large animals can carry his bones away.'

Peter weighed up the situation. He knew nothing about her tribe's customs but somehow felt obliged to help.

'There's a narrow ravine, more like a crack in the earth,

about fifty yards north of here. We could drop him in there.'

The girl stared at Peter for several seconds; Peter's simple solution followed her tribe's customs. How did he know?

'Back into the earth from where he came,' she said. 'Sounds OK. Show me.'

Peter turned and walked northwards. He scanned the trees and strained his ears looking for signs of danger. He walked silently, avoiding twigs and fallen branches. Much to his relief, the girl did the same. Mishka patrolled the area, ranging both sides of them. They soon came to the fissure in the earth. They stared into it with solemn expressions.

'It will do,' she said. 'His body will get wedged where the crack narrows. No large animals will be able to get to him.'

Peter carried the body fifty yards from the clearing to the fissure. His knees almost buckled a few times under the heavy weight of the inert body. The girl kept her eyes open for trouble but the mountain man was thankful that Mishka was looking out for them both. Peter's chest heaved for air as they arrived at the crevice. He placed the body as gently as he could on the ground, took a deep breath and straightened.

'Do you want to say a few words?' he asked the girl.

She knelt by her brother's body and fingered the black-beaded necklace that hung around her neck; she began to speak in a quiet but clear voice that sent shivers down Peter's spine.

'Great Spirits, accept my brother's body back into the earth from which it came to complete the circle of life. Welcome his spirit and guide his path in the afterworld. See that the sun always shines on his face and the rainbow touches his heart keeping his life force strong so that I may see him in every sunrise and feel him in every raindrop. May his spirit live forever in the winds that blow on this sacred mountain, home of our ancestors.'

Peter continuously scanned the area while the girl prayed. Mishka sat a few yards away watching the young woman as if she knew what was taking place.

She finished the prayer, kissed her necklace, stood and nodded at Peter. He bent and used his hands to roll the body, as respectfully as he could, over the edge and into the crack in the earth. The body fell noiselessly until it wedged about twenty feet from ground level. Peter looked at the girl for approval but she turned away and bowed her head.

'Where will you go from here?' Peter asked.

'I don't know. My brother knew of a safe haven. High in the mountains is a sacred place of our ancestors. He was taking me there until things settle down.'

'You had better go back to your folks.'

'That's not possible. They're too far and I don't even know if they're still alive. Our community was under attack and we only just escaped with our lives.'

'You can't stay here on the mountain. There are a lot of crazy and desperate people about.'

'*You* stay here.'

'Well, maybe I'm a little crazy.'

'No. If you were crazy your dog would tell me.'

'Now you're scaring me.'

'Don't worry about me. I can take care of myself. I'm not your responsibility.'

Peter remained silent. He had already spoken more in one day than in the previous six months.

'I'll just keep climbing. I'm sure the higher I go the safer I'll be.'

Peter seemed calm and relaxed but that belied the turmoil taking place in his soul. This girl was not his responsibility and she'd held a gun on him less than ten minutes ago. He'd refused to help the storekeeper with his son and felt no remorse, but somehow this was different. She didn't have a father at hand like the storekeeper's son. His crazy neighbor had killed her only protector in front of her eyes. What's more, he could still be in the vicinity. Still, the girl was determined and independent enough to tell him she wasn't his responsibility. So be it.

'Do you have a compass, miss?'

'Yes, and I have good sense of direction.'

'From here, take a north-east route until you find a small river. Then follow that upstream until you hit the tree line. That will keep you safely off the land occupied by your brother's killer. Once you get above the trees, you can pick your spot. You got that?'

'Yes.'

'Good luck, miss.'

'Thanks.'

Peter whistled softly to Mishka, adjusted his backpack and began the long hike up to his cabin. He took ten steps before he realized that Mishka hadn't followed.

'C'mon, girl. Let's go.'

The big dog looked at Peter then at the girl then back to Peter.

'Suit yourself. I'm going home with or without you.'

Mishka seemed reluctant to follow. Eventually she stood, shook herself and followed Peter while casting frequent glances back at the girl. The man and his dog fell into a comfortable stride as they left her further behind.

The two of them made good time. When he'd been alone,

Peter had moved with caution. He'd constantly been on the lookout for danger. The mountain man could afford to move faster now that he could rely on Mishka to warn him of strangers.

'How did you find me, girl?' he asked his furry companion.

The big dog didn't break stride but wagged its tail in reply. Peter fell silent. He marveled at Mishka. Never before had his canine friend met him so far from the cabin, and he wondered what had driven the dog to such lengths this time. He caught Mishka looking at him with an expression on her face that could have been a smile. *Damn dog knows what I'm thinking!* The dog looked away and Peter's thoughts returned to the more mundane.

The light faded; they needed to make camp soon. As if on cue, Mishka found a small gully sheltered by a thick tree and promptly lay down in its shade. Her tongue hung out and she panted to cool herself. She looked at Peter again as if to say, 'This is the place to camp.'

Peter laughed aloud. *I've been alone with this dog too long. I'm going crazy like old Ben. The next thing, I'll be hearing her talk!*

Peter didn't risk a fire. He shared some beef jerky and canteen water with his canine companion and settled down under the tree for the night. Peter curled up next to Mishka, for warmth, and soon fell into a trancelike sleep. His subconscious mind took over.

Like an eagle, he flew high above his mountain kingdom. He looked down and saw his inert body curled up with the great dog. He felt a sense of freedom he'd never experienced before. He soared over the trees without conscious effort. He found himself over the sleeping form of the Indian girl. She was just a tiny bundle huddled under a bush but he somehow knew it was her. She gave off a blue glow, which he knew was good.

He looked to the northwest and his form took him in that direction. He was capable of incredible speed and instant changes of direction. He felt euphoric. He soon came upon another sleeping bundle, which gave off a red glow that unsettled Peter. It was Ben Atwood. Peter knew by the color emanating from Ben that he was sick, not in a physical sense but a spiritual way. An evil madness held Ben in its vice-like grasp.

Peter found the Spirit Bear. It glowed the same blue as the young Indian girl. It dozed peacefully in a small hollow far from any other living creature. He came across many sleeping animals and some that were hunting and foraging in the dark of night. They all gave off various hues of blue.

Peter circled the great mountain taking in every sleeping bundle. Most were huddled in groups. A glow of mixed colors muddied his impressions. He felt fear, confusion and desperation in varying amounts from the different groups. One large group differed from the rest. A strong glow from one individual dominated them. It was an unsettling deep orange glow and it enveloped and dominated the entire party. It scared Peter to his very soul. He felt himself shrink and lose control. He found himself sucked back to his sleeping body in less than a heartbeat.

He woke with a cry. His pulse raced and he gasped for breath. He sat up in a panic. He checked for Mishka, but the big dog was gone. He took several huge breaths and steadied himself.

Damn! What sort of dream was that?

Somewhere, deep inside, Peter knew it wasn't a dream. He knew where everyone was on the mountain. The Indian girl would call it a vision. Others would call it a revelation. It should have scared him. It didn't. The only thing that scared him was the individual with the orange glow leading the group to the north.

Peter sat with his back against the big tree. He felt different, enriched in some way. He tried to analyze his feelings. His subconscious had invaded his conscious mind. For a few minutes, he'd been enlightened and almost godlike. He knew where everyone was and what they were feeling.

Yeah, right! I don't even know where my dog is. It was just a crazy dream!

He tried to convince himself. His experience the previous day had affected him more than he thought. The strange encounter with the girl and the bear had started the whole thing. After that, it seemed that his communication and understanding with Mishka had moved to a new level. That had been swirling in his head when he'd fallen asleep. Hence the dream. He'd woken and the dog was gone. *So much for a closer relationship. Ha!*

Peter checked the sky. He couldn't see the moon anymore but he could see the soft glow in the distant sky that hinted at the morning to come. He tightened his bootlaces and drank from his water bottle. He chewed on a strip of pemmican as he put on his pack and prepared to move out. He gave a soft whistle and waited for a response but Mishka never appeared, so Peter started up the sloping terrain towards his cabin. He would make it by nightfall if he pushed hard.

Chapter Three

Peter woke, in his own bunk, as the first signs of dawn colored the landscape. He'd had a dreamless night. He felt relieved but a little disappointed that the visions of the previous night had not returned. He felt a little out of touch, as he didn't know where people were on his mountain. He called out for Mishka, but the big dog never responded. Peter scowled as he walked to the stream to bathe.

As usual, the cold running water made Peter gasp. It was the perfect way to kick-start his mind and body for the coming day. As his body adjusted to the chilled water, he relaxed and enjoyed the sensation.

Fully awake, he began to assess recent events. His refuge on the mountain was under threat. His dog had gone AWOL. There were possibly two dead men in the area and many gun-happy bands of refugees from the town. He had a feeling that many more would die in the coming days. He determined that he would not be among the dead.

As was his habit, he walked naked back to the cabin carrying his freshly washed clothes. He felt exposed as he walked across the clearing to his cabin; not because he was nude but because Mishka was absent and he carried no gun. Circumstances had changed dramatically in his peaceful and safe world. He was no longer isolated and he would have to change his lifestyle to compensate for the danger. Someone could be hiding in the brush with a gun aimed in his direction. The skin on the back of his neck crawled and he increased his pace to a jog.

Safely back in the cabin, Peter cursed himself for his mini panic attack. He pulled on a pair of shorts and ducked outside to hang his wet clothes from the previous day over the porch rail. His mind worked overtime as he reviewed his defenses. He had many items blocking the line of sight from his cabin to the tree line - skins hanging out to dry along with strips of bear meat and fish from the stream cluttered the clearing. He would bring the hides and some of the meat into the cabin. The flesh that wasn't cured, and still smelt strongly, would go on the roof. A large pile of logs surrounded his chopping block. He would have to do something about that, as it would provide cover for an intruder.

Peter's military background kicked into overdrive and he spent the morning clearing sight lines and storing food inside his cabin. Finally satisfied, he walked several feet into the trees and found the distinctive white rock that marked his emergency supplies. He'd buried a fifty-gallon drum with spare rations and a survival tent in case a fire or other mishap overtook his cabin. He reassured himself that it wasn't detectable to an outsider and turned his thoughts to the hunger that had crept up on him during the day.

He dug in his small vegetable patch and returned to his cabin with some potatoes and turnips, which he'd prepare with some dried meat. He propped his shotgun inside the door of his cabin along with a loaded hunting rifle. While he waited for the water to boil on his stove, Peter checked through the medical kit he had retrieved from the ranger's SUV. It was comprehensive, as far as first aid kits went, and he decided to leave it intact inside its original box. He found a place on a shelf for it and returned to the stove.

He kept an eye on the tree line from his open door and the small window. Just as steam began to rise from the pot, he saw movement in the trees. He moved quickly, grabbed the rifle and knelt down inside the doorway, focusing the sight into the trees. He steadied himself against the doorframe and locked his elbow onto his thigh to give the barrel a steady base. He forced himself to breath slow and steady. He was as ready as he would ever be.

Mishka broke through the trees into the clearing and Peter almost yelled with relief and joy at seeing his canine companion. The trees moved again and another figure emerged into the weak sunlight. Peter groaned. It was the girl from the previous afternoon. Mishka had led her back to his cabin.

Peter waited until it was obvious there was no one else with them and then stepped out onto his porch. Mishka ran to him. A peculiar sound of joy and greeting escaped her throat as she ran towards her master, like a baby keening for its mother. Peter knelt, without his rifle this time, and the big dog almost knocked him over in greeting.

'I see she missed you,' the girl said, as she approached the cabin.

'Yeah, well, the feelings mutual.' Peter's tone was gruff and unfriendly. He stood, as she neared, and looked at the young woman.

Deep circles ringed the girl's eyes. Her shoulders stooped and her feet dragged as she walked. Without warning, she caught her foot on a rock and stumbled. Instinctively, Peter reached out and grabbed the girl to stop her from falling. As he held her, he felt a sideways lurch and a strange tingling sensation as if he were falling. He briefly saw the blue aura surrounding the girl and something more. He knew. She was with child. The girl's eyes widened as she sensed his knowledge.

'Yes, I'm pregnant,' she said, then fainted in his arms.

Peter carried her inside, struggled to remove her backpack and laid her on his bunk. He saw the slight swell in her abdomen through her clothes. He laid his hand on her belly and again felt the sideways lurch. It was a boy. A boy with a strong spirit. Peter removed his hand as if burnt. He looked at his hand in wonder. It was shaking slightly.

What's going on? I'm not asleep. This isn't a dream. How can I know these things?

The girl opened her eyes and saw the look of wonder on his face.

'It's the Gift, Peter. You have the Gift. Don't fight it.' She closed her eyes and drifted into a deep peaceful sleep.

The Gift? What the hell does she mean?

Mishka barked to draw Peter's attention the stove. The pot boiled over and steam rose from it like smoke from a locomotive. He cursed, grabbed a cloth and removed the pot from the flames. There was barely any water left and he would have to start over. This time he would be cooking for two. He rummaged through his sparse food supplies for some herbs or spices to make his meager fare more palatable for a pregnant girl.

He needn't have worried. The girl slept deeply throughout the morning, and as afternoon became evening, her breaths were long and rhythmic. Peter fussed over his simmering pot until the food was ready and still she slept. Peter ate mechanically while his mind pondered the latest developments. He tossed some dried meat to Mishka as he retired to the porch and sat in his customary position with his feet on the rail. It was his favorite time of day. It was that moment just before twilight when the light seemed mystical and the trees turned auburn with the dying sun.

So, he had the Gift. What was it and how could he use it? For the first time he wished he could turn it on at will. He wanted to know where potential threats came from. He tried to relax and open his mind in the hope that it would descend upon him. He sat immobile, feeing ridiculous and self-conscious. Nothing happened. Contact with the girl had started it and maybe it would again. He took his chair, made his way into the cabin and sat beside the sleeping girl. He tentatively took her hand and waited.

The big man's eyelids closed and he dozed. Suddenly, the lurching sensation hit him. He didn't fight it. He was above his cabin. Twilight filled the sky as the light faded quickly. Once again, his slightest thought dictated the direction of his flight. Only wildlife shared the proximity of the cabin. There was no sign of human life in the immediate vicinity. He soared higher and looked further. Groups of humans were scattered over the terrain like balls clustered on an undulating pool table. There were fewer individuals than before. Either they had assimilated into the groups or they were dead.

Peter sought the orange glow he'd seen previously. He soon found it. The group had moved closer to his sanctuary and seemed to have swelled in numbers. He flew until he was above them and tried to discern the numbers and make up of the party. It was impossible as darkness descended and the strong orange glow of the leader dominated the rest. Once again, he felt a sense of fear but this time he accepted it and didn't panic.

Some distance away, he caught sight of Ben's red aura. It was if the mad mountain man stalked the group but kept at a safe distance.

A flurry of air and a buffeting assaulted his senses. An eagle flew so close that Peter fancied he felt the touch of its wings. Startled at the unknown presence, the eagle screeched and flew off at an oblique angle. Peter found himself back in the cabin in an instant. His heart raced and he gasped for breath. The girl was awake and staring at him.

'I see you're learning the way of the Gift. That's good.'

Peter stared vacantly at her, not sure where he was. The assault on his senses was almost too much to comprehend.

'It will become easier as you begin to understand more.'

'What's happening to me?'

'The spirits have chosen you. To my knowledge, it's never happened to a white man before.'

'Why's it happening to me?'

'I'm not sure. I have an idea, but it's only a theory.'

'Well, tell me.'

But, exhaustion overcame the girl and she slept again. Peter clenched his fists in frustration. He felt like shaking the girl awake to find out more but didn't have the heart to disturb her.

Reassured of their immediate safety from intruders, Peter turned his thoughts to other issues. What was he going to do about the pregnant girl? It was as if the gods were punishing him for turning away John's son.

So, you don't want to take care of a little boy? So, now you have a young woman and her unborn son to take care of!

The thought swelled in his head until he fought it down. It was just fate. Things happen for a reason, or so his grandmother was fond of saying. That didn't help him much. His medical training in the Corps hadn't extended to childbirth. That's if they lived that long. Peter decided that he would keep them alive until the time came - then it was up to her. Just like that, Peter accepted his unexpected house guest.

He used blankets to make an impromptu bivouac near the stove and settled down for the night. Mishka lay down beside him. The big dog was subdued, as if she knew her master had a lot on his mind. Peter slept and dreamt of eagles, bears and babies, none of which he remembered in the cold light of day.

***

The girl woke just before dawn. As her eyes adjusted to the dim light, she saw the unfamiliar wooden ceiling and sat bolt upright in surprise. It had been many days since she had slept indoors and she felt disoriented. Realizing where she was, she climbed out of the comfortable bed and smiled at the sight of Peter curled up in an untidy bundle by the stove. Mishka raised her head from her position beside Peter and stared at the girl. Suzie could hear the big dog's tail thumping against the floor as she wagged it in greeting.

Suzie put her finger against her lips to signal the dog to remain quiet as she tiptoed past the sleeping man. She had no idea if Mishka understood the sign but the dog followed her quietly outside.

The young woman gazed to where the sun signaled its arrival with an amber glow in the morning sky. She needed to come to terms with the loss of her brother and to understand this strange white man whom the spirits had blessed. She stepped off the porch and felt the earth of the Sacred Mountain beneath her feet and between her toes. Her spine tingled. All answers lay buried in Mother Earth. She would seek knowledge from the Spirits that lived here.

Suzie sank to a cross-legged position and placed her hands on her knees. She lifted her face to the morning sun and closed her eyes. She cleared her mind of mundane thoughts and left it uncluttered and empty, ready for insight. She felt her weight upon the earth and imagined herself bonding and becoming one with it. Mishka gazed at the girl and, deciding she was safe, trotted off into the tree line to hunt for breakfast.

The wise ones cooperated with the young girl in her search for enlightenment. They didn't always. She saw the white man dressed in a green uniform training for war. He was younger but his physique was the same. She saw him killing in the name of his country and realized the pain it caused in his spirit. She saw him seeking solace in the wilderness and finding the sacred mountain. She saw him hunt for food. He took only what he needed to survive, no more no less. He seemed genuinely grateful for the gifts that Mother Earth bestowed upon him.

He lived in the way of the people. He lived the way her ancient people had lived for eons. The way they had lived before the white man came and some of the tribes had moved south to the plains and adopted the culture of the horse. The way her obscure tribe had continued to live throughout the twentieth century and to the present. She saw the man find the abandoned puppy and nurture it until it grew into a fine strong hunting dog and companion. She saw him grow closer to the environment and Mother Earth. His love for the mountain matched that of her people.

He was a warrior and a hunter just like her brother. But, there was more to him. He was tougher and harder than her sibling. The cauldron of war had tempered his toughness and pangs of hunger and starvation had sharpened his hunting skills to perfection. He was a survivor. Years of solitude on the sacred mountain had cleansed his mind and attuned his senses. The Spirits had chosen wisely.

* * * *

Peter woke at dawn, stiff from the night on the floor. He checked his bunk but the girl was gone. He found her outside on the earth beside his porch. She sat cross-legged, meditating. Peter shrugged and boiled water for tea. The girl must be hungry but he had nothing to offer except cold potatoes and dried meat or fish. The girl sat apparently in a trance while Peter drank his tea and started on a second mug. He was about to go to the stream to wash when she roused.

'Good morning, Peter.'

'Good morning, miss.'

It seemed strangely formal and she laughed.

'My name's Suzie.'

Peter didn't reply.

'I've been doing some searching. I believe I know why you've been given the Gift.'

Peter waited but said nothing.

'When I was a young girl, a Shaman in my tribe told me that I would give birth to a special child during a time of upheaval and danger. He also told me that the spirits would send a powerful, mystic warrior to look after the child. As I grew, I came to believe that it would be my brother. He was strong and a natural warrior and hunter. He was leading me to the spiritual home of my people where he planned to sit in solitude and seek the vision that would bring the gift of mysticism. He died, and you were there, so the spirits chose you. You, with your years of solitude on the sacred mountain, will fulfill his destiny.'

Peter stared at the girl. He heard her words but they made no sense to him. Shamans, mystic warriors, sacred mountains - they were all foreign to him. This could not be his destiny. His was a doctrine of God, The Marine Corp and his rifle. He had turned his back on all that. But, still, this could not be his destiny. Could it?

More confused than ever, Peter asked the only thing that made sense to him, 'Are you hungry, miss?'

'Suzie! And yes, I'm starving.'

Chapter Four

Suzie followed him inside and shook her head when she saw the leftover food from the night before.

'You reheat that while I go foraging,' she said and ducked back outside.

The stove was still hot though the embers were low – the perfect temperature to heat leftovers. He put his all-purpose pot of stewed potatoes and meat on to simmer while he hurried to the stream to bathe. He'd seen the girl heading downstream away from his usual bathing area. This time he took a spare pair of shorts so he wouldn't have to walk back naked.

Peter felt strange. He was so used to being alone and just catering to his own wants and needs. If he felt like walking naked all morning then it had never been a problem, until now. He had mixed feelings. He should have felt invaded or violated. The girl had stolen his privacy. But, somehow he didn't begrudge her. It was as if this is what he had been waiting for. The years of solitude on the mountain had been solely for this purpose. He had been waiting for the girl. He couldn't shake the feeling.

Sweet Jesus, I'm going nuts. Where are these ideas coming from? How could I wait for someone I didn't even know existed?

Peter snorted and hurried to the stream kicking up small

clouds of dust on the way. The cold water would wash away these crazy ideas along with the dirt. He stripped, spent a few minutes soaking his clothes and rubbing them together to release the dirt before laying them on a rock to drain off. He entered the water with slight shiver and waded until he was waist deep in the refreshing stream.

The cold, running water had its usual effect on him. It was more than just a means to wash off grime. It was a morning ritual that cleansed his body, mind and soul for the coming day. He ducked under the water, rubbed his scalp and poked around his ears with experienced fingers. He stuck his head above the water and relished the feeling of the rushing current over his shoulders as he remained on his haunches. He glanced up and saw the girl. She stared at him for a few seconds, bent and placed some items on the ground, quickly disrobed and stepped into the icy water with him. The roaring of the water seemed to intensify to a new level that overwhelmed his hearing.

The girl spotted something on the far shore and quickly waded to the middle of the stream. Her son's presence was just discernable by the slight swell of her belly. She moved without inhibition and seemed oblivious to Peter's presence. The middle of the stream was deep enough for her to lift her feet from the ground and swim a few strokes. Regaining her feet, she waded to the opposite shore and bent down to the shrubbery that clung to its edge.

The young woman pulled something from the riverbank and peeled some green skin from it. She began to rub it between her hands and then over her body. Even at that distance, Peter could see lather forming on the girl's skin. It glistened white against her brown complexion and intrigued and perplexed him. Was there a soap-like plant growing on the banks of his stream that he had been ignorant of for all these years? What else could he learn from the girl? His curiosity overcame his awareness of his nakedness and he quickly made his way to her side.

'Is that soap?' he asked.

'It's close,' she replied. 'You have to rub it hard and it's not as foamy but it works well and grows all year.'

She showed him how to identify the right part of the plant and how to peel off the outer layer. He was amazed at the feeling it produced on his skin and how fresh and clean he felt afterwards. They waded back across the stream together seeming to synchronize the point at which they swam. Her clothes were still dry on the bank and she quickly pulled the chamois smock over her head. Suddenly aware of his nakedness, Peter reached for his dry shorts and spent a few seconds hopping around on one foot as he tried to maintain his balance to get his second leg into them.

She watched him with a grin on her face, which gave her an impish look. Peter ignored her and began to wring the excess water from the clothes he had washed.

'You don't call that clean, do you?'

'What do you mean?'

'Give them to me,' she ordered.

She took the wet clothes from his hands and knelt down by the rocks that bordered the running water. She began to beat the clothes on the rocks then spread them out and used the soap plant, which Peter hadn't realized she still held. As the girl used the ancient method to wash his garments, he felt a tingling followed by the sideways lurch.

Peter found himself in a different reality. The sound of

voices and laughter mixed with the gurgling of the stream. The smell of wood smoke filled his nostrils. Dogs barked and children squealed as they played in the stream near their mothers. He looked up and saw the village of skin tents and cooking fires. Old women sat around the fires cooking, while young women washed at the stream. Children and dogs were everywhere. Peter knew the men were out hunting. He found himself splashed with water and saw a young boy in a loincloth laughing at him. He splashed the child back and squealed with laughter. A woman slapped some cloth loudly on the rocks close to him and he lurched again.

He was back at his stream and Suzie was looking at him as she squeezed water from his clothes.

'What did you see?' she asked.

At first, he didn't reply. He was not sure what he had seen. He gazed into the distance as if recalling every detail.

'I saw a village. With tents and fires. Women cooking, children and dogs playing. Young girls washing by the stream. I think it was this stream but I don't know.'

'It was a vision. The spirits were showing you how it was in the old days.'

'No, I was there. I was a child myself, playing in the water.'

She looked at him with wide eyes. Could his spirit have lived before in the village on the sacred mountain? The wise ones had not shown her that.

'I'm hungry,' she said.

Before they could head back to the cabin, Mishka ran to them from the tree line. Blood discolored the white patch of fur on her chest. Her morning hunt had been successful. She ran by Peter, jumped into the water, swam and attempted to drink at the same time. Peter shook his head at the dog's antics.

Mishka hauled herself from the stream and shook herself vigorously to dry. The bloodstains had vanished. The stream cleansed everything.

Suzie retrieved the vegetation she had gathered and the two of them walked to the cabin while the dog ran back and forth to burn off excess energy.

'What did you find to eat?'

She showed him the roots and leaves that she had gathered along the banks of the stream and moss she had scraped from rocks. Peter turned his nose up at the sight of the moss.

'The moss is similar in nutritional value to seaweed and has a high sodium content. Perfect to season a stew if you don't have salt,' she informed him.

Peter reddened and turned his face away as they approached the cabin. Was she deliberately trying to embarrass him? He glanced at her. She had no idea that he had ran out of salt. She was just teaching him her knowledge and ways. She had sought him out for protection but he might end up benefiting more in the end. They arrived at the cabin and he stepped aside to let the girl in first.

She added some of her haul to the simmering pot and he stoked the fire to prolong the cooking. The girl retrieved a mirror and comb from her pack, and sat on the porch to fix her long hair. Peter followed and sat close by her.

'I'm worried,' he started.

She remained silent waiting for him to express his concerns.

'These visions and dreams I'm having. I can't control them. They come whenever they want. I'm afraid one will come at the wrong time. Maybe when I'm defending you or the baby. I know people are on the mountain and some mean us harm. What if they attack and I have a vision?'

'The Spirits would not place you in danger.'

'You have great faith in something you can't see.'

'Can you see the moon right now, Peter?'

'No.'

'Do you doubt its existence?'

'That's not the same thing.'

'How do you know there are people on the mountain who would hurt us?'

'I saw them in a dream. They're coming closer.'

'Do you believe the Spirits showed you them?'

'I have no other explanation.'

'Then you must accept that the Spirits are there to help you, not put you in danger.'

Peter could not fault the girl's logic. He just found this new ability disconcerting. His furrowed brow amused the girl.

'Your Gift isn't unique, Peter. You're like a child learning a new language.'

Peter snorted in disgust at her comment. She put him in his place.

'Even Mishka knew I was pregnant the moment she saw me. That's why she came back for me. She was more attuned than you when we met. The Spirit Bear came to protect me from you before it realized you were one of the people.'

'One of the people?'

'Yes, whether you realize it or not, you're one of my people. The custodians of the Earth. Maybe not by birth but by heritage and custom. You instinctively chose to live as my people have lived for centuries. You're one with nature and the spirits recognized it. There's no escaping your destiny, Peter.'

He fell silent as he contemplated her words. The girl combed her hair and gave him time. The smell of cooked food filtered from the cabin and Peter roused himself to go and check the stove. The stew seemed thicker than usual with an aroma that teased his nostrils and set his mouth watering. He dipped a spoonful and blew steadily on it to cool it down. The first taste exploded in his mouth with flavors that he'd never experienced. *Damn! It might be worth it to have the girl around if all my meals taste this good!*

Peter had trouble finding an extra bowl for Suzie's share of the stew. He was used to a solitary life and barely had one of anything. There were times when he ate his meals directly from the pot and didn't even bother with a bowl for himself. After all, he was not one to stand on ceremony, and who was going to question his manners? He managed to rustle up two bowls but only one suitable spoon. Suzie came to his rescue by producing a compact cutlery set, designed for campers, from her backpack. They sat on the porch and ate in comfortable silence. Mishka sat close by waiting for any leftovers.

Peter savored the stew's flavor and distinctive aroma with the added ingredients that the girl had contributed. His sense of taste and smell seemed enhanced. He heard birds singing from the trees and smelt the wood smoke from his stove. Suddenly, he sat bolt upright…

'Damn!'

He dropped his bowl of stew, grabbed the small barrel of water from the corner of the porch and ducked inside the cabin. Intrigued, Suzie stood and, with bowl in hand, followed him inside to see what the fuss was about. She found Peter by a hissing stove with an empty barrel dangling from his hand. Steam rose from the pot-bellied stove as the water evaporated into the cabin.

Suzie chuckled, 'Are you trying to create a sauna, Peter?'

He glared at her and shut the flues of the stove to prevent the flow of air to any remaining heat. He said nothing.

'Peter?'

'I've been stupid. I've put us in danger.'

The girl swallowed her last drops of soup straight from the bowl and looked at him quizzically.

'Don't be so dramatic. What are you talking about?'

'The smoke from the stove can be smelt, and seen, for miles. I've been advertising our position.'

The girl stared at him. She seemed lost for words. Mishka stuck her head in the door with an expectant look on her features. She had licked up the remains of Peter's dropped stew and held his empty bowl in her jaws. She wagged her tail and put on her best hungry face in the hope of a further helping. The girl giggled at the sight of the dog.

'It's no laughing matter!' Peter was angry. The truth was he was angry with himself for his lapse in security.

'Would it be so bad if others came here, Peter?'

His eyes widened, 'Look, we need all the food I have just for the two of us to survive. I never planned on a winter for two so it will be a struggle with what I have. I can't let them take it from us.'

'Who's "them", Peter?'

'The people on the mountain looking for food.'

'You would deny them what Mother Nature has given up?'

'I hunted it myself. It's for my survival. It's for you too, now.'

'You wouldn't share? After all, it's the way of the people.'

'They're not my people, Suzie.'

'Yesterday I was "not your people", Peter.'

'That's not the same.'

'Isn't it?'

He stared at her.

'You can't live your whole life alone, Peter.'

'I've been doing OK until now.'

'Already I've shown you herbs and plants that you knew nothing about. There are many things for you to learn. Each person you meet will teach you a little more as you will teach them.'

'Look, that's all very high-minded of you, very magnanimous, but these people want to take our food from us!'

'Peter, it's not *our* food. Mother Nature gives up her bounty for us to share with our brothers and sisters. There's so much more here. You've only scratched the surface. This ground can support a whole village.'

'The hell you say!'

'You saw it in the vision you had by the stream. You described it to me. It was a vision of how things were here a long time ago'

'A lot of things have changed since then. Man's moved on. He's progressed.'

'Has he really, Peter?'

Her words struck home. He sat in silence. She had a point.

'Peter, the Spirits chose you but you're still a baby. You have the right instincts but you must lose the ways of the modern world that you've been brought up in.'

'I've left that behind.'

'Maybe physically, Peter, but not spiritually.'

'What do you mean?'

'You've survived on the mountain by bending it to your will. By using rifle and shotgun and tearing from the earth what you need. She gives it grudgingly. It's been hard for you.'

'What's your point?'

'Learn to live in harmony with nature, Peter.'

'I do!'

'Only up to a point. Learn to listen to Mother Earth. Learn to share with you brothers and sisters. There's a natural flow to life that you must tap into. You need your brothers and sisters for the people to survive. If everyone isolated themselves like you then the people would perish in one generation.'

He measured his response carefully, 'Suzie, I know, from the visions, that there's a group of people on the mountain led by an evil force. It's hard to describe the malevolence I feel coming from that source. I know they mean us harm.'

'You know that all of them mean us harm, Peter? Take away the evil leader and see what happens. People are inherently good but sometimes get led astray.'

He raised his eyebrows and took a deep breath. 'You are idealistic, lady. I've seen what humans are capable of. I've seen war, death and atrocities you wouldn't dream of. You saw your brother struck down in cold blood only yesterday, killed for no good reason.'

'I also met a stranger who took me in, gave me shelter and his own bed to sleep in. I met a stranger who offered me protection and a share of his food. I met a stranger who is willing to risk his safety and possibly his life for me and an unborn child not of his blood.'

Embarrassed, Peter bowed his head. The girl waited to see what effect her words would have.

'OK, maybe there are some good people out there. But, I know there's a least one evil son-of-a-bitch on the mountain and I believe he's coming for us.'

'So, deal with that evil one. The Spirits brought us together for you to protect my son from evil - not for you to deny food to the people.'

Once again, Peter looked to the heavens.

'You are infuriating, woman!'

She smiled. She knew she was getting to him. Peter changed tactics.

'It's almost impossible for me to protect you on my own.'

'What do you mean?'

'I have to sleep at some stage. Plus, there are a lot of people in the group and many approaches to the cabin. There are blind spots at the back of my cabin and the roof's vulnerable. I can't protect you from an all-out assault from every direction.'

'I have faith in you, Peter. Sleep on it. I'm sure you'll find a solution.'

'Ha! I guess you think the Spirits will show me the way in a dream?'

'Yes I do.'

'Well, unless they can show me how to be in four places at one time, we're buggered.'

'Have a little faith, Peter.'

The faithless one shook his head in frustration. It would be a long afternoon in the company of this cantankerous woman.

Chapter Five

Later that night, Peter once again made a bed on the floor by the stove. He slept and he dreamed. He dreamed he was a teenage boy, running. He ran with the ease and energy of one born to run.

*　*　*　*

The youth ran at a steady pace and his stride ate up distance at a deceptive rate. A thick layer of skin covered his soles from years of walking and running barefoot. On this day, light moccasins further protected his feet from the sharpest shale and broken roots. Sixteen summers had weathered his skin to a deep red brown. The arduous route challenged the boy to his limits and he faced gradients and constant changes of direction to avoid rocks and small trees. He ran on the balls of his feet with the grace and power of a mountain lion. He read the faint trail with ease and never hesitated.

He had set out from the camp at dawn with three other boys of the same age. A young warrior had given them each a mouthful of water colored with beet juice. They had to carry this water in their mouths and spit it out upon reaching their destination. The temptation to swallow the liquid, and breathe through the mouth, had overcome two of the boys. Nevertheless, the four youths ran on, each taking turns to lead in the fashion their elders had taught them.

The morning passed and the sun rose higher, blazing directly overhead. The air shimmered with heat making distant objects dance in the bright sunlight. Sweat glistened on the teenagers' skin and soaked their loincloths. The boy took the lead more often as the temperature rose. They were close to their goal and he increased his pace leaving the others behind. He heard one of the boys stifle a choke as he half-swallowed and half-spat his water. The boy suppressed a smile. He was the only one who still held the water in his mouth.

The incline grew steeper as he caught his first sight of the hunting party. He lengthened his stride and the others fell back. He ran to where the Hunting Chief stood to greet them, stopped, bowed his head and allowed the pinkish water to trickle from his mouth onto the dusty ground near the warrior's feet. A light sheen of perspiration covered his dark skin and his breaths were deep but even. The man nodded and waved him to join the hunting party. He strode up the rest of the slope relishing the pleasure of breathing through his mouth.

The other boys came to a breathless stop in front of the implacable warrior. Their chests heaved with effort as they sucked air through their mouths and one of them bent with his hands on his knees. Stone-faced, the older man looked at them, raised his arm and pointed over their heads back down the trail. Without protest, they turned and began the long run back to the village. They knew they would go to sleep hungry if they arrived after sunset. Only the strongest survived the harsh customs of the tribe.

The boy's chest puffed with pride as he waited with the

warriors. This would be his first time with the tribe's main hunting party and his first opportunity to pass from a boy to a man. The Hunting Chief, Running Bear, approached and stood in front of him.

'Don't be so proud, young brave. You pushed your companions too hard. It was unnecessary. You'll need the help of your brothers if you're to bring down a moose or bison. You'd do better to help them, not crush them. They're not your enemy.' The boy hung his head as he absorbed the first of many lessons he would learn that day.

The party sheltered in the shade of a maple tree while they waited for scouts to return. It made no sense for all of them to tire themselves spotting prey. They sat and told stories of earlier hunting trips and poked fun at each other good-naturedly. The young brave hung on to every word. Years from now, he would have his own stories to tell in the time-honored tradition of his people.

Running Bear led the boy from under the tree and gave him a chance to show his prowess with a bow.

'I will show you how to select the tree and limb to make your first real bow. In the meantime, use mine. I want you to aim for the big knot in that tree yonder.' The warrior pointed to a tree fifty paces away. The boy's eyes widened. It was the limit of his range with the bow he'd been using.

He selected an arrow from Running Bear's otter-skin pouch. It was true, straight and perfectly balanced. He slotted the arrow into the bow and, using two fingers, drew back as far as he could. His shoulders were wide and powerful for one so young, and he drew the bow to its limit. He carefully sighted his aim above the target allowing for the arrow to fall as it sacrificed height for distance. He let fly. The arrow flew from the bow with a hissing sound the boy had never previously heard. The bow was more powerful than he'd possibly imagined. The arrow flew past the tree line, gaining height until it disappeared into the bushes behind the target.

'That's a valuable lesson, boy. If you're not sure of the power of your weapon, aim short not long.' Running Bear pointed into the trees. 'Wake me when you've found the arrow.'

The abashed young man ran to find the offending shaft.

The afternoon progressed with each hour bringing a new lesson for the boy. His second attempt was a watershed moment in his life. Once again, he drew back the bow to its limit but aimed straight and true for the target. He'd quickly learnt not to over compensate for gravity at that distance. He let fly and heard the hiss for the second time. Almost simultaneously, he heard the satisfying *thunk* as the arrow found its target. With a huge smile, he turned to his mentor for approval.

'Good shot. But, you wasted both your energy and the bow's. Wake me when you've dug the arrow from deep in the tree.'

So, the early afternoon passed. The pattern set. The Chief never gave instructions. He let the boy teach himself by making mistakes. After each mistake, Running Bear gleefully pointed out the error and the boy retrieved the arrow. Slowly but surely, the boy made fewer misjudgments. The Chief increased the distance to each new target as the afternoon progressed, and the boy learnt to control the power and accuracy of the potent weapon. The curious boy peppered the chief with questions.

'When are we going to hunt real game?'

'We are hunting.'

'We are waiting.'

'A scouting party is stalking a herd of Waapiti. Together

with the dogs, they will drive them back through that narrow gully to where we wait.'

'How will we know when they approach?'

'Ha! By the noise and the scent. You will hear and smell them long before you see them. It's almost mating season and the bulls urinate on themselves to attract the females. The smell makes warriors vomit like pregnant squaws.'

'Why do we come so far from camp to hunt? We have a stream full of fish and small game everywhere we look.'

'You have much to learn, my son. Winter approaches and the stream will freeze and the game will disappear. We need the elk to see us through the winter.'

'Why the elk?'

'A bull elk is a great bounty for the entire village. The meat is lean and can be dried and turned into pemmican for the winter months so we don't starve. The skin makes a handsome teepee covering and the offcuts make the best moccasins. The medicine men fight over the antlers to grind into healing powders. You can't get these things from fish and small game, little one.'

The boy absorbed the elder's knowledge like sand absorbing water.

The Chief set a target at one hundred paces. The boy made the shot with ease. He ran to retrieve the arrow with an energy that seemed inexhaustible. A warrior approached the Chief.

'The young brave does well.'

'Yes, he has good hands and eyes like an eagle. We'll wait and see how he performs with a live target.'

A rumble of hooves and the bark of a dog signaled the wait was over. The party took up positions facing the gully just as the boy returned. His eyes shone with excitement as he notched the arrow into the big bow in anticipation. The Chief took the arrow from the young boy's grasp and gave him a fresh one with a razor-sharp flinthead. They locked eyes and the Chief nodded, the boy smiled.

'Let the young brave take the first animal,' the Chief ordered in a loud voice. The hunters remained impassive as the boy took up his stance facing down the gully.

A huge bull elk ran into the mouth of the gully and stopped suddenly in a swirling cloud of dust. Steam rose from its heaving flanks. The animal was the biggest any of them had seen. It weighed as much as six men, maybe seven. Each antler had seven or eight spines and velvet dangled from them like old cloths drying in the wind. It was too big and powerful for the boy to take down. The warriors turned to the chief with questioning eyes. He raised his eyebrows and pointed to the boy. His order stood.

This elk had few natural predators. It was too large and powerful for packs of coyotes or wolves that chose weaker targets in the herd. The bull feared no living creature except a grizzly. It snorted and scooted its back legs in the earth, marking its territory. It raised its head and sniffed the air. It could escape the trap by climbing the sides of the gully, but it would be hard to drag its bulk up the steep sides. The huge beast signaled its intentions with a great bugling roar that echoed from the sides of the gully. It lowered its head and made its choice. It charged the weak two-legged creatures clustered at the head of the gully.

It made directly for the boy who stood his ground with bow drawn. The bull started quickly for such a large beast. It soon ran at full speed its hooves beating the ground like war drums. The boy did not move. The bull shortened the distance with terrifying speed despite the gradient. Still the boy did not flinch. The warriors again stole glances at their chief in agitation. He remained as still as stone.

The boy waited until the beast was almost upon him. The huge animal was about to lower its antlers for the collision when the boy let fly. The arrow took the animal flush in the chest at point blank range. The shaft buried itself almost to the feathers and pierced the heart clean through. The animal's front legs crumpled, as if chopped off at the knees, and the beast fell into the dirt. The animal's forward momentum barely slowed at first. Its great weight kept it sliding along the ground. The boy did not move. The carcass slithered to a stop, barely inches from the boy, showering his feet and ankles with dust and grit. The warriors stood in awed silence unsure of their own eyes. Running Bear spoke.

'Good shot, young brave. But you waited too long. Wake me when you've dug the arrow from deep in its chest.'

The assembled hunters let out a warbling cry that reverberated in the air. It was a spontaneous outpouring of glee and relief; a tribute to the incredible feat they had witnessed. Movement, noise and scent cut short their celebrations as several young elk ran into the far end of the gully. The hunters quickly notched their bows and prepared to shoot. Adrenaline pumped through their veins and testosterone filled the air.

'No!' the Chief's voice was like thunder.

'We have more meat than we can carry. Let the rest go. Let them mate and grow bigger and we will come for them another time. Mother earth has given us enough bounty for today.'

Seeing the wisdom in his words, the warriors lowered their bows. They gathered around the young brave in wonder and stared at the great beast lying at his feet. Once again, Running Bear spoke.

'Young brave,' he began, 'today you became a man. From now on, your name is Charging Bull.'

The hunters looked upon the newly christened warrior with grudging respect. This story would become part of the history of the tribe. Charging Bull would become a legend as tales of his valor swept through the villages.

'The bull elk is renowned for its courage and sexual prowess, Charging Bull. The last thing to decay from the body is the teeth. You will wear the largest tooth from this bull's mouth around your neck. Wear it with pride and in the knowledge that the great elk sacrificed his life for the benefit of the people. Wearing it will give you long life, courage and many children in the years to come.' With that, the Chief used a stone tomahawk to dislodge a large tooth from the mouth of the dead animal and presented it solemnly to the new hunter.

The men set about skinning the animal and preparing a fire. They expertly divided the carcass into sections a man could carry. There was more than enough. They cooked what they couldn't carry and sat around the fire eating their fill.

Charging Bull sat some distance from the fire in a cocoon of solitude. He stared into the distance as he played with the elk's tooth turning it over repeatedly in his hand. The Chief approached and sat beside him.

'What troubles my young warrior?'

'Why did the elk attack? He could have escaped. He had the choice to climb the side of the gully but chose to charge instead. I sensed it.'

'That is a good question, Charging Bull. A chief needs to be wise as well as brave and today you have shown me you posses both these qualities. The elk made a mistake. Remember this if you forget everything else about today. This is the most valuable lesson you can learn. **A hunter may make many mistakes but the hunted, only one.** Always seek to be the hunter and not the hunted, Charging Bull.'

With those words, he slapped the new warrior on his shoulder, stood and left him to absorb the most valuable lesson he would ever learn. The boy, who would be a man, had passed his first rite of passage.

* * * *

Peter woke refreshed in mind and body. He had felt everything in the dream as if he'd lived it. He had been Charging Bull. He'd felt the joy of hitting his first target. He'd felt the sinewy power of his shoulder muscles as he'd pulled the bow. He'd felt the fear as the huge elk charged him but he'd controlled that fear. He'd felt a sense of pride as he saw the warriors looking at him with admiration. Most of all he felt awareness. He was part of a great tradition that had its roots in the ancient past. He could not shirk his responsibility. His duty was to protect the girl and her unborn son and to use the knowledge and customs he had learned from the ancient ones.

What had he learned? The chief had told him that he needed his brothers, echoing Suzie's words. But, what was the most important lesson from the dream? *Always be the hunter and never the hunted.* He realized the spirits were once again guiding him. He would no longer stay in the cabin waiting for danger to come. He would go out onto the mountain, hunt down the danger, and eliminate it.

Chapter Six

The morning light angled through the tall trees shooting beams of light into the clearing like inquisitive fingers. Smoke rose lazily from the remains of the previous night's fire. The occupants of the camp still slept off the effects of the alcohol and marijuana they'd consumed. Under a grubby blanket, a large bundle squirmed, coughed and settled again. Birds sang a morning chorus and one fluttered to the ground, snatched a morsel of bread and flew away. Nothing stirred. It was a signal and others soon followed to pick up what sustenance they could find.

A head poked gingerly out from under a large blanket and looked around, blinking in the morning light. It belonged to a long-haired young woman. She sat up and eased out from under the cover, careful not to disturb its other occupant. She was naked and shivering but not from the cold. Bruises and welts stood out starkly on her pale flesh and leaves clung to her blond hair as she fumbled around for her clothes and shoes. The bundle she'd escaped from moved and she froze, eyes wide, and sent up a silent prayer. The movement stopped, she breathed again and finished retrieving her clothes, shoes and a canteen of water. She held them in an untidy bundle in her arms as she crept from the camp, ignoring the macabre sight of a dead body pinned to a tree by several arrows. She held her breath until she reached the relative safety of the surrounding forest. Then she was gone; birds fluttered back to earth and pecked at the ground as if she was never there.

The sun climbed higher, sent a shaft of blinding light through a gap in the trees and into the bloated face of a sleeping figure. He stirred, coughed and opened his eyes. He blinked several times in quick succession to adjust his sight to the dazzling brightness and moaned as a shooting pain racked his skull. Dehydration, from the alcohol, had shrunk his brain and caused his headache. The harsh smoke from the cannabis had left him with a sore throat, dry mouth and cracked lips. He sat up, fighting dizziness, and looked around for a source of water to relieve his woes. The noise he made roused a mangy dog that'd been asleep by the fire. The dog stood on shaky legs and stretched its sinewy body. Birds flew off in a flurry of squawks and fluttering wings, disturbing another sleeping figure into life. Slowly, the camp came awake.

A man rose from under the blanket the blonde-haired girl had shared. He stood, stretched and yawned in the morning sun. He stood several inches over six feet and with his muscular, tattooed arms stretched above his head he looked like a statue of a war hero celebrating victory. He let out a huge growl and dropped his arms, shattering the illusion. The bearded giant wore dirty jeans and oil stained boots. He wore no shirt but sported a denim vest with the colors of his motorcycle club covering the back. His patch identified him as a member of the Predators. Nazi emblems adorned his colors like Boy Scout merit badges. A 9mm pistol protruded from his waistband and a red bandanna held his hair from his eyes. He noisily cleared his throat and spat a glutinous glob onto the forest floor.

'Where is that whore? Hey, Julie, bring your ass here, now!' His deep voice rose to a shout. He glared around the clearing, looking for the girl. Julie had vanished.

'Bitch,' he muttered. He took two huge strides and kicked an inert bundle on the forest floor. The figure rolled and thrashed, fighting to extricate itself from the blanket before another vicious kick arrived. A tousle-haired girl, dressed in the Predators' colors, rose from the tangle and looked fearfully at the giant.

'Spice, go find that blonde witch and make her fix me some breakfast.'

The girl stared at him in a show of defiance, 'What d'you need her for? She's flabby and soft. I'm all the "old lady" you need.'

He glared at her, took a step closer and clenched his fists. It was all he needed to do.

'OK, Mitch, I'll find the skank. No worries.'

She ran off before he used his fists on her.

The yelling woke the whole camp. It came to life as figures emerged from under blankets like corpses rising from shallow graves. Three more Predators in full colors emerged into the light blinking like vampires scared of the dawning sun. Two bearded men, almost as big as Mitch, gathered around the fire together with a shorthaired brunette whose jeans seemed painted onto her long, skinny legs. All sported tattoos; the girl had nose and eyebrow rings to complete her ensemble. They kicked at the fire, trying to elicit some extra warmth.

The rest of the party contained a mixed cross-section of all ages and both sexes. Some, like the Ranger, had joined the bikers against their will but many gravitated to them for protection, seeking a strong leader in uncertain times. One sleepy-eyed young girl of three clung to her mousey mother as if her life depended on it. It probably did. The Ranger stood off to one side, the holster on his leather belt empty as air. Downtrodden and forlorn, his shoulders slumped as he yawned and rubbed the sleep from his eyes.

Mitch spotted him, 'Hey ranger, collect the canteens, go to the stream and bring us water. Hurry up, I'm thirsty. And, if you even think about spitting in them, I'll kill you.'

Ranger Martin retained a small vestige of pride, so he didn't run to obey the order. He strolled across the clearing to collect Mitch's canteen. One of the Predators took a run up and booted him hard in the backside.

'Run, boy, don't keep your master waiting.' Humiliated and beaten, the Ranger scurried to pick up the canteen. Mocking laughter followed him to the nearby stream.

The Predators dominated the group and Mitch was their nominal leader. People dressed and prepared for the day in nervous silence, careful not to catch the attention of Mitch or his cronies. Some felt safe under the protection of such strong leaders but others would swap places with Julie in a heartbeat if they had the courage to go it alone. The tousled-haired girl returned alone and attempted to avoid Mitch's attention but to no avail.

'Hey, Spice, don't think I don't see you. I can smell you! Where's the girl?'

'There's no sign of her, Mitch. She's gone.'

'She'll be back. The first sniff of a bear and she'll come scurrying back begging for protection. Now, fix me some breakfast like a good old lady.'

Mitch joined the gathering by the dying embers of the fire. He poked a stick at the fire in a desultory fashion. Sparks rose and crackled in the morning air but no flame caught. The fire had run its course. The biker pointed to the nearest youth.

'Hey, you, get this fire going and boil some water.'

The youth rushed to obey. The gang soon lost interest in him. Mitch looked around his fellow bikers.

'The body of that old madman's gonna start stinking the place out. We should bury him.'

'Nah, fuck that, this place is a mess now. We'll move on today and make another camp further up the mountain,' the brunette declared.

A biker with Jeb stitched on his colors spoke up, 'Me and Billy-Bob was thinking the same thing. We still looking for that fella the Ranger told us about?'

'Yeah. He's s'posed to have a lot of food stored for the winter. We need it more than he does.'

'The Ranger says he's ex-military so he might not be a pushover.'

'So am I. You think I can't take him?' Mitch stared hard at Jeb.

'No man. I didn't mean that. I know you can take anyone.'

'Well stop worrying about it. We'll tie him to a tree and have some fun, just like we did with that other mountain freak last night.'

The Predators laughed and the rest of the group relaxed a little. Their day would be a lot less stressful if the bikers were in a good mood.

The youth re-kindled the fire and Spice and the brunette called Cydney bullied some of the women into making coffee and heating some of the leftover bear meat from the night before. Billy-Bob rolled a huge joint and soon the camp echoed to laughter and loud voices.

Julie was still close enough to the camp to hear the laughter and smell the acrid smoke from the fire mixed with the sweet smell of marijuana. Although she was petrified of Mitch, she was hungry and wary of the forest. She'd avoided Spice with ease; the girl hadn't really searched that hard for her. She hung around, hoping the group would break camp and maybe leave some food behind. She'd heard Mitch talking to the Ranger and knew he was on the trail of some mountain man with a supply of food and a safe cabin somewhere high up the mountain. Julie knew he would break camp soon to go in search of it. She also figured that there wouldn't be enough food for all the group and wondered what Mitch's solution would be. She had a pretty good idea. Once the group became a liability, he would kill them. She had come to know how cold and cruel he was.

She pulled her jacket tighter around her shoulders and waited to see what would develop as the day wore on.

In the camp, the three-year-old began to cry. The mother was frantic. She could tell by the way her daughter cried that it was serious. The young girl was in pain. Maybe it was the water from the stream or the half-cooked bear meat. Suddenly the girl vomited, caught her breath and wailed even louder. Ignoring the sticky mess, the mother hugged the girl tightly in an attempt to sooth her and silence her cries. It didn't work. The mother stared glassy-eyed as Mitch walked over with a dark look in his eyes.

'What's wrong with that brat? Can't you keep her quiet?'

'I'm sorry. She's sick. I'll take care of her.'

'Stop her crying or I will,' he said with menace dripping from every syllable.

The woman knelt, placed the girl gently on the ground and began to clean away the vomit from her face using the hem of her blouse. The girl stopped crying. Mitch turned away and the woman breathed a sigh of relief. It was short lived as her daughter began to wail louder than before. Mitch turned and in one smooth, unhurried motion pulled his pistol from his waistband and shot the three-year-old girl between the eyes.

A silence fell over the forest as if nature gasped in shock at the callous, evil deed that had unfolded in the clearing. No one in the camp moved. Mitch tucked his gun back into his pants, turned and walked away as if nothing had happened. No one else moved. It was like a bizarre movie scene where everyone froze in place while the villain moved about free to rob and pillage. The Predators were used to violence but even they stood and gaped at the bloody sight of the slaughtered child.

The mother broke the silence with a chilling scream of anguish and anger. She rose and ran at the retreating Mitch raining blows ineffectually on his broad back. He stopped, turned, struck her to the ground, pulled his gun from his pants and shot the mother in identical fashion to her daughter. He glared at the dead woman for a few seconds and then looked up at the people staring at him. He waved the gun for them all to see and challenged them.

'Is there anyone else, while I've got my gun out?' They looked away. 'I didn't think so. Now pack up and get ready to leave. This place is getting real messy.'

The group hurried to obey Mitch and one teenager called out for the skinny dog that had attached itself to the group. The dog had disappeared after the first shot and hadn't returned. The youth shrugged. The dog had sense enough to run and keep on running - maybe he should do the same.

Julie heard the shots but couldn't see the results. She could only guess that some unlucky souls had met their fate. Maybe they weren't so unlucky after all, she mused. Surviving in the shadow of Mitch and the Predators was a living hell and she was glad to be free of it. She shuddered as she recalled the previous night's rape and felt anger and hatred swell in her chest. Somehow she would kill that evil bastard Mitch. Quite how she would manage it she didn't know. She was alone, defenseless and no match for the giant biker.

Julie longed to see into the camp. She recalled her childhood when she had played in the tree house adjacent to her parent's property. From its vantage point, she could see into her neighbor's yard and knew all their business. She looked up at the tree she was hiding behind and cast an appraising eye over the trunk. She worked out the first several foot and handholds, stood and began to haul herself the tree.

Some time later, she found a sturdy branch with good foliage and settled herself onto the wide limb. She could see into the camp and watched the group preparing to leave. She felt safe for the first time in days and allowed herself to relax. The tension drifted from her leaving her drained; her body shut down and she fell into a deep healing sleep.

Chapter Seven

Peter managed to bathe, wash his clothes and prepare tea before Suzie woke for the day. She found him sitting on the porch with Mishka at his feet.

'Good morning, Peter.'

'Good afternoon, sleepyhead.'

Suzie managed a weak smile at his attempted humor. The sun wasn't even above the tree line and she guessed it was around five am.

'Any more tea?'

Peter rested his cup on the porch rail, ducked inside and fixed her a fresh cup of tea. He returned to the porch where she had purloined his chair. He gave a rueful smile to Suzie as he passed her the cup, 'I hope you're comfortable.'

'Yes, thanks. Did you sleep well?' she asked, her eyes full of innocence.

He looked sideways at her. She had a habit of getting in his head. Could she possibly know about his dream? He thought not.

'I had a dream,' was all he offered.

'So, are you any clearer about what you should do?'

'Yes. I'm taking the initiative. I'm going after them. I'm not waiting for them to find us.'

'Good. I told you things would seem easier after a good night's sleep.'

Peter raised his eyes to the sky.

'I do hate an "I told you so".'

Suzie smiled.

'So, when are you going?'

'I'm heading out this morning as soon as I've eaten. I want you to keep Mishka here.'

'I'm not sure she'll stay. Why don't you want her with you?'

'I don't know how she'll react if I get close to strangers. She might get over-excited and give away my position.'

'Well, I'll try. But, I'm not sure she'll listen to me if she wants to follow you.'

Peter said nothing. He sharpened a Bowie knife on a grinding stone while she finished her tea. She could contain herself no longer.

'It must have been some dream you had.' She looked away suppressing a smile.

'Yes it was,' he said and left it at that. She shrugged and remained silent. He would tell her in due time. Peter filled up on some cold potatoes for energy and set off as the sun's rays rose above the tree line.

He headed to the area where he'd last 'seen' the large group in his vision two days previously. He set a course to approach their camp from below, so took a circuitous route. It was a crisp, clear morning and he made good time. He traveled light, carrying water, Bowie knife, shotgun and ammunition. He moved through the trees using years of hunting experience to become invisible and silent.

The rising sun told him it was mid-morning when he heard the first shot. It was a pistol shot and the crack of it sent startled birds high into the sky to fly in confused circles. A deathly silence followed and Peter felt sorrow grip him as if a great tragedy had occurred. He felt a sense of sadness greater than he'd ever experienced before. He shared an immense loss with the forest and felt the acute pain of Mother Earth in every fiber of his being. A second shot echoed off the mountain and the feeling of anguish turned to anger. Evil had manifested itself on the mountain and left a scar that only time and retribution could heal. He wanted to be the instrument of retribution. He felt compelled to redress the balance in the forest. He pushed on, anxious to meet the evil head on.

His heightened senses helped him avoid twigs and fallen branches that threatened to trip him or crack and give away his position. Sure-footed as a mountain goat and quiet as a cat on a hunt he sped down the trail towards the enemy. He accepted his supernatural awareness of the forest as part of his development. The sun rose to signal the approach of midday and he smelled the scent of the camp for the first time. He was five hours from his cabin.

As he approached the camp, a silence fell over the forest. The smell of wood smoke mingled with the scent of death to produce a perfume of unadulterated evil. The overhanging trees cast dark shadows that reflected his somber mood. It appeared the forest wore mourning black for the occasion. He found Ben's body first. He picked up a bow and otter-skin arrow pouch about twenty feet from the tree where Ben sat. As he approached, he saw the grisly details and his stomach lurched. Someone had tied the old man to the tree and used him for target practice using his own arrows. Only God knew how much he'd suffered before one of the arrows took his life.

The monstrous sight repulsed Peter. Somewhere in the back

of his mind, alarm bells rang. Despite his madness, Ben was a skilled tracker and vastly experienced on the mountain. His knowledge and skills were superior to Peter's. How had they caught him? How had they trapped the best trapper on the mountain? A chill ran down Peter's spine. He looked around the clearing. He wished he had brought Mishka. He placed Ben's bow and pouch beside the tree and scouted the rest of the camp.

He soon found the dead woman with the body of her child mere feet away. He realized the significance of the two shots he'd heard earlier and why he'd felt such a sense of loss. The death of the small child had torn at the soul of the forest and he'd experienced the feeling.

With the familiar lurch and tingling sensation, he fell under the spell of another vision. He witnessed the slaying. He saw the callous way the big biker dispatched the girl and the indifference he showed in killing her mother. His legs weakened, as he returned to the present, and he collapsed onto the ground next to the stiffening bodies. He could have done without the spirits showing him that. The gift was truly a curse. At least he knew the source of the orange glow and the significance of the shots he'd heard earlier. The neo-nazi biker oozed evil from every pore.

Oblivious of potential danger lurking in the woods, Peter buried the two females in shallow graves, which he covered with rocks to keep them safe from small scavengers. It was the best he could do under the circumstances. Remembering Suzie, he recited the Lord's Prayer over the pathetic mounds as he gave in to the tears that welled up. It seemed a trivial tribute to an innocent child with her whole life ahead of her, but it was the only prayer he knew.

Peter turned his attention to Ben. Regardless of the man's madness, it was a horrible way to die. The growing heat made Peter strip to his waist as he prepared the old man for burial. Anger slowly built up in Peter as he removed each arrow from the stiffened body with tenderness and care. He turned the old man on his side and covered him with earth, leaves and rocks. He looked down at the mound and once again said the Lord's Prayer. He added a few words at the end.

'I'll get him for you, Ben. I'll make him pay.' Peter shocked himself with the venom of his words. He had no doubt that the big biker he'd seen in his vision was responsible for Ben's fate.

He collected the arrows, took them to the nearby stream and washed the last vestiges of Ben's blood from them. He filled the pouch with the arrows, cast around behind the tree and found several more that had missed their target. He thought about the hours of craftsmanship that had gone into making each arrow and marveled at the old man's patience and expertise. Without making a conscious decision, he placed his shotgun on the forest floor and emptied his pockets of shells. He slung the pouch over his shoulder using the leather strap and picked up the bow. He felt comfortable with the light weight of the ancient weapon. It would be fitting to use the bow to exact revenge for Ben's death. It made no sense to swap his powerful and deadly shotgun for the unfamiliar bow but it felt right and Peter was at peace with his decision.

He'd heard the shots around mid-morning. Assuming that the group had broken camp soon afterwards, they had about three hours' head start on him. The group would struggle with the uphill trail and Peter felt sure he could catch them in short order, but they were much closer to Suzie, and his cabin, than he was. He cast a last look around the camp and prepared to pick up their trail.

He took note of the damage they had inflicted on the surrounding area. The indifference to nature appalled him. They had chopped down a tree to make a fire when fallen branches were available everywhere he looked. Empty spirit bottles littered the forest floor together with plastic packaging that would pollute the environment for eons. They had hunted and killed a small bear and left meat and fur to rot in the clearing. None of this compared to the three corpses they had left but it further enraged Peter. These well-armed, extremely dangerous men had no regard for life or nature. They were a formidable enemy - but so was Peter.

He selected a charred piece of wood from the ashes of the campfire and rubbed it into his skin to blur the outline of his body. He drew marks on his face similar to the camouflage paint he'd used in the Marines. Unknown to him, it was also a technique that Suzie's ancestors had employed many centuries in the past. He found the trail of his quarry at the northern end of the camp and set off to track them down. With his painted torso and bow in hand, he looked for all the world like a native warrior, a modern version of Charging Bull.

Silence descended on the camp. Seconds passed, then minutes. Sometime later, Julie broke free of the trees and entered the clearing, rubbing sleep from her eyes. She had awakened in time to watch Peter from her vantage point high in the tree and had fought the temptation to join him at the graveside of the young girl and her mother. She wasn't ready to risk her life with another strange man just yet.

She found Peter's discarded shotgun and shells. She felt the weight of the weapon in her hands and smiled with satisfaction.

Her brother had shown her the rudiments of shooting and she was somewhat familiar with the pump action and the loading mechanism. She pocketed the shells, made sure the safety was on and cradled the weapon in her arms as she followed Peter's trail from the clearing. She now had the means to kill that bastard, Mitch. She strode with purpose and determination.

* * * *

Suzie had distracted Mishka to allow Peter to leave the camp. She'd spent the morning playing games with the exuberant dog and feeding it tidbits from Peter's stock of provisions. Now girl and dog sat on the porch and caught their collective breaths. Suzie ruffled the big dog's fur as Mishka took noisy breaths through her open mouth to cool herself after the morning's exertions.

Two shots echoed faintly in the distance several seconds apart. Mishka jumped up and barked a loud warning. Her tail stood to attention, her ears twitched and the fur rose on her hackles.

'It's OK, girl. It's nothing. Come here and sit down.' Suzie beckoned to the dog with shaking hands. The shots had come from the general direction Peter had taken. The dog ran to Suzie with eyes wide, stopped and ran a few paces away and looked back at the girl. She repeated the exercise three times before grabbing the girl's arm in frustration and tugging fiercely. It was obvious the dog wanted to investigate the shots and needed Suzie to accompany her. Suzie took a firm hold on the fur above the dog's neck.

'It's OK, girl. Hush.'

She rubbed the animal's chest to reassure and calm it. The

dog's sides heaved and Suzie could feel its heartbeat racing. A soft whine escaped from Mishka's throat. She was concerned for her master. It took the girl many minutes to calm the animal. No more shots echoed in the distance and the dog settled after several minutes. It lay down and the girl released her hold. Mishka remained alert. The loyal dog sat on its haunches with ears pricked and stared into the forest.

The shots worried the girl and left her restless. She needed to meditate. The dog seemed calm so Suzie stepped off the porch and sat cross-legged on the bare earth. She closed her eyes and cleared her mind. Within minutes, she drifted into a deep trance and tranquility descended on the small clearing.

Mishka seized her chance to slink away while the girl was distracted. She picked up her master's scent at the edge of the tree line and set off at a steady lope to find him.

* * * *

Peter ran, bent at the waist, at a fast pace. He easily followed the trail the Predators left. He felt the familiar tingling sensation as he ran and seemed to drift between two realities. He was Peter but also Charging Bull. He stopped, scared. He pinched himself and slapped his own face. He was Peter Friel and this was the 21st century. He fleetingly regretted leaving his shotgun behind. He couldn't afford to slip into a fantasy world while he hunted. He could end up being the hunted himself. Maybe that's what happened to old Ben.

Despite the dreams and visions, he was not Charging Bull. But, why did he find himself half naked with a bow and tracking like a native? He remembered Suzie's words to him. Maybe this was the natural flow of life that he must tap into.

Anyway, it was too late to go back for the shotgun. Besides, in the hands of an expert like Charging Bull, the bow was more accurate over long distances. He looked up at the sky, let out a war cry and resumed his run. The tingling soon returned but this time he didn't fight it.

* * * *

Peter's quarry stopped for respite at mid-afternoon. The constant partying each night had taken its toll on the Predators' stamina and they found the uphill trek draining. Once again, Ranger Martin found himself ordered to fill the canteens while the rest of the party collapsed in the shade. He walked thirty yards through trees and bush to a small tributary of the main stream. They had been walking parallel to it for some time. He carried over a dozen assorted water bottles and canteens.

He'd worked out a simple system to fill the canteens with water and add a purification tablet to each one. It didn't pay to keep Mitch waiting. He cursed as some small floating debris found its way into the neck of one of the canteens. Before he could tip it out, a hand clasped around his mouth and a knife pressed against his throat. His bladder emptied. His time was up.

'Don't struggle, it's Peter Friel,' a voice whispered.

Strong hands flipped him onto his back and a knee pinned him to the ground while one hand remained over his mouth. Martin looked up and saw the blurred tip of the biggest knife he'd ever seen floating just above his left eye. Through his right, he saw the face of a determined and fierce man who resembled someone he knew.

Peter's eyes bored into the ranger's skull, 'Tim, calm down.

It's me, Peter. Do you recognize me?' He kept his voice to a whisper.

Tim Martin nodded. His eyes bulged and a vein stood out on the side of his forehead but he didn't struggle. Peter took a quick tally of the water bottles.

'Is it one water bottle for each person?'

The Ranger nodded.

'So, there are fourteen people including you?'

The Ranger gave a nod in response.

'Do you know where they're leading you?'

Once again, the Ranger nodded.

'Are you heading for my cabin?'

Tim Martin hesitated, weighed his options and nodded again. Peter looked deep into the man's eyes and saw fear growing there.

'You told them about me.'

It wasn't a question. Peter hadn't realized, until now, just how expressive human eyes could be in isolation. He saw the fear in the ranger's eyes turn to desperation. He was convinced that Peter was going to kill him. Desperate men can do dangerous things.

'Listen carefully. I'm not going to kill you. Do you understand?'

The uniformed man nodded as tears flooded his eyes.

'I'm going to release you in a few seconds. I want you to take a canteen of water for yourself and run like hell back down the mountain. Don't stop until you collapse. You got that?'

The man nodded so hard Peter thought his neck would break.

'You make any noise or call out and I **will** kill you.' Peter pushed the knife close to the ranger's throat for emphasis. The tip pressed against soft flesh.

He released the trembling man. For a few seconds, Martin remained frozen to the ground. Then he swiveled, snatched a canteen, and scrambled on all fours until he was out of sight. Peter left the spare water bottles for the gang to discover but pocketed the purification tablets the Ranger had dropped. It might work to his advantage if the gang couldn't boil their water and ended up with dysentery. He scanned the far bank for cover, waded across the small stream and hid himself in the bushes on the other side. He settled himself into a comfortable position and waited to see who would come looking for the Ranger.

He had a rough idea of the breakdown of the party after tracking them all morning. There were five bikers including two females. Peter assumed they controlled the group. That left eight other people once he took the Ranger out of the equation. There were no small children but he'd seen a couple of teenagers. The three male bikers were the main danger but he could not discount the rest out of hand. Everyone in this part of the country had a casual familiarity with guns. Whether the bikers allowed them all to carry was another story. Martin had been unarmed. He focused his attention over the stream. They would come looking for the Ranger soon now.

Chapter Eight

Mitch sat down in frustration, picked up a rock and hurled it with all his might. It hit the base of a tall tree many yards away and startled a critter, which scurried away. They had travelled less than two miles since breaking camp that morning. The terrain was steeper than it looked and had soon taken its toll on the motley group. They'd slept rough for several days and most of their calories had come from alcohol. Even the Predators suffered and they were hardened drinkers.

Mitch's stamina was unaffected and he cursed everyone around him for their weakness. He should get rid of the dead wood. They'd travel faster without the soft civilians. Besides, what good would they really be in a fight? Would they be useful against the army vet they sought? Just having sheer numbers might give them an extra edge. So, he would tolerate them for now.

He stood, as Cydney marched up the incline to confront him. She came to a halt just feet away; arrogance manifested itself in her stance despite the fact that the steep slope forced her to look up at him.

'We're not making good time,' she stated.

'I know. There's too many of us, Cyd'

'I'm gonna take Jeb, push on ahead and find this guy's cabin.'

'How you gonna find it?'

'I had a nice long talk with the Ranger and he was very co-operative,' she said with a grin. 'It's simple as long as you know the right tributary to follow up the mountain. Besides I took this from him.' She brandished a small hand-held GPS receiver, 'The battery's about gone but the cabin's position is recorded clearly,'

Mitch knew how Cydney persuaded people to be "co-operative" and felt almost sorry for the Ranger. Almost but not quite.

'We should all go together. This guy's supposed to be able to handle himself,' Mitch said.

'Really? You mean like that other mountain man I captured?'

The big man stared at the wiry girl. She matched his stare with blazing eyes. He towered over her but seemed to shrink under her gaze. As always happened, he dropped his eyes first.

'What guns are you taking?' He almost whispered the question.

'I'll take my favorite pistol.' She held out her hand.

Without fuss, Mitch pulled the weapon from his waistband and handed it to the girl. She took it from him and held out her other hand. He reached into his vest and passed her two spare clips.

'Jeb's taking the hunting rifle we stole from the supply store.'

He nodded; she turned on her heel and walked off leaving Mitch staring at her colors as she strutted away. He sat brooding for ten minutes. She always pushed his buttons but he could never deny her. It had been that way since they were kids.

Where was that idiot Ranger with the water? He'd been gone long enough to drain the entire river. He didn't have the balls to take off - or did he? Mitch looked towards the stream. He saw most of the party but none of them held a canteen.

'Hey, Spice, go find our Ranger friend and bring the damn water back,' he shouted.

He watched the girl walk towards the stream and, once again, his thoughts turned to Cydney. Where was Billy-Bob? He was master-at-arms and Mitch needed another weapon. He stormed through the temporary camp and found the bearded biker sitting against his backpack on the mountain floor.

'Give me another gun. The Luger will do.'

Billy-Bob struggled to his feet and searched through his pack until he found the black gun. He checked it was loaded and offered it to Mitch who snatched it from his grasp twisting his finger in the process. Billy-Bob grimaced in pain.

'What's the matter, Mitch? Her Highness took your gun?'

The punch took Billy-Bob on the point of the chin. He never saw it coming. He regained consciousness a few seconds later. Mitch had vanished. He picked himself off the ground and cursed his big mouth. He knew how sensitive Mitch was about his sister, Cydney. She was the only person in the world who scared the big biker. He wondered what hold she had over him.

* * * *

Peter saw the girl emerge from the brush and look up and down the stream with a frown on her face. She wore the denim jerkin of the motorcycle gang but it seemed out of place on her. She walked a few yards downstream, stopped and turned. She found the abandoned water bottles and looked upstream shading her eyes from the afternoon sun. She then did something that Peter found strange. She called out in a soft voice.

'Ranger Martin, where are you? Are you OK?' she seemed more concerned than frustrated. She scanned the riverbank again without success. She cupped her hands in front of her mouth to call out again but another loud voice disturbed her.

'Spice! Where are you?' She turned and responded.

'Over here, Mitch.'

Peter removed an arrow from the pouch and notched his bow with a smooth deliberate action. He was low to the ground and held the bow horizontally. He kept his mouth closed and breathed slow and even through his nose. Mitch emerged onto the riverbank. Peter recognized him at once. He'd seen him in the vision butchering the young girl and her mother. Did he trust the vision enough to be judge and executioner? Should he shoot the man in cold blood? He had to decide soon and act fast. He would have to break cover to use the bow. Once he did, he would be committed. There would be no going back. Charging Bull would not hesitate - but Peter did.

'Where's that fool Ranger?'

Spice looked up at Mitch, 'I think he took off. There's no sign of him, just the canteens.' She held them up by their straps to show him.

Still Peter hesitated.

'That crazy bastard. I never thought he had the gumption to run for it. At least he's unarmed,' said Mitch.

Peter agonized. He fought an internal battle with the spirit of Charging Bull and lost. He rose to one knee, turned the bow upright, pulled back on the bowstring and sighted the arrow on Mitch's heart. It felt the same as the dream. He felt the tension in his back muscles and the power of the bow. He knew with absolute certainty that he would not miss.

A movement to his right broke his concentration and he

lowered the bow. A girl had appeared from nowhere. How had she got so close without Peter hearing her? Her long blond hair hung over her shoulders as she held Peter's shotgun and pointed it across the stream. Time stood still for the mountain man as he stared at the girl's profile. He found her strikingly beautiful and noble. She spoke and ruined the impression.

'Mitch, you bastard! Die!'

Peter could see that the girl didn't have a proper hold on the shotgun. She aimed at the biker's heart and pulled the trigger. The gun bucked in her hands; the recoil slammed the butt into her shoulder sending her to the ground and the buckshot high and wide of its target.

Mitch snatched the Luger from his waistband with a snarl. Spice grabbed his arm but he shook her off and brought his weapon to bear on the fallen girl less than fifteen feet away. In his anger, he either didn't see Peter or chose to ignore him. It was a fatal mistake. Spice's action had given Peter time to re-adjust his bow and he let fly. The arrow hit Mitch in the throat so hard it stuck out the back of his neck.

The biker sank to his knees. Gurgling noises escaped his throat as blood bubbled out. Shouts came from the camp as people responded to the noise of the shotgun. Peter could hear people running towards the stream. Spice yelled across the water at the girl.

'Julie, run!'

Spice glanced behind her as people approached then she looked back and appeared to see Peter for the first time.

'Go,' she hissed.

Peter didn't stop to wonder at the girl's behavior. He shouldered his bow, ran to Julie, grabbed her by the arm, dragged her off into the trees and ran for all he was worth towing the girl behind him. Too late, he realized he'd left the shotgun behind for a second time.

* * * *

A quarter mile to the north, Cydney paused and smiled at the sound of the shotgun blast. She had pushed Mitch's buttons as she always did. He'd obviously taken a shotgun from Billy-Bob and relieved his frustration on one of the civilians in the party. She looked at Jeb.

'I wonder who Mitch shot this time?'

Jeb laughed as they started up the trail again. He suspected it was the Ranger.

* * * *

Peter took pity on the girl after a long ten minutes' hard running. He stopped and listened hard for signs of pursuit. All he could hear was her gasps as she fought for breath. She collapsed in a heap as he let go of her arm. Julie turned her back to Peter and threw up onto the forest floor. Peter didn't know whether it was a reaction to the violence or the effort of the forced flight down the mountain. The blonde didn't have much in her stomach and dry heaved several times. He tapped her on the shoulder and gave her his canteen.

Drinking silenced the girl and Peter heard no sounds of pursuit. He leaned against a tree and looked at the blonde woman as she brought her breathing under control.

'Are you OK?'

Her eyes widened, 'Oh yes. Just perfect.'

Peter scowled, he'd deserved that response. *What a stupid*

question. She rubbed her shoulder and winced. He reached out a hand.

'Let me look at that.'

She pulled away. He dropped his hand.

'Sorry, I didn't mean anything. The recoil from the shotgun's gonna leave a nasty bruise, miss.' He experienced déjà vu. This was the second time he'd used the title 'miss' in as many days. There were too many people on his mountain.

'Tell me something I don't know.'

Peter's expression hardened. He'd just saved her life and she was giving him attitude. He didn't need this even if she was beautiful. Suzie was alone in the cabin and he was further away than before after their headlong flight down the mountain. *Thank God, she has Mishka,* he thought. He reached out, took the canteen back from the girl, put the stopper in and slung the strap over his shoulder.

She sensed he was going to walk away and her attitude changed in a heartbeat.

'Thanks for coming to my rescue back there.' She seemed suddenly vulnerable. Her hard shell evaporated and Peter softened.

'That's OK. We were both after the same person and the enemy of my enemy is my friend, as they say.'

'Do you think he's dead?'

'If he's not, he soon will be. He's hit bad and there aren't any hospitals up here. He'd have to be one tough hombre to survive that.'

She looked at the ground, 'His name's Mitch - he's a bastard and real tough, trust me.'

'Well, I don't think he's so tough right now. What were you doing trying to ambush him and where did you get my gun?'

'I escaped from that damned rapist this morning' Julie almost spat the words, 'I watched you bury the girl and her mother from a nearby tree and I picked up the gun you left and followed you. I figured you were going after them.'

Peter stared at the girl with an appraising look that made her uncomfortable.

Her eyes widened as a thought struck her, 'Are you the guy with a cabin up the mountain?'

Peter remained stone-faced.

'Why do you ask?'

'We, well that is they, are coming for you. They want your food. They'll take it from you, mister.'

'Yeah, I know. But, now that I shot their leader it should take the wind out of their sails. I'll be OK for a while, until they regroup. My dog's up there guarding the place anyway.' Peter kept Suzie a secret from the girl.

As if on cue, a rustle of leaves and a bark signaled Mishka's breathless arrival from behind a clump of trees. She ran full pelt at Peter, breaking fallen branches like twigs in her haste. She knocked Peter off his feet and they ended up in an untidy tangle on the ground. Peter settled the dog and it lay panting on the ground looking warily at Julie.

'I guess my dog's not guarding the cabin after all,' Peter said with a grin. The girl's next statement wiped the smirk from his face.

'There's more bad news. Mitch acts tough but the ultimate power belongs to his sister, Cydney. She's real evil and manipulative. She pulls his strings like a puppet-master. You should see the pleasure she took when they were using that old guy as target practice last night.'

'You're not serious!'

'I wish I wasn't. She orchestrated the whole thing. She went out in the forest and tricked him somehow. She and a biker called Jeb brought him back all neatly tied up last evening. I saw her and Jeb leave the camp and head up the mountain ten minutes before I took the shot at Mitch.'

Peter's face turned white, he had been convinced that Mitch was the source of the orange glow. It seemed he was wrong. The spirits had sent him mixed signals.

'I've gotta go.'

'Let me come with you,' she pleaded.

'You'll slow me down.'

'No I won't. I've hunted with my brother since I was a little girl. I can move quick and silent.'

With sudden insight he understood how she'd come so close to him by the stream without his knowledge. He re-assessed the girl. She looked athletic and fit.

'Look, it's like this - there's a pregnant girl sheltering in my cabin. I must protect her. I need to get there before this Cydney does. You can't help me.'

'I'm a nurse.'

Peter froze. She was a nurse? God, he would need her when the baby came. He made an instant decision.

'Drink some more water now. We're gonna move fast. We won't be stopping to rest. If you get left behind, wait where you stop. I'll come back for you later. Do you understand?' He wasted no words, rattling out orders military style.

She nodded and bent down to tighten her bootlaces. Peter cinched the straps holding his canteen and arrow-pouch. Sweat had made the charcoal on his torso smudge a little but he ignored that. He glanced down at Mishka. The dog had incredible stamina and would range far and wide as the two humans struggled up the mountain. She would find her own water and food on the way if she needed to. Mishka was the least of his worries. He looked at the girl.

'I'm Peter.'

'Julie.'

'You ready?'

She nodded. They set off.

* * * *

'Shut up!' Billy-Bob yelled.

The civilians fell silent as Spice attended to Mitch. He'd passed out allowing the girl to examine the wound without fuss. She'd had medical training and knew the wound would probably be fatal. But, she had to try. She pointed at a young woman, who didn't seem too shaky.

'Grab one of the boys and get a fire going. Boil some water. Billy-Bob, bring me the strongest bottle of spirits we've got left and don't drink any! We scored some penicillin and morphine when we raided the pharmacy, didn't we?'

Billy-Bob gulped and nodded.

'Bring those too - and hurry!'

She looked around the subdued group.

'Anyone who has any clean linen left is to bring it to me now. Any of you ladies have a needle and thread? Does anybody have any first-aid kits? Bring it all to me now. Quickly!'

Mitch lay where he'd fallen. He was too big to move even had Spice wanted to risk it. The initial rush of blood had slowed to a trickle, which told her the arrow had somehow missed any arteries. That was a miracle in itself. The next miracle would be to remove the arrow without killing Mitch.

She crossed herself and took a deep breath. She hadn't trained for this.

Billy-Bob grabbed the bottle of 151-proof rum from its hiding place in the bottom of his backpack. His hands shook. His whole world had turned upside down. He was a follower - not a leader. He was muscle not brains. He was master-at-arms but way down the pecking order in the club's hierarchy. Cydney had gone off up the mountain and taken his mentor, Jeb. Some crazy mountain man had shot Mitch with an arrow. A fucking arrow, for God's sake! Now, that little timid bitch, Spice, was giving orders. She'd never said boo to a goose until now. Who died and put her in charge? She wasn't even a full member of the club. He defiantly unscrewed the top of the rum and took a huge swig. He choked and coughed. Damn, that was strong. He found the penicillin, morphine and several syringes in a plastic bag in the outside pocket of his backpack and grabbed them ready to go. He heard Spice calling to him from the stream. He took one more gulp of rum, replaced the bottle top and set off at a jog. Deep inside he was glad someone had taken charge even if it was that little shrew, Spice.

Chapter Nine

'Hit me harder.'

Jeb hesitated. She slapped him.

'Hit me harder. Make me bleed.'

Jeb tightened his fist and hit her flush in the mouth. His tacky skull-ring opened a gash under her lip and she tasted blood. Her breath became ragged.

'Harder!'

This time his fist caught Cydney high on the temple and she staggered. He saved her from falling by grabbing her upper arm. She brushed his hand away. Again she slapped him; trying to provoke a violent response. It worked. He backhanded her across her left cheek and, once again, his ring opened a gash. He followed up with an immediate right hook that dropped her to the ground.

She fell on her back. He bent to help her up.

'Leave me,' she ordered.

Jeb watched Cydney with caution. She rubbed the back of her hand across her bloodied mouth and grinned up at him with devilment in her eyes. Her denim vest hung open at the front and he saw her erect nipples through her grubby T-shirt. Jeb caught his breath. Violence excited her, sometimes to the point of climax. He felt himself harden. She sat upright, took off her colors with an awkward shrug and handed them to him. She lay back and writhed on the ground as if trying to make a dirt angel. Jeb shook his head, puzzled.

She got to her feet and looked at him. Dirt and blood fought for attention on her white tee shirt. Her faded, oil-stained jeans completed the bedraggled image. Blood seeped from gashes under her eye and lip. One eye was almost swollen shut.

'How do I look?' Blood dripped from her nose.

'Like you been trampled by a bear.'

She grinned wolfishly through the blood and caught him with a roundhouse right that span his head and knocked him back a step.

'What the fuck was that for?' He felt his mouth, checking for loose teeth.

'For hitting me.'

'But, you told me to do it!'

'Yeah, but, you enjoyed it too much.'

He glared at her and her eyes narrowed. She stepped forward, grabbed the hair at the back of his head, pulled him close and kissed him full on the lips. Her tongue forced its way into his mouth, making him grab for her. She pulled away, biting his lip as she pushed him off.

'Later, big boy. It's getting dark. I'm gonna flush him out now. Wait for a head shot and take him out. Tonight, we sleep in his bed.'

They'd found the cabin late in the afternoon and had sat and watched from behind the tree line. Wispy smoke rose from the cabin's single chimney. They'd waited for the occupant to venture outside. The Ranger said that the cabin's owner was an ex-marine. The plan was to take him by surprise in the open clearing. The lack of cover would leave him exposed and vulnerable. One good shot would do it. Evening approached and he remained inside. Their patience reached its limit. Cydney decided to entice him out.

She waited while Jeb lay down and took a bead on the cabin door. She took her pistol from her backpack, jammed it down the back of her pants, turned her back to Jeb, pushed through foliage and walked into the clearing with an exaggerated limp.

'Hey!'

At the sound of her cry, birds exploded from a nearby tree and dispersed with a chorus of squawks. She saw movement at one of the windows.

'Help!' She staggered and fell. Jeb shook his head and smiled grimly. She was good.

Cydney struggled to her feet, held her side and winced.

'Anyone in the cabin? Please help. *Please!*'

The cabin door swung open with a faint creak. A Native American girl emerged holding a shotgun. She squinted her eyes against the setting sun and focused them on the bloodied girl.

'Stay where you are. Who are you?'

Cydney sank to her knees as if in supplication. 'Please, help me. I'm thirsty.'

Jeb had a rifle but he didn't have a target. He stared at the stocky girl. Who the fuck was she? Where was the legendary mountain man? He examined the cabin for any further sign of life. Nothing moved in the doorway or at the windows. He waited.

Suzie stared at the woman. Her face was swollen and bloodied and her clothes worn and dirty. She looked a forlorn figure.

'Please help me, miss. I'm hurting bad.'

Suzie kept the heavy gun pointed unwaveringly at the girl

who swayed in the fading light. Keeping her focus on the girl, Suzie cast quick glances towards the tree line in case danger threatened from that direction. She approached Cydney with caution in every step. As she walked, she changed the angle of her body to allow herself to view the perimeter of the clearing without losing sight of the girl. The growing child in her womb made her ultra cautious.

Cydney sensed the girl's suspicions and sought to distract her. She swayed theatrically, ran her fingers under her nose and examined the resultant blood on her hands. She allowed her legs to buckle and sank to her knees leaning forward on one hand. As she bowed her head, a large drop of blood fell from her nose and landed in the dirt.

Compassion overwhelmed Suzie's sense of danger. She bent, placed the shotgun on the ground, leaving the safety off, cast one more glance towards the trees and moved to the stricken girl. She helped Cydney to her feet and allowed the taller girl to use her as a human crutch as they made their way to the cabin. Still Jeb waited.

Suzie could smell blood and stale sweat and felt the heat coming from the girl. Cydney looked skinny but she leaned on Suzie who staggered along with bent knees struggling with her weight. Jeb watched from his hiding place and frowned. If anyone else was in the cabin, they would surely have come out to help by now. But, still he waited.

Cydney came to the same conclusion as Jeb at about the same time. The girl was alone. The cabin was empty. Using her free hand, she reached around her back, removed the pistol from the waistband of her jeans and jabbed it into Suzie's ribs. At the same time, the arm that she had around Suzie's shoulder tightened to trap the shorter girl in a vise-like grip.

'Where is he, bitch? Where's your man?'

Suzie squirmed in an attempt to break free. She couldn't move. The girl was strong like whipcord. Unable to fight or flee, Suzie controlled her bladder, which threatened to betray her.

'I don't have a man,' she responded, 'I don't need one.' Suzie surprised herself. How could she sound so calm and confident?

'Ha! You definitely need a man, sister.'

Cydney twisted Suzie so that she formed a shield between herself and the cabin. She held the gun against Suzie's head.

'Come out from the cabin or I shoot the girl,' she shouted.

She didn't expect a response. She was sure the cabin was empty. Anyone in the cabin would have covered the girl from behind as she emerged to confront the unexpected visitor. She still erred on the side of caution. She lifted her head and shouted over her shoulder.

'Jeb, come out from there. Come and check the cabin while I hold the girl. Bring my colors. Any surprises and I shoot her.' The last statement was for the benefit of anyone still lurking in the darkness of the cabin.

Jeb had waited behind the tree line like a good soldier obeying orders. He'd fashioned a sniper's nest from their two rucksacks and had an uninterrupted view to the cabin. He'd not seen the slightest sign of life from the cabin since the girl had emerged. He rose to his feet, picked up Cyd's denim vest, draped it over his left shoulder and broke cover. He kept his gun pointed at the cabin door as he closed the distance. He strutted past the two women, sure in the belief the place was empty. Just for the hell of it, he fired a shot into the centre of the door. It hadn't been latched and it swung open in a shower of splinters. The sound of the shot echoed around the mountain.

'You stupid son-of-a-bitch, what are you doing?'

'Relax, Cyd. Just making sure no one was hiding behind the door.'

Cydney cursed under her breath. Why were men so stupid? Jeb might as well have sent out an engraved announcement to the whole damned mountain. Keeping the girl close, she made her way past Jeb and entered the cabin. The sun had long faded and her eyes took a few seconds to adjust to the dim interior; she saw that it was vacant. She pushed the compliant girl onto the bed at the far end of the cabin and turned as Jeb entered the doorway. She walked up to him, snatched her colors from his shoulder and put them on.

'Go get our backpacks and try not to attract any more attention.'

Jeb grinned and ducked out the doorway. Cydney was anal-retentive. So, he had fired the rifle? Big deal. What if the man did come? They would have to face him sooner or later. Might as well get it finished. He tried to remember if there were any flares in his backpack. Firing one off would drive Cydney crazy. He grinned as he pictured her reaction. She would slap him silly, probably become quickly aroused and ride him like a rodeo horse for the rest of the night. The idea suddenly became irresistible and he burst out laughing. He loved to live life on the edge of danger.

Jeb passed the shotgun that Suzie had left on the ground making a mental note to collect it on his way back. He had a good sense of direction and knew unerringly which bush sheltered his sniper's nest. He made a beeline for the backpacks. He pushed through the brush, shouldered the rifle and bent to pick up the packs. It was going to be awkward carrying both bags and the gun.

He heard and saw nothing. The blow came as a shock. His last image was of the bags. Then everything turned black and silent. He had finally met the legendary mountain man.

* * * *

Peter was close to the cabin when he heard the rifle shot echo around the mountain. Despite his exhaustion, he managed to sprint close enough to see the clearing and its occupants. Julie was a couple of hundred yards down the trail and Mishka accompanied her. Peter saw a tall girl in a dirty white tee shirt bundle Suzie into the cabin. A large bearded man carrying a rifle stopped in the doorway behind them. The silhouette of the man revealed much to Peter. Despite the fading light, he clearly saw the colors on the man's denim vest. It was one of the bikers. The tall girl must be Mitch's sister. He was too late.

Peter didn't waste time berating himself. He ruled out charging across the clearing to rescue Suzie as rash and risky. He assessed the terrain and picked the best vantage point. He skirted the clearing to reach the area he had chosen and soon found the two backpacks. They'd return here for sure. He cast around, found a fist-sized rock and melted into the brush to wait.

The biker left the doorway and made straight for the rucksacks. The light was nearly gone and Peter was almost invisible. The man came close and Peter tensed, gripping the rock tightly in his right hand. Jeb bent over and presented an easy target. The rock caught him just below the ear and he fell like a dead tree landing with a resounding thud. Peter stole a glance at the cabin but there was no reaction from that area. He breathed a sigh of relief. It was not a scientific way to render the

93

biker unconscious, and could have killed him, but Peter didn't really care.

He picked up the fallen man's rifle with one hand and with the other dragged the inert figure by the collar to a nearby tree. Peter struggled for several minutes to remove the big man's belt. Night arrived with a vengeance, and Peter used his tactile senses to compensate for the darkness. He felt like a blind man fumbling his way in the inky black. He propped Jeb into a sitting position and looped the belt around his neck and the tree. Using his fingers to feel where the holes were, he tightened the belt enough to secure the biker to the tree without strangling him. He made sure the buckle was as far from the man's reach as possible. Just as he finished, he heard noise on the trail. He picked up the rifle, released the safety and melted into the nearest shadow. Mishka wasn't fooled and found him within seconds. The panting dog licked his face until Peter silenced her with a curt word. Julie shouldn't be far behind. He waited. He could hear the sound of someone coming up the trail. It was dark and someone unfamiliar with the terrain was bound to make a lot of noise. He saw a shadowy figure moving closer. The dark shape stumbled.

'Damn it!' Julie swore in a loud whisper. She had caught up with Peter at last.

He let out his breath, engaged the safety and stood up tall.

'Julie, it's Peter. Follow the sound of my voice and tread softly,' he hissed.

She paused, orientated herself and uncertainly crept the last few yards to him. He reached out, took her arm and gave it a squeeze. She tensed a little and he realized that her night vision was not the best. She hadn't seen him at all.

'I've got one of the biker guys unconscious and tied to a tree.

The girl has my lady-friend prisoner in the cabin. I don't think the bitch knows her friend's missing yet,' He said, summing up the situation neatly for Julie. He led her by the arm to where Jeb sat strapped to the base of the tree trunk. The moon came out from behind heavy cloud cover and bathed the scene in pale white light.

'What's your plan?'

'Off the top of my head, I'm guessing the girl might come out to look for her friend and I may be able to take her.'

'That's not much of a plan.'

'I know. If you think of anything better, do tell.'

* * * *

Cydney soon ordered Suzie off the bed to light the cabin. The blackness of the night had fallen quickly. Peter had a small stock of candles and even a kerosene lamp he rarely used. He usually got up at the first sign of dawn and went to bed at sunset so didn't use much of his precious kerosene reserves. Suzie lit the lamp, trimmed the wick, and hung it from a convenient hook in the ceiling. It gave off enough light to illuminate the whole cabin and cast shadows into the corners.

Suzie said nothing to the girl. She guessed that she was part of the group that Peter had gone after and studied her without being obvious. Her tee shirt exposed her arms and midriff. The sleeveless vest didn't cover much more. She had a slim frame covered in sinewy muscles with prominent veins that hinted at a hidden strength. She had several tattoos that Suzie couldn't make out in the shadowy light. Her stomach muscles were well defined and a piercing highlighted a neat belly button. She looked fit, healthy and strong apart from the superficial injuries to her face. Suzie mentally kicked herself for allowing the girl to trick her so easily. The girl noticed her staring.

'What you looking at, bitch?'

'Nothing. Nothing at all,' Suzie said.

Cydney snorted. She looked around the cabin and spotted the length of cord that Peter used as an indoor clothesline when it rained. She snatched it from the hooks attaching it to the ceiling.

'Sit down on the floor by the bed,' she ordered.

Suzie didn't move. Cydney took two steps and floored her with a backhand slap. She lay there stunned, her head spun and her thoughts swirled. The casual way the girl had used violence shocked Suzie more than the slap itself. She felt strong hands manipulating her like a rag doll and soon found herself bound to the wooden bed frame unable to move. She opened her eyes in time to see the girl open the shutters and look out of the window.

'What's taking that asshole so long?'

Suzie didn't think the girl expected an answer so she didn't reply. She felt very tired as if a huge weight sat on her shoulders. Just formulating thoughts seemed a huge effort. She watched as the girl closed the shutters and moved to the door. She opened it just enough to look out. She waited for Jeb to return, tapping her foot with impatience. Suzie summoned up the energy to speak.

'What do you want? If it's food, I'll gladly share what I have. There's no need for violence or to hold me prisoner.'

'Really, is that why you greeted me with a shotgun?' She opened the door wider.

Before Suzie could think of a suitable reply, a shot rang out.

* * * *

Peter had seen the light come on in the cabin. He settled himself into the same position that Jeb had occupied only minutes before. Mishka lay beside him passive but alert. Julie took a long swig from her water bottle, pulled off her boots and massaged her feet; a soft groan escaped her. Peter had a clear line of sight to the cabin door. He saw the benefits and drawbacks of all the clearing away he had done the previous day. It may have improved the defensive sight lines but it also benefited a sniper. He kept his attention focused on the door. He was sure the girl would soon grow impatient and come looking for her partner.

He watched as the window shutter opened. He saw a silhouette framed in the window but couldn't be sure it wasn't Suzie. Just like Jeb had done, minutes before, he waited. The shutters closed and Peter returned his attention to the door. Cydney rewarded his vigilance within seconds as she slowly edged the door open and peered out. Peter waited for a clear shot.

The door inched open and Cydney's unmistakable figure stood in the doorway. The lamp illuminated her from behind, making her an easy target. Peter went for the kill shot and sighted the rifle on the centre of her head. He let out his breath and squeezed the trigger smoothly. The rifle bucked in his grip and let out a familiar crack as he fired at point blank range. He couldn't miss. Once again, a shot echoed around the mountain and disturbed the wildlife, sending birds flapping skywards.

Chapter Ten

Spice fought to keep her eyes open. Mitch lay where he had fallen. It was dark, and Billy-Bob had built a fire close by. It was more to keep the animals away than to keep the patient warm. Spice had removed the arrow, stopped the bleeding and dressed the wound. She'd shot him full of the penicillin and morphine that Billy-Bob had produced from his backpack. They'd broken into a pharmacy the previous week and emptied the place. Billy-Bob knew almost as much about pharmaceuticals as he did about guns.

It had been a long afternoon. Her medical training at Quantico hadn't prepared her for the trauma of field surgery. Mitch's super-human strength had played a major part in his survival. Her ministrations had only played a minor role. The stress involved had drained her last resolve. This latest drama had come after months of non-stop pressure and anxiety. She was at her breaking point.

Spice was an undercover ATF agent. She had spent two years working her way into a position of trust inside the Predators Motorcycle Club. It had been a long and dangerous two years. From hanging around and performing demeaning tasks she'd finally become an associate member. Being a woman had precluded her from becoming a full member. Her mandate was to clarify Cydney's role in the club and identify the source of its weapons. The agency had been astonished at the incredible power that Cydney wielded within the macho world of the bikers. In the entire country, she was the only fully-fledged female member of the gang - which included more than twenty chapters nationwide. Spice did her best to befriend the girl but although she tolerated her, Cydney preferred the company of men.

Recent events had turned her mission pear-shaped. The worldwide oil crisis had destroyed communications. She was an agent without an agency, alone in the gang, without back up. She had no alternative but to stay. It was better to be a member of a strong group in these uncertain times than to be a woman alone. It was just a matter of survival. Law and order, as she had known it, had broken down. She had participated in a homicide back in the town when the gang had killed a woman in the supply store. That would cause the agency to pull her out of her deep cover if they still operated. They didn't and she was stuck.

'Hey, Spice. He gonna live?'

She looked up and saw Billy-Bob towering over her. He had a shotgun in his hand, a pistol tucked in his waistband and a joint dangling from his lips. He was an accident waiting to happen.

'I don't know. I thought he'd be dead already. It's out of my hands. It's in the lap of the gods now.'

'You talk real strange sometimes,' he said, looking suspiciously at her. 'Where did you learn to doctor?'

Spice's antenna pricked up. She was tired of all the lying and subterfuge. However, she had no choice but to keep up the façade.

'My sister's a surgeon,' she said in a tired voice.

'I never knew you had a sister. You never talked about her before.'

'We didn't get along.'

Billy-Bob grunted. He knew all about that. The Predators were his family now, as his real kin weren't worth shit. He sat down beside the sleepy girl and rested his shotgun on the ground.

'You did real good,' he said.

She looked at him, her eyes widening: she hadn't expected a compliment, 'Thanks.'

He reached out and put his arm around her. She stiffened. The last thing she needed was to fight off his advances.

'Hey, big guy, do me a favor.'

'What?'

'Keep an eye on Mitch while I get some sleep. I'm good for nothing right now. Wake me if there's any change.'

He looked searchingly at her for some seconds, 'OK, I can't sleep anyway.'

Spice checked Mitch's pulse one last time. It was steady and strong. She shook her head in wonder. The guy had the constitution of an ox. She hid the plastic bag of drugs under her vest as she passed Billy-Bob on the way to her bedroll.

'Keep the fire going, man.'

'Sure.'

'Goodnight.'

'Yeah.'

Spice stumbled off to get some sleep while Billy-Bob stoked the fire until it crackled and popped. He sat cross-legged, rolled a joint, took a long drag and stared into the fire. He heard a single rifle shot in the stillness of the night. He fancied he'd heard one earlier but wasn't sure. He listened for several minutes but heard nothing more except the sounds of the forest. He took another deep toke on the joint, relaxed and forgot all about the gunfire.

* * * *

The shot missed. Mishka barked and Peter cursed. The bullet somehow killed the light in the cabin and plunged the clearing into darkness. Peter grabbed Mishka's collar.

'Steady, girl.' His voice was hoarse and shaky. How the hell had he missed? Where had the girl gone? Was she in the cabin or on the porch? Clouds obscured the moon and it was impossible to see anything at all.

'Did you get her?' Julie asked. She sounded panic-stricken.

'No.'

'Are you sure?'

'No.'

'What do you mean?'

'For Christ's sake! What do you think I mean? It's dark. I'm not sure, but I think I missed.'

Tension crackled in the air and Mishka growled at Julie. The blonde women wisely stayed silent. Peter watched the cabin and waited. As the hunter, he could wait.

* * * *

Cydney lay in the doorway unable to move. Her pulse raced. Her heart pumped so hard she thought it would burst from her chest. It was pitch black. The bullet had taken a tiny slice from her ear before knocking the lamp from its hook on the ceiling. Suzie had trimmed the wick low and the fall extinguished the

101

flame before it could ignite any spilled kerosene. Cyd knew the moon could emerge any second, bathe the porch in its eerie light and expose her. She had to move.

Should she go or stay? Should she crawl back into the cabin or disappear into the forest? Where was Jeb? Who had fired at her? How many people were out there? She felt alone, vulnerable and exposed. She detested the feeling. She liked to be in charge. Anger and frustration took over as hatred began to build for the unseen gunman. She had to move, and she had to do it soon. As the hunted, she couldn't wait.

* * * *

Ranger Martin heard a faint rifle shot echo down the mountain. It was the second he'd heard in five minutes. He had a gut feeling that Peter Friel was somehow responsible. Single rifle shots were not the bikers' style. Their tactics were less subtle and usually involved safety in numbers, several weapons and multiple shots. He remembered the look in Peter's eyes from earlier that day and shuddered. He suddenly felt a little sorry for the Predators. He pictured Peter stalking them, picking them off one by one, creating fear and confusion. He felt strong admiration for the mountain man and wished he could help.

* * * *

Peter wasn't quite living up to the Ranger's image of him. He waited and worried. Was Suzie safe? Would the girl use her as leverage? Where was the girl? Why didn't the damn moon come out from behind the cloud cover? Should he let Mishka go? *Damn, Peter, think!*

He took a deep breath and glanced at the sky. He could see clouds moving and tried to gauge when the moon would next break through. He released his grip on Mishka and crawled forward on his belly while it was still pitch black. He wanted to be a lot closer when the moon flooded the porch in its glow. Mishka, sensing his caution, lay where he left her.

* * * *

Cydney was nobody's fool. She knew when to cut her losses. She was a sitting duck on the porch. Locking herself in the cabin wouldn't be much better. She briefly considered using the girl to bargain her way out of her predicament. But, who was she gonna bargain with and did they even care about the girl? Jeb could fend for himself. She would melt away into the night and reunite with her brother and the rest of the gang. She'd live to fight another day. Then she'd find the bastard who'd taken a lump from her ear and flay him alive.

She rolled off the edge of the porch and dropped the few inches to the ground. She squirmed on her stomach away from the direction she believed the shot came from. Cydney tasted dirt in her mouth and felt her anger build. Whoever had shot at her would pay. She'd teach him a painful lesson for making her crawl like a snake on her belly. He would beg for mercy long before he died. She wouldn't show him any. She felt her hatred simmering like a stew coming to a boil. She could smell and taste it. It fed her evil spirit and festered in her malicious mind. Her lips pulled back from her mouth and her face contorted into a malevolent mask. Madness shone in her eyes turning them red like fire. She was the devil's daughter. She made it to the tree line without incident. The clouds still shielded the moon as she rose to a crouch and started back towards her brother.

* * * *

The moon finally broke free from the cloud cover and cast its bleak light over the clearing. Peter strained to see a figure on the porch. Nothing.

'Shit.'

Peter's whispered curse acted like a command to Mishka. She ran past him and bolted for the open cabin. She disappeared into the darkness of the doorway before Peter could react. He stood to follow but felt a tingle and the familiar sideways lurch. As his body sank to its knees, his spirit soared above the mountain.

He'd kept his feet solidly on the ground all afternoon, and fought the spirits so he could focus on getting back to the cabin. Peter now realized the mistake he'd made in pushing the influence of Charging Bull to the furthest corner of his mind. He'd behaved as he'd been trained in the military. With dogged determination, he'd single-mindedly tracked up the mountain to his objective, blocking everything else from his mind.

As his spirit soared above the ground, he had an insight. He'd missed with the rifle because the sight hadn't been calibrated properly. The gun was unfamiliar to him and he should never have relied on an untested gun. He should have used the bow. Since Julie had informed him about Cydney, he'd stopped placing his faith in the spirits. He'd gone against the natural flow of things and ended up blind and groping in the dark, in more ways than one. It was time to let go and seek the help of the spirits.

He saw Cydney's aura moving away from the cabin at a fast rate. It pulsated with a brilliant orange hue more intense than before. He decided to get closer to the fleeing girl. As he descended, he saw her outline surrounded by the light. He moved as close as he could until he realized that she sensed his presence. She stopped, stared upwards straight at him and seemed to snarl. He could not know this because her face was a mere silhouette but he sensed the hatred coming from the figure. Suddenly, a huge black crow flew at him screeching and buffeting him with its wings. Peter quickly retreated upwards and the crow fell away below him. He flew away from the cabin to seek the rest of Cydney's group.

It didn't take him long to find them. The pattern had changed with the absence of the evil girl's aura. Still, an orange glow emanated weakly from one of the figures. The life force was low but steady. The man was fighting for his life and Peter realized that it was Mitch. His aura wasn't strong enough to dominate the group so Peter had a better idea of its character. He saw fear, confusion, excitement and a whole gamut of conflicting emotions given off by individuals within the group. Before he could investigate further, several huge crows attacked him and drove him away from the camp. They buffeted him with large wings, tore at him with their razor-like talons and used their beaks to try to spear him. He felt no pain in the physical sense but felt panic growing slowly as the birds tightened their circle. The noise they made invaded his entire being and added pressure to his attempts to escape. He tried everything to evade them but could find no respite. There were too many for him to overcome and he returned to his earthly body in an instant.

'Peter? Are you there?' Suzie called from inside the cabin.

Mishka barked. Peter found himself on his knees, in the clearing, with Julie staring at him with a puzzled look on her face. The moon filled the clearing with ethereal light that made it clear as the brightest day.

'Are you OK, Peter?' Julie asked. He nodded but remained silent. She shrugged, stepped on the porch and ducked through the open cabin door.

Peter tried to adjust his thoughts back to reality. It was difficult. Where had those damned crows come from? Had the girl sent them? What sort of unearthly power did she possess? He needed to speak to Suzie. He rose, stepped onto the porch and followed Julie into the cabin.

He found Julie untying Suzie from his bed lit by the moonlight pouring through the window. Mishka stood to one side, wagging her tail and growling at the same time, unsure how to react to the evening's events. Peter knew how she felt.

'Are you OK, Suzie? Did she hurt you?'

'I'm fine, Peter. I'm just embarrassed that I let her fool me so easily.' Suzie rubbed her wrists, nodded her thanks at Julie and looked at Peter with a quizzical expression.

'Oh, this is Julie. She's a nurse. She escaped from the same people that were here tonight. Julie this is Suzie.'

The two women appraised each other in the dim light. Suzie tried a tentative smile.

'Thanks for untying me.'

'You're welcome.'

An awkward silence followed as each woman assessed the other and tried to decide the pecking order. Oblivious to the silent drama taking place between the two females, Peter began lighting a few sputtering candles before the moon decided to hide behind another cloud.

'Thank God you came back when you did. I've never been so pleased to see any living creature as I was when Mishka came running into the cabin. I knew you couldn't be far away.' As Suzie mentioned her name, Mishka approached the girl and licked her hand. Suzie ruffled the dog's furry neck.

'Trust me; I was far away at the time.' A look of understanding passed between them. Julie frowned at the exchange.

'Where's the girl, Peter?' Suzie asked.

'She's hightailing it back down the mountain to her friends.' Once again, Julie frowned. How could Peter know that?

'What about the big man? What did you do to him?'

'Oh, shit!' Peter had become so swept up in the vision that he'd forgotten about the biker tied to the tree.

He ducked through the door with Mishka close on his heels. Moonlight bathed the clearing in silver light and stars carpeted the sky; the clouds had gone. He found the shotgun lying on the ground, picked it up, checked the safety and carried on towards the big biker. Mishka kept pace with him and made no attempt to go on ahead. That should have warned him what to expect. He broke through the bush and found the area empty of the biker and both of the backpacks. He saw the belt on the ground, cleanly cut through. He cursed himself. The biker's hands were free when he'd left him attached to the tree, by his neck, and he clearly had a blade in his possession. Peter stood still and listened. He heard nothing. Mishka remained calm. The biker was long gone.

It had not been a good night for Peter. He'd had the biker in custody and the girl in his sights only to lose both. They were back on the loose and still a danger to him and the two women. He would have to do better. He slouched back to the cabin in a dejected mood. Suzie had the stove fired up and looked up when he returned, her eyes full of cheer, in stark contrast to Peter's mood.

'You must be hungry. I'll reheat some stew I made earlier. Where's the biker?'

'I had him tied to a tree but he freed himself and disappeared. I should have checked him for a knife.'

'That's OK. What would you have done with a prisoner anyway? You don't have anywhere to keep one. Besides, you would've had to feed him. We're better off without him.'

'But now he's out there and a danger to us. The girl too. I was really careless.'

'Peter, less than ten minutes ago, I was helpless, trapped in the cabin with two armed strangers and you were somewhere out on the mountain. Now, they're gone, you're here and I'm safe. I think you did real good.'

Peter snorted in disgust, but the girl's words mollified him somewhat. He could always rely on Suzie to look on the bright side of things. He looked at Julie and saw the grim look on her face. She knew how dangerous these people were and wasn't looking on the bright side. Peter knew he had to be more ruthless if he got another chance at the bikers.

Chapter Eleven

Tim Martin's tongue stuck to the roof of his mouth and his shoulders drooped with weariness. He'd heard nothing after the second shot twenty minutes earlier. It was dark and he'd not prepared a suitable place to sleep. He shivered as he felt the cold night air seep through his clothes. Should he risk a fire? Could he start one? He'd had all the training and now it was time to put it to the test.

He tipped his water bottle almost vertical and sucked hard, his Adam's apple frantically working to swallow non-existent water. The empty flask summed up his predicament. He cursed himself for not taking more bottles when he had the chance. He needed to get a grip and apply his training. Otherwise, he would die.

He was the local Forest Ranger and had been a respected and well-liked leader in his small community until the Predators came to town. He'd been trained to protect the forest against environmental threats and save errant hikers from getting lost or eaten by bears. His uniform gave him a certain authority and he'd doubled up as the local peace officer. This entailed occasionally rescuing Lee, the town drunk, from the worst excesses of the demon drink and renewing gun licenses. Nothing had prepared him for the vicious biker gang. He felt helpless and ashamed after capitulating so easily in the face of their casual violence.

Like all fallen heroes, Tim craved redemption. The only way back for him was to face up to the gang and retrieve his weapons. He fantasized about helping Peter Friel, who obviously would defend his cabin against the assault from the bikers. Tim felt responsible because he'd told the Predators about Peter to ingratiate himself and save his life. He'd promised to lead them to the mountain man's cabin in return for his life. He didn't believe for one minute that they'd really honor the bargain.

He owed Peter but also owed himself. He needed to restore his self-esteem. He wanted to join the mountain man and help him overcome the threat from the bikers. But, he needed to bring something to the table. He couldn't turn up at the man's cabin hungry, thirsty, tired and weaponless. The last time he'd seen Peter he had cried and wet his pants, so he had a long way to go to impress him. He also had a long way to go to impress himself. He needed to rest, find sustenance and arm himself before he could approach the veteran with an offer of help. He sat, gathered his thoughts and began to formulate a strategy.

* * * *

Despite her exhaustion, Spice couldn't sleep. Every muscle ached as she tossed and turned on the hard earth. Every stone on the ground seemed to torture a different place on her weary body. Miniscule pebbles became giant rocks that tormented her bones and disturbed her rest. It wasn't just physical hardships that kept sleep from claiming her. A crisis of conscience assaulted her spirit.

Spice was a trained law enforcement officer. But, now

she was a member of a lawless gang who thought nothing of gunning down women and children for no reason. Spice had managed to save the life of the Ranger by suggesting he carry some of their load and was glad he'd managed to escape. But, she'd also saved the life of a cold-hearted murderer. Should he survive, she had little doubt that Mitch would kill again without remorse. The gang planned to assault the cabin of an innocent man, kill him and steal his food. She should be defending him - not attacking him. She should sneak away from the camp with every weapon she could carry, warn the guy and offer her help if he would take it.

Her thoughts turned to Julie and the strange man she'd seen at the stream. She'd been shocked to see the blonde women appear on the other side of the creek with a shotgun. Interfering when Mitch pulled out his luger to shoot her was the last decent thing Spice had done. Who was that scary looking dude who shot Mitch with the arrow? She'd seen him grab Julie and drag her away to safety before Billy-Bob and the rest showed up. What was his relationship with Julie? Had they joined forces? If he was the man the Predators sought then she definitely should try to help him and the brave blonde girl.

Julie not only had the ingenuity to escape and find a weapon but also the courage to return and attack Mitch with it. If Julie could do it then so could she. She needed sleep to pull it off. She had to force herself to rest in order to summon the strength she would need. Mitch was out of the picture for the time being. Cydney and Jeb were God knows where and Billy-Bob was sure to be stoned by now. There would never be a better time to make her escape. But, she was so tired. Maybe she should stay and try to sabotage the gang's efforts. She lost her train of thought. She tried to keep her ideas in order, but it was like grasping at smoke. Her eyelids drooped and she blinked several times. Finally, mercifully, sleep overcame her.

* * * *

Jeb's head pounded with waves of pain. There was a lump the size of half an egg behind his ear where Peter had caught him with the rock. His back stiffened with the weight of the two backpacks and soreness turned to pain. The throbbing in his head seemed to diminish as his back worsened. He sat down to rest. He'd been conscious when Peter missed his shot at Cydney and was certain the girl had escaped into the darkness. With Peter and Julie's attention fixed firmly on the cabin, he'd managed to slip the knife from his boot, cut the belt around his neck and escape.

He knew Cydney would return to her brother and so would he. They'd regroup and take that crazy bastard. Jeb had a score to settle with the sneaky son-of-a-bitch who'd blindsided him. He would make him suffer before they killed him.

So, Julie had joined forces with the mountain man. There was the native girl to consider as well. She didn't seem much of a threat and Cydney had handled her like a small child. Then again, Cydney was one dangerous bitch who could handle just about anybody, man or woman. He had to get back to warn Mitch that he would be up against three people and not one. He struggled to his feet, manhandled the packs onto his shoulders and set off down the mountain.

* * * *

It was like a bad acid trip. Cydney's mind boiled; thoughts

112

bubbled to the surface and disappeared before they properly formed. Somewhere deep inside, where the child still lived, she realized that she was close to madness. She fought for control. If actions define a person then she knew she was evil, but something else had entered the battle for control of her soul - something dark and wicked. Just for an instant, she'd lain on the porch feeling vulnerable and afraid. Her spirit had reached out for help, and something evil and malicious answered her call. She'd left the door ajar for a fraction of a second, and a spawn of Satan had walked right in. The evil essence that had tormented Ben Atwood to the edge of madness for so many years had finally found a perfect conduit in Cydney.

She didn't realize what had happened. Had she really seen a spirit flying overhead? Had she changed into a crow and driven it off? Had she summoned help from the nether regions to defend the camp from its prying gaze? Had she really done these things or was she hallucinating? Was she just having an acid flashback? She didn't know the answers. She felt like a passenger in her own body; just there for the ride. It went deeper than that. She'd lost control of her mind and soul. Something was fighting to take her very essence from her and she was losing her identity.

Her tortured mind drove her down the mountain at breakneck speed. At last, the adrenaline wore off and she collapsed in a breathless heap onto the forest floor, shaking and shivering with exhaustion and fear. What had possessed her? Where had it gone and when would it return? She felt abused. Her mind craved solace and her body yearned for respite. She curled up in a fetal position and slept like an innocent baby. A malevolent dark presence kept a protective watch over her sleeping form.

✷ ✷ ✷ ✷

After Peter returned without Jeb, Suzie insisted they all eat. Tiredness overwhelmed Julie after the traumas of the day and the others suggested that she rest on Peter's bed. She dozed off as soon as her head touched the pillow. Sometime later, she woke to the sound of soft voices coming from the porch. Through the open shutters, she could hear Peter and Suzie's muffled conversation in the still of the night. She lay still and tried to make sense of the exchange. She had so many questions. Peter had captured her heart from the moment she'd watched him bury the young girl and her mother with tenderness and compassion. She was curious about his relationship with the strange native girl? She strained to catch every word. She heard Peter's deep voice and her chest tightened.

'What about the crows? Why did they attack me and where did they come from?'

Julie didn't understand. What crows? When did that happen? She waited for Suzie's answer.

'Peter, just as our world has balance and harmony so does the spirit world. For every action there's an equal and opposite reaction. This also includes good and evil.'

Suzie paused but Peter didn't respond. She continued.

'Have you heard of Shapeshifters?'

'No, and I don't think I want to either.'

'My people believe that in ancient times wise men called Shamans could inhabit the bodies of animals. They flew like birds and swam like fish. They used this art to see over great distances and to foretell of storms that could endanger the people. They could tell the hunters when the salmon would run. But… some shamans perverted the art to gain power and make war.'

'Ha, that sounds familiar. Just like warplanes and submarines today.'

'Yes, the comparison is apt, something that so benefits mankind used to kill and maim. My people called those evil Shamans, Shapeshifters.'

'My people call them politicians.'

'Yes. Well, I believe a Shapeshifter has chosen the girl, Cydney, in the same way the good spirits have chosen you.'

'So, this Shapeshifter used crows to attack me?' Peter sounded doubtful. Julie drew in a sharp breath; what were these two babbling about?

'Yes, Peter. The world's going through a crisis. Humankind's on the brink of a new age. It could go in many directions. In times such as this, when humanity is most vulnerable, the spirits wage a struggle for control. My son has been sent to play a role in the future of mankind and the evil ones want to stop him. You've been chosen to protect him.'

Julie's heart raced. What were these two lunatics talking about? She'd escaped the clutches of the Predators only to find refuge with a couple of nut jobs.

'Come on, Suzie. You make it sound like the Second Coming. You're gonna have a baby. I promised to keep you and the baby safe. You don't have to convince me with some pseudo-religious nonsense.'

'You're the one having the visions, Peter. You're the one being attacked by crows. You asked me for an explanation and I gave you one. I'm sorry if you don't like it.'

Julie sat on the edge of the bed deciding what to do. She was tired and not just physically. First came the fuel crisis and she'd dealt with it. She'd dealt with a lot of things; she'd lost her job, her savings disappeared. The electricity had failed and, without fuel, her car became a useless chunk of metal, plastic and rubber. She'd gone looking for food and been taken by the Predators. She'd endured humiliation, beatings and rape. She'd finally broken free and seen some light at the end of her personal tunnel of hell. She'd pinned her hopes on the resourceful man with the humanitarian streak she'd observed burying the dead at the Predators' camp. Now he turned out to be a candidate for the funny farm and possibly more dangerous than anyone she'd experienced so far. Where would it all end?

She looked up. Peter stood in the doorway staring at her. She hadn't heard him enter the cabin. The look on his face told her that he knew she'd been listening. Her heart raced.

'We need to talk,' he said.

'Yes.' She couldn't think of anything else to say.

* * * *

Mitch's body slept but his mind dreamt with an intensity that made the images seem real. He chased the blonde bitch through the forest. She was quick and nimble and he felt clumsy and slow in comparison. She dodged low-hanging branches and evaded rocks and stumps as he powered through the trees and scrambled over the terrain. He used his great strength to bludgeon his way through the obstacles she easily avoided. His power ate up the distance between them and he gained ground on her but it took forever. He came within arm's reach and grabbed for her. Spice appeared from nowhere, blocked his path and knocked his hand from the bitch's shoulder. He stumbled and fell.

Now, he saw the blonde again. She pointed a shotgun at him and fired, but he felt nothing. He aimed his gun at the girl but she changed into Spice before he could pull the trigger.

Spice pulled at his throat. It hurt. What was she doing? She tipped a bottle of liquid but it missed his mouth and splashed over his neck. It burnt his flesh and hurt so much that he woke with a start. He saw red flames rising into the air giving off sparks that crackled and popped in the darkness. Was he dead? Was he in hell already? His throat hurt but he couldn't muster enough saliva to swallow. He closed his eyes to the flames and tried to turn his head but it wouldn't move. He opened his eyes to mere slits and slowly accustomed them to the light from the fire. After agonizing seconds passed, he saw Billy-Bob's figure illuminated in the firelight.

Billy-Bob stared into the flames and held a burned-down joint between his stained fingers. His eyes were glassy. Mitch tried to speak but could only summon a dry rasping sound. Billy-Bob's eyes flickered in recognition. Their powers of deduction and communication were at the mercy of morphine and marijuana, two intoxicating mistresses. Mitch summoned up all his will and managed a one-word question.

'Spice?'

Billy-Bob stared at Mitch trying to comprehend the meaning of the word. Mary Jane had a grip on his thought process and he struggled to find a suitable response. The last joint had hit him hard. Finally, he had an epiphany.

'Doctor,' he responded, amazed at his own insight.

They stared at each other for seconds that could have been minutes or even an hour. Eventually, Mitch opened his dry lips one more time.

'Cop,' he managed.

The effort was too much for both of them and they each descended into their own temporary oblivion.

* * * *

Julie listened as Peter and Suzie explained their version of the previous few days' events. At first, she had a dozen questions on the tip of her tongue, but as their astonishing story unfolded, she fell silent. They seemed so inextricably linked that Julie found it hard to believe the odd couple had only met a day or so beforehand. It seemed too much to take in at one sitting. She felt jealous of their close, almost telepathic, relationship. She pushed the feeling aside and held up her hands.

'Stop, please. You're scaring me. I've heard of stuff like that but always thought it was nonsense. You know the sort of thing I mean - some fake medium conning a little old lady out of her savings, claiming to be in contact with her dead husband. You're telling me you can do that, Peter?'

Peter smiled, 'I'm not after your money, Julie. There's nowhere to spend it anyway.'

The look on Julie's face told him that his attempt to relieve her fears with humor had fallen on deaf ears.

'Seriously, this is all new to me as well. The last few days have come as a real eye-opener to me. I had no idea that I was capable of stuff like this. But, I'm not a freak. It all seems so natural if I relax and let it happen.'

Suzie reached out, took Julie's hand and looked into her eyes, 'I've been very lucky. Fate brought Peter into my life at the exact time that I needed help.'

'By fate you mean the spirits, right? That's what Peter said. Don't try to sugarcoat it now.'

'Sorry, I didn't mean to be condescending. I know it must be hard for you to accept all this.'

'I'm trying.'

'Stop and think for a minute. The same spirits brought you together with Peter just when you needed help.'

Julie looked at the native girl, 'You don't believe in coincidence or luck?'

'You can call it luck in the same way I called it fate. It all comes back to the same thing. The spirits have brought us all together for a reason.'

The three sat in silence as the stillness of the night enveloped them in a protective shroud that sheltered them from the perils lurking beyond the clearing. Mishka sat facing the tree line with her back to them watching for danger. It seemed they were in a little peaceful island of their own in the midst of a sea of turmoil and danger. Julie felt safe from harm for the first time in many days.

These were good people, albeit a little strange. She knew the feeling of safety was an illusion. Mitch, Cydney and their friends hid in the darkness waiting to pounce at any opportunity. Somehow, this couple managed to shield her from her fears. Maybe it was more than just the couple at work. Maybe there were spirits that turned the darkness from something to fear into something to embrace. Maybe there was something to what they said after all.

Julie realized that Suzie still held her hand. She reached out and took Peter's hand and he smiled. He moved closer and took Suzie's free hand to complete the circle. They sat serenely in the night, at peace with themselves and the world.

Chapter Twelve

At first, Spice thought she was dreaming. She felt rough hands shaking her. It wasn't a dream. She fought to remain asleep. She was so tired. A stinging slap to her left cheek broke the chains of slumber and she woke with a racing heart and adrenaline pumping though her veins. Jeb held her shoulders and stared into her eyes with a wild and angry look.

'What the fuck happened to Mitch?' he shouted so hard that spittle flew into her face.

Spice's insides shrank to the size of a pea as she looked into Jeb's eyes. She felt like screaming: *It wasn't me. I didn't hurt him. I saved him.* Whatever she said wouldn't matter. Spice knew that Jeb needed an outlet for his rage and she would suffer. The petrified girl lay on her back as he leant over her. She had never felt so vulnerable in her life.

'A stranger shot him in the throat with an arrow,' she said. *Please don't kill me, I'm only the messenger,* she thought.

He didn't kill her but he did hit her. He hit her hard and his ring drew blood. She fought to remain conscious and flinched as she anticipated a second blow. It never came as a dawning understanding replaced the wild look in Jeb's eyes

He knew who the stranger was; the same sneaky bastard

who'd blindsided him earlier. The Ranger had been right. The veteran was dangerous and unpredictable.

'Cydney's gonna go crazy when she gets back. We're gonna skin that son-of-a-bitch alive. We'll barbeque his balls and feed them to him one at a time.' He stood, turned and left Spice alone on the ground with one eye closing fast.

So, Jeb was back and he expected Cydney to return. Something had separated them. Spice guessed that their private foray had not gone as planned. Maybe the stranger with the bow had thrown a spanner in their works. Spice had to make a decision. Mitch's condition had Jeb distracted and Billy-Bob was, in all likelihood, still stoned. It was now or never. She had to leave now before Cydney returned and Mitch regained consciousness. Ignoring the pain from her face, she began to collect her gear together. She secured the plastic bag from the pharmacy in a safe place in her backpack and thought about weapons.

The moon bathed the camp in a silvery glow and Spice could hear the gentle sounds of the river. She could feel dampness in the air and a slight chill as if rain threatened. It was a peaceful night but she didn't have time to appreciate it. Everyone was asleep except for Jeb and he waited for Cydney at the riverbank with Mitch and Billy-Bob for company. Spice doubted he would get much conversation from either of them. She needed to find the gang's supply of weapons and arm herself. Despite her fast-closing eye, Spice's night vision was good. She'd been awake long enough to adjust to the weak moonlight.

Billy-Bob had left his backpack in the main camp area. Spice found it next to the pack containing the gang's ammunition, with which the Ranger had struggled for so long. No one in the party had touched either of the bags. It was a telling sign of the fear instilled in them by the Predators. Spice had slept while Mitch lay comatose, Billy-Bob got stoned, Cydney and Jeb reconnoitered the mountain, and yet no one in the rest of the party had dared disturb either of the bags.

Billy-Bob wasn't the world's best master-at-arms and most of the weapons were distributed amongst the senior members already. Billy-Bob carried a shotgun and pistol at all times. She only found one weapon in the bags; a standard police-issue 9mm, with which she was familiar, together with several clips of ammunition. She took a few seconds to think about the gang's supply of weapons. Could she account for their whereabouts? Was there anything she was overlooking? Something nagged at the edges of her mind.

She contemplated trashing the ammunition in the other backpack. She could throw it in the river. The gang would struggle to find all of it and it might give her an edge. She grabbed a box of shotgun shells and froze. Shotgun! Julie's shotgun! That's what had been nagging at the edge of her thoughts. The blonde had messed up her shot at Mitch and been knocked off her feet. When the stranger had dragged her off, she hadn't taken the gun. Her hands were empty. Somewhere on the riverbank, opposite where Mitch lay, was a shotgun. She had to find it.

She stuffed two boxes of shells in her pack along with the clips for the 9mm. She'd cross the river downstream and slowly work her way to where Julie had stood. She had no idea if Jeb could stay awake through the night but couldn't take any chances. She slipped out of the camp without disturbing any of its sleeping occupants.

Spice found a suitable crossing half a mile downstream. She crossed at a spot where the stream widened, the current slowed and the water was shallow. She hid her backpack under a bush. Hopefully, she would stay alive long enough to retrieve it. The stream gurgled and bubbled as it made its way down the mountain. It wasn't loud, but it dampened the soft sounds that Spice made as she negotiated her way upriver.

She moved at a snail's pace and scrutinized the opposite bank for signs of the bikers. She walked on tiptoe and placed each foot down as if walking on eggshells. She knew she was being over-cautious but wasn't in a hurry to be discovered. She saw the glow from the dying embers of the fire that Billy-Bob had set. The fire helped illuminate things for her and would impair the bikers' night vision if they stared into it long enough.

Spice's eye had swollen shut and she'd lost her depth perception. She was in a surreal dream in which she moved in slow motion and saw everything through a backward telescope. In her dreamlike state, she saw Billy-Bob staring at her from across the stream. He sat propped up by a tree and looked straight at her. She froze, her heart racing, and waited for him to yell out an alarm. He didn't move and he didn't yell. His face didn't change expression not even a blink. She realized he was stoned and on a different planet. She breathed a huge sigh of relief.

Spice gathered herself. The optical difficulties had affected her perception of reality and she needed to check herself. She took several deep breaths and waited until her heart slowed to normal. Mitch lay where he'd fallen and that was opposite where Julie had stood to take her shot. Spice resumed her stealthy progress until she was opposite Mitch. She saw the outline of a second figure lying next to the stricken biker and hoped that it was Jeb sleeping. She examined the ground around her feet but saw only shadows and darkness. She sank to her knees and felt around for the shotgun.

Rocks of all sizes covered the ground. They were typical smooth river rocks, worn down by eons of flowing water. She slowly circled on her hands and knees. She winced as the hard stones dug into her knees. She ignored the pain and increased her circle. To add to her discomfort, rain fell. It started slowly but with large drops. Spice's head dropped and she groaned to herself. The rain would help dampen any sound she made but could wake Jeb and rouse Billy-Bob from his stupor. She had to hurry.

The rain intensified and threatened to turn the ground to mud. Spice feared the gentle river would turn into a raging torrent at any moment. She scrabbled around for the shotgun as panic rose in her chest and her breath shortened. She picked up movement from the corner of her one good eye as she saw Jeb struggle to shelter Mitch from the elements with a sodden bedroll. Billy-Bob still hadn't moved. Sheets of rain fell and obscured them from view. The rain made her invisible and therefore bolder. On her haunches, she cast around, desperate to find the weapon as rain found its way inside her clothes and trickled over her skin with intimate fingers.

Her hand moved over something cold and cylindrical. Her breath caught as she tried to relocate it… *Please God, let it be the gun!* It was, and she pulled it free from the shallow mud that fought stubbornly to keep it from her. Her emotions spilled over into tears. They ran down her face and lost themselves in the muddy streaks of rain.

The relentless rain pounded down in waves and soon became a deluge. She could barely see. She stumbled along the edge of the fast moving stream that threatened to obliterate its banks. She followed its path downstream as best as she could. She'd found the gun but it would take a miracle to recover her backpack. She prayed one more time to a God she'd long neglected. She tripped and fell headlong into a bush. She struggled to rise and found herself tangled in something that gripped her hand. It was a strap from her backpack. She didn't stop to marvel at her good fortune but shouldered the bag, struggled to her feet, tightened her grip on the gun and continued to put distance between herself and the camp.

She didn't remember finding the hollow. The thick foliage of the overhanging tree sheltered the small depression from the worst of the rain. In a trance, she fell exhausted to the ground, crawled under a low branch, and using her pack as a pillow, fell into a deep dreamless sleep.

* * * *

Finding the cave had been a turning point for Tim. His experience told him that rain threatened the area and he'd gone looking for shelter. He sought a dry haven under the trees and found a sheltered hollow that seemed suitable just as the heavens opened and rain poured down. He cracked a smile at his good fortune and realized it was the first one since his encounter with the Predators. He explored the little hollow to its edges, looking for kindling, and spotted the opening. Local legends told of caves on the mountain but he'd never found one before. The entrance hid behind a thick gorse bush and showed no signs of recent passage. He crawled on all fours through the narrow gap and into the cave beyond. Darkness enveloped him like a death shroud and he shivered as the temperature dropped several degrees.

The Predators had relieved him of his Government Issue shotgun, pistol, mace and handcuffs as well as his personal hand-held GPS. They had left him with only a compass and a small metal flashlight in a pouch on his belt. He blessed them, as the other items were useless to him now. He carefully unbuttoned the flap securing the torch and prayed he wouldn't drop the slippery cylinder before turning it on. He flicked the switch and for a brief moment, nothing happened. His heart missed a beat, for a split second, he thought the battery was dead. Much to his relief, white light flooded the small cave. He let out a whoop of delight.

It took him only a few seconds to ascertain that the compact cave was vacant. There were no signs of recent habitation. The cave was too small to keep a fire going for any length of time and the battery in his flashlight wouldn't last forever. He turned off his only source of light and sat in the darkness for several minutes waiting for his night vision to adjust.

He'd never been afraid of the dark but this was altogether a new experience. He waved his hand in front of his eyes and saw absolutely nothing. His grip on the flashlight tightened as his heartbeat increased. His spatial awareness deserted him and he realized he was so disoriented that he didn't even know where the entrance was anymore. He resisted the urge to turn on the light and forced himself to relax and face the fear that threatened to overwhelm him. No light penetrated the cave whatsoever and his night vision was useless.

Logic told him the entrance was behind him. He knew it without looking. He'd only crawled a few feet inside and hadn't turned around at all. He felt a cool breath of damp air on the back of his neck and heard a muffled sound from behind. His nose picked up the familiar smell of fresh rain mixed with rotting vegetation. His other senses were making up for his lack of sight and he'd overcome the sense of panic. He took a deep breath and felt a smile of satisfaction break out on his face. It was a small but important victory.

His ears picked up a tiny sound for a second time. He couldn't identify it. It wasn't exactly a noise but more of a muffling of the background; like he'd put his hand over his ears and blocked out the silent white noise of the night. Something or someone had disturbed the peace of the hollow. He turned and crawled in the direction of the entrance to investigate.

He peered out from the cave into the hollow and saw a figure lying huddled on the ground. His heart missed a beat as his eyes strained to make out details. The rain eased and he saw the moonlight reflecting from its wet clothes. He waited several minutes but the intruder's figure didn't stir in the slightest. He crawled closer relying on the rain to muffle any sound he made. He made out the silhouette but struggled for details. He weighed up his options. Should he risk the flashlight or not? The huddled figure seemed small and he had the advantage of surprise. He compromised by cupping his hand over the lens before flicking the switch.

He allowed the light to escape through his fingers and cast its glow onto the figure. *Jesus H Christ! It's Spice, what the hell is she doing here?* In sleep, she looked innocent despite the fact she held a shotgun in a lover's embrace.

He removed his hand from the flashlight and ran the light over her entire body. It would take flashing lights and a siren to wake the girl. A nasty purple swelling, complete with a deep gash, distorted the left side of her face. He doubted if she could open her eye. Her bloody knees poked through rips in her jeans and she was soaked through to the bone. Despite the circumstances, he felt sympathy for the girl.

Her denim vest rode up her back and exposed the gun tucked in her jeans. Tim managed to slide it out without waking the girl. He recognized it at once. He smiled again; it was becoming a habit. He checked the clip, found the gun was fully loaded and slid in firmly into its rightful place in his holster. Step one was complete and he had his weapon back. Now he had to find Peter and offer his help. What about the girl?

She shivered in her sleep. Under the bruises and swelling, Tim could see the haggard look on Spice's face. Her features were drawn, she had a dark circle under her remaining good eye and she'd bitten her nails to the quick. Tim wasn't the only one who'd suffered at the hands of Mitch and his gang.

The rain stopped and Tim cast around the hollow for some dry materials for a fire. The girl shivered again and gave a small moan. Tim decided to build a fire, wait for the girl to wake and find out what had driven her to desert the Predators in the middle of a wet and cold night. It promised to be an interesting conversation.

* * * *

Spice woke from her exhausted sleep as the first tentative rays of sun filtered into the hollow to signal a new day. She felt damp but warm and she stretched her aching limbs before her eyes adjusted to the weak morning light. She felt the hard cold metal of the shotgun she'd cradled in her sleep and the numbness down the left side of her body, which she'd slept on during the night. The girl winced as she straightened her legs and felt the soreness in her knees. The last embers of the fire that Tim had kindled during the night still gave off a faint but comforting warmth. As her brain adjusted to the unfamiliar sensations, she jolted awake in fear at her strange surroundings. Spice jerked upright and took stock of her situation.

Tim Martin dozed a few feet away; she saw the effort he must have made to nurture the fire for her benefit, and she relaxed a little. She noticed that the Ranger had positioned an open canteen underneath a dripping leaf to collect rainwater. Her neck ached from the unnatural angle caused by using her backpack as a pillow and she massaged it to no avail. She felt the fresh morning air as it chilled her kidney area, which her short denim vest exposed. She shivered, moved closer to the fire, tucked in her tee shirt and rubbed her hands to generate some warmth. The rain had left the morning air fresh and the surrounding ground sodden with water. The hollow was dry in comparison. She laid the shotgun down, careful not to disturb the sleeping ranger, found a charred stick and poked some life into the sputtering fire. She saw extra kindling that the Ranger had gathered before sleep overcame him, and added it slowly to the fire. Fresh flames rewarded her efforts but they would soon disappear without fuel.

She looked around for something substantial to burn and finding nothing, she removed her denim vest and dangled it over the flames until the bottom edge caught fire. She slowly manipulated the vest until flames licked higher and threatened to burn her fingers whereupon she dropped it onto the fire and spread her hands to catch the heat. The movement disturbed Tim from his fitful sleep and he woke with a start and eyed the girl with suspicion.

'Good morning, Tim,' she said, her voice soft in the intimate hollow. 'Thanks for making the fire.' She tried a smile and Tim responded in kind.

'You're welcome.'

'How did you find me?' she asked.

'I didn't – you found me.'

She frowned but didn't pursue the topic. The fire popped as metal studs on her vest succumbed to the intense heat. Tim noticed the smoldering garment and raised his eyebrows.

'Burning your colors? I thought they were sacrosanct to you bikers.'

'I'm not a real biker. I couldn't wait to get rid of them. Burning them's like setting myself free.'

'OK,' Tim sounded dubious.

'Look, you may find this hard to believe, but I'm an undercover federal agent.'

'I suppose you can't prove that,' Tim said.

'No, you're right, I can't.'

'No ID taped to the bottom of your foot or anything like that?' he asked, failing to keep the sarcasm from his voice.

'That's only in the movies. Something like that could have gotten me killed.'

'It seems, from your face, that someone tried anyway,' he said, more sympathetic this time, 'Does it hurt?'

She reached up and touched her swollen cheek with her fingertips, 'At least the swelling has gone down enough for me to see out of the eye this morning.'

'We can't stay here much longer,' said Tim, 'we don't have any food and very little water.' He leaned over and lifted the canteen from under the dripping leaf. He shook it and grimaced. 'Only half full.'

Spice unzipped her backpack and produced a canteen of water.

'I'm not sure if it's clean enough to drink. We lost the purification tablets when you took off, but we did boil some water to treat Mitch.'

'What happened to Mitch?'

'Some half-naked mountain man shot him with an arrow.'

Tim's eyes widened; he realized that Peter must have wounded Mitch just after his own encounter with him at the river. He remained silent as he remembered the circumstances surrounding his flight down the mountain. He would keep that to himself for a long time. He replaced his open canteen under the dripping water, took the water bottle from Spice, unscrewed the top and took a tentative sip. He followed it with two more then offered it to the shivering girl.

'It smells and tastes OK. I'd take the risk rather than get dehydrated,' he said.

She smiled, and accepted the bottle with a grateful 'Thanks'. She took three gulps and handed it back to the Ranger.

'So, what are your plans?' she asked.

He tapped his holster.

'Well, now that I have my weapon back, I want to offer my help to a friend of mine up the mountain.'

'You're talking about the army vet with the cabin?'

'Yes. Mitch is hunting for him and it's my fault.' He looked away from the girl to hide his shame.

'I'd planned to help him as well. I think that Julie has already joined forces with him. He must be the same guy who shot Mitch. Maybe we could go together?' She looked at him with anxious eyes.

Tim stared at the girl for several seconds and then his mouth formed a small smile.

'Maybe we could at that,' he said.
'That would make four of us.'
Tim laughed, 'The four Musketeers.'
'Yes, but there's still a dozen of them,' she pointed out.
Tim stopped laughing.

Chapter Thirteen

The sudden heavy rain drove them off the porch and into the cabin. The two girls made an amicable arrangement to commandeer Peter's bed and left him to sleep on the floor once again. Mishka put on her most forlorn face; Peter relented and let her in to shelter from the rain, despite the cramped conditions.

The rain pelted onto the roof and against the shutters with a constant drumming. The cabin was a little cocoon of comfort to Julie. She felt warm and safe inside with her new companions. She ached all over and tried to ignore the nasty welts and bruises that Mitch had inflicted. She was aware that she must smell bad even if she couldn't detect it herself. She fought an urge to go outside naked and let the rain wash the dirt and pain from her body. She would have to wait until morning. Meanwhile, she prayed that Suzie didn't find her odor too offensive.

Julie woke in a panic. She relaxed when she realized the warm body next to hers belonged to Suzie and not Mitch. The rain had stopped and the cabin was so quiet she could hear the others breathing. Their breaths were deep and even. They still slept. She slid from the bed and, in the dim light, found her way to the cabin door. She found the latch and gently lifted it.

As she opened the door, Mishka eagerly pushed past her legs, raced across the clearing and disappeared into the trees. The sun was just making its first appearance of the new day but the weak morning light still made Julie blink after the darkness of the cabin. She glanced back inside; both occupants were still asleep. Julie closed the door without disturbing them.

She took a deep breath of clear air and stretched like an athlete preparing for a race. She winced as her sore muscles complained about their recent overuse. The flight down the mountain and the subsequent long climb had left her stiff. She needed to soak in a nice hot tub. The thought brought a wry smile to her face. The nearest stream would have to suffice. She cocked her head and listened. She heard the faint sound of running water and stepped down from the porch to check it out.

She discovered Peter's stream and sat looking at it for a long time. She found the sight and sound of the flowing water relaxing and almost hypnotic. She roused herself, stripped off her clothes and braved the cold water. The initial shock of the icy water astounded her but she gritted her teeth and plunged in as far as she could. She rubbed herself hard to circulate the blood and remove the grime. After a few minutes, she stopped shivering and began to unwind. The pure water washed the aches and pains from her body along with the dirt. Mitch's excesses began to fade from her thoughts and she allowed herself to think about Peter for the first time.

She loved the tender side he'd displayed when attending to the people Mitch had butchered. From her position high in the tree, she'd heard him weeping for the slain child. His gentleness when handling the young girl's body was in stark contrast to Mitch's handling of her own. She began to wonder what it would feel like to have his gentle hands touch her. She shivered again but this time it wasn't because of the cold water.

The sun rose above the tree line and made the river sparkle like liquid diamonds. She saw a fish leap from the water and land without making a splash. A flock of birds passed overhead in perfect formation. She saw the stunning natural beauty of the mountain for the first time. The river had worked its magic on the beautiful blonde girl as it did every morning on Peter. The dawn had not only produced a new day but also a renewed Julie.

* * * *

Peter's bladder roused him from a deep slumber. He rubbed the sleep from his eyes, let himself out of the cabin, walked a suitable distance and relieved himself onto a random patch of the clearing with a sigh of satisfaction. He didn't like using the clearing around the cabin for a toilet and usually used the stream's flowing water for his morning ablutions. He looked at the sun's position and realized that he'd slept later than usual. He let himself back into the cabin to collect his grubby clothes and realized that Mishka was missing. He didn't remember letting her out. He shook his head, *Damned dog's getting sneaky, maybe she let herself out.* He stepped back outside, shut the door and made his way to the stream.

A surprise waited for Peter at the stream. He'd assumed that Julie still slept in his bed. Only her blonde head was visible above the water and the reflection of the sun on the fast moving surface hid her body from his curious gaze. He scanned the bank for signs of her clothes and saw a neat pile a few feet away. His pulse quickened at the thought of her nakedness. He felt guilty and hoped it didn't show.

'Good morning, Peter,' she called. Her eyes sparkled and the sun bounced off the water casting hypnotic, dancing shadows on her neck and under her chin.

Peter felt the red flush invade his face; it soon moved south to warm his groin. He groaned to himself as his body betrayed him. He felt a tantalizing stirring between his legs that threatened to grow into an embarrassing bulge in his shorts.

'Morning,' he managed. 'Sorry, I didn't realize you were bathing. I'll come back when you're finished.' He turned to walk away.

'Don't be silly, Peter. Carry on like I'm not here.'

Peter stopped. He didn't want to leave. He wasn't sure what would happen if he stayed but he knew he couldn't leave. Why was this so difficult? He'd had no problems when Suzie disrobed and joined him naked in the stream. This was different. He turned around and stared down at the pretty, bobbing face.

'Bit hard to pretend you're not here.'

'True. Would it help if I told you that I was waiting for you?'

Peter's thoughts swirled faster than the river's current. His tongue stuck to the roof of his mouth. He hadn't flirted with a woman for several years, and he'd forgotten the art. Not that he was ever good at it to begin with.

'Come on in, the water's great once you get used to the cold.'

Peter stood frozen on the bank. He held his previous day's clothes in one hand and was dressed only in a faded pair of denim shorts. The early morning sun highlighted his muscular physique and drew Julie's eyes to his chiseled midsection. Remnants of the charcoal, embedded in the deep ridges of his abdominals, emphasized each muscle of his six-pack.

She had visited Florence, as a nubile teenager, and marveled at the beauty of Michelangelo's David. The perfectly formed representation of the male form had stirred the adolescent Julie's sexual awakening to new heights. She'd ended up with wet panties and rubber legs. This morning, Peter looked even more beautiful, to her, than the iconic statue. Her heart raced and she struggled to fill her lungs with air as she stared at his tanned and touchable body. A rush of warmth invaded her pelvis and she shivered. She could almost feel his skin under her fingers; so much better than David's cold marble.

Peter dropped the grimy clothes he held and took a hesitant step towards the fast-flowing stream. Julie's breath stopped; her head spun. Two steps, then three, then he was thigh deep in the water. Goosebumps erupted over his torso and Julie's nipples responded in kind.

He smiled. She giggled. No words were necessary. The water darkened Peter's shorts as he moved closer. Faces only inches apart, they stared into each other's eyes. Julie's lips quivered as if she would cry and Peter reached up to touch them with a shaking hand as she grasped his hand in hers. No earthly force could stop them now. Their bodies came together like two magnets and he finally confirmed her nakedness.

Her tongue investigated his mouth with delicious intimacy as his hands explored her body. Julie moaned and his breath became deeper. Two bodies entwined like one as the water flowed sensuously over them both. He ran his fingertips down her back and caressed her satin skin. She shuddered and gave in to the irresistible urge to slide her hand down his abdomen and inside his tight fitting shorts. As she squeezed, he groaned.

'Take them off,' she whispered in his ear.

He did.

Much later, they dried off, dressed and lay on the riverbank in satisfied silence. Mishka appeared and sniffed them so intimately they laughed in embarrassment.

'Do you think she knows?' Julie asked.

'She was probably watching from behind a bush.'

Julie slapped him, Mishka barked and they both laughed. The playful mood infected the dog, who took off running in circles. As they watched Mishka's antics, they lapsed into silence and lay back on the grassy shoreline holding hands.

'What are you thinking?' he asked.

'I'm thinking we don't have much time until they get here.'

Peter let go of her hand and sat up. He knew who 'they' were. For a few precious moments, he'd forgotten them. The couple had snatched a little piece of heaven and held it between them for a brief but precious moment. It would have to do for now. Maybe, if they were lucky, they'd be able to hold onto it longer in the future. That's if they survived the coming days.

'Well, life's not all fun and games. We have to pay for our sins at some stage.'

'What sins? You speak for yourself, Peter. I'm not a sinner!'

He looked at her and laughed when he saw the look of mischief on her face.

'You're lucky Mishka's here, otherwise I'd make you sin again.'

'We could always send her away,' Julie said with a twinkle in her eye.

Before Peter could reply, Suzie yelled from the direction of the cabin. Mishka broke off from her latest circle and bolted towards the sound of her voice. The couple scrambled to their feet and followed at a sprint.

They found Suzie standing on the porch pointing a shotgun

at two people standing in the centre of the clearing. Mishka stood by her side, tail and ears erect, growling a warning. The couple stood with their hands above their heads. Peter recognized them both. So did Julie.

Tim Martin and Spice stood as still as a pair of Florentine statues, though neither as majestic as David. Peter was impressed with the change in the Ranger since he'd last seen him. There was no sign of fear in his eyes. His holster now contained a gun and he looked very professional and businesslike. The girl also looked transformed since Peter had first seen her. Julie spotted the difference too.

'What happened to your colors, Spice?' asked Julie, 'I thought you bikers never took them off.' Peter tensed; he didn't like the tone of her voice.

'They weren't my true colors, if you'll pardon the pun. I'm an undercover agent. Well, I was. I guess I'm a free agent now.'

'Enough with the puns.' Peter placed a restraining hand on Mishka's head; he sensed no threat from the couple in front of him. 'What are you guys doing here?'

Tim answered, 'We're here to offer our help. The Predators are coming to take your food and your cabin. We want to join forces with you.'

'Why?'

'I owe you. And, I have unfinished business with them.'

The two men stared at each other and a look of understanding passed between them. Peter nodded at the Ranger and switched his gaze to the girl.

'What about you?'

'I gotta finish what I started. I want to bring them down. I stood by and watched them kill two women and a child. I can't stand by any longer, but I can't do it on my own. I guess I need you more than you need me. We both do.' She glanced at Tim as she finished and he nodded in support.

Peter cast his mind back to the stream where he'd first encountered Julie. The biker girl had puzzled him with her behavior on that occasion. She'd saved Julie's life by obstructing Mitch and she had urged them to escape while they had time. She'd behaved like an undercover agent and actions spoke louder than words to Peter. It all made sense and he wanted to believe the girl. But, it was no longer just his decision. He looked at both his companions in turn.

'What about it, ladies? Do you believe them?'

'The last time I trusted someone and dropped my guard, I ended up tied to the bed,' Suzie said. Peter blinked at the hardness he saw in her eyes.

'I've known the Ranger for years, Suzie. And, I saw the girl prevent that biker from shooting Julie. I believe them. Remember what you said about people being basically good?'

Suzie glanced at him with a surprised look on her face. A half-smile formed on her lips. She lowered the shotgun but before anyone else could react, Julie grabbed the weapon from her and pointed it straight at the two newcomers. Nobody moved. It seemed the whole forest held its breath, waiting. Peter broke the silence.

'I guess *you* don't trust them, Julie.'

'They sat around and did nothing while Mitch raped me. How do you think I feel about them?'

Tim dropped his head in shame at the memory. Spice opened her mouth to speak but Julie cut her off.

'Don't say a word. Nothing you say can fix what happened.'

She stared at the abashed agent with a venomous glare. A tense few seconds passed while they waited for Julie to make the next move. A wolf howled in the distance and Mishka stood with her hackles raised. A sudden gust of wind blew a cloud of leaves across the clearing and still nobody moved. At last, Tim lifted his head.

'We're sorry, Julie. You'll never know how sorry we are...' His voice trailed off and he looked back at his feet.

'Aw, fuck it,' Julie said. She loosened her grip on the gun, letting it drop to the ground, turned on her heel and marched into the cabin closing the door behind her. Spice and Tim stood still for seconds that seemed like hours then lowered their hands.

Peter bent and picked up the gun. Tim looked at Spice with raised eyebrows and she shook her head. Neither could put their feelings into words. Suzie turned and, without a backward glance, followed Julie into the cabin.

'I appreciate you coming and welcome your help,' Peter said, 'but I guess you're gonna have to wait for Julie to come around and accept you.'

'What if she doesn't?'

'Suzie will talk with her. She has a way of making you see things from a different angle. It'll be OK. Now, what's happening with those damn bikers? Did that big bastard rapist survive?'

'Mitch? Yeah, he was alive when I took off. Weak but alive.'

'I'll make sure I finish the job next time. What about the girl? Did she make it back yet?'

'Not when I left but she'll be back there by now. She'll be out for blood when she sees Mitch's condition.'

'Ha! That one doesn't need an excuse to look for blood.'

They sized each up in uncomfortable silence for several seconds.

'I'm Peter; I've known Tim for years. Who are you?'

'My real name's Tiffany. As I said, I was an undercover agent for the ATF until the oil ran out. I've been living as "Spice" for so long I'm not sure I'll answer if you call me anything else.'

'Tiffany? You never told me that,' said Tim, 'I like it.'

She looked at him and smiled, 'Don't say it suits me. It used to, but that was in another life.' Her smile faded and she looked into the distance.

'We all had other lives before we came to the mountain. Some better and some worse. But, we're all here now and have to make the best of it,' said Peter. 'As for me, I'd rather be here than anywhere else on Earth.'

They stared at him in silence, lost in their own thoughts. He took in their haggard features and slumped postures and realized they were dead on their feet.

'You guys look worn out. You'll be no good to me in that state. When did you last eat?'

* * * *

Suzie found Julie sitting on the edge of the bed using a comb to tidy her hair. Recent events had reduced her once silky smooth mane to a mass of tangles. Tears of frustration welled in her eyes as she fought a losing battle with a small plastic comb. Suzie knew that it wasn't just the hair that caused the tears.

'I have something that might help,' Suzie said. She opened her backpack and, after a few seconds searching, retrieved a brush and a small dark bottle. She placed the brush onto the bed, beside Julie, and unscrewed the bottle-top. Julie dropped her comb onto the bed and watched the young native girl pour some of the contents into the palm of her right hand.

'What's that stuff?'

'It'll help with your tangles… if you'll let me…'

'It smells nice.'

Suzie smiled, lifted a section of Julie's hair and began working the sweet-smelling oil into her tresses.

'It's such a mess. It's gone from bad to worse since the electricity went off.'

'You're talking about your hair?' Suzie asked.

'I was, but I could have been talking about my life I s'pose.'

'Well, I can fix your hair but I'm not so sure I can do anything about the rest.'

The two girls said nothing more as Suzie worked the contents of the bottle deeper into the roots of her friend's hair using slow movements designed to calm and sooth. Eventually, Suzie moved onto the brush. She used long, relaxing strokes that untangled the long blonde hair. Julie relaxed and enjoyed the sensation of having someone pamper her hair. Suzie began with a soft voice.

'You were brave to break away from that gang,' she said, 'it took a lot of spunk.'

'It was horrible. I felt helpless. I didn't know what to do when Mitch killed that girl and her mother.'

'It seems you weren't the only one to feel that way.'

Julie digested the meaning of Suzie's words. She realized what she was trying to say. Were Spice and the Ranger scared too? Did they feel as helpless as she did? Each of them had suffered indignities and cruelty of their own. Each of them had broken away and wanted to fight. She shared a lot with them both. With each stroke of the brush, she felt her anger and frustration diminish. Minutes passed before she lifted her hand and stopped Suzie in mid stroke.

'Thanks, it's better now. The tangles have gone. You're a miracle worker.'

'You'd have untangled them yourself in time. I just gave you a little help.' They both knew it wasn't just the knots in Julie's hair that Suzie had untangled.

Julie reached out and hugged the smaller girl in a comforting embrace. She spoke softly into Suzie's ear.

'I'd better take the first aid kit and go sort out that cut on Spice's face before it gets infected.'

Suzie broke the embrace, 'Yes, Nurse, you'd better do that.'

The two of them laughed as they prepared to go back outside.

Chapter Fourteen

Cydney strode into the camp as dawn broke and cast its weak rays over the sleeping occupants. She'd slept through the rain and woken stiff but somehow dry. The stiffness had eased as she'd stretched and begun to walk with a surprising spring in her step. She felt strong and vital but hunger gnawed at her stomach, making her irritable.

The previous night's rain took everyone by surprise and left the camp in a sodden mess. She found Jeb shivering by a sputtering fire, which he tried to kindle using the last of the over-proof rum. Mitch and Billy-Bob lay by the fire, still asleep.

Jeb looked up, as Cydney arrived, just in time to take a vicious slap across his face. He fell back onto the ground tired, cold, hungry and angry.

'What the fuck's your problem?'

'That's for running off and letting some prick take a shot at me!'

'I didn't run off. The fucker ambushed me, knocked me out and tied me up. I came to and saw him miss his shot and you got away. I cut myself loose and followed you. What happened? Did you get lost?'

'No I didn't get lost. I stayed dry and slept which is more than you did. Wake my lazy brother and get some food on the go; I'm starving!' She picked up the bottle of rum, took a quick swig and made a sour face. Jeb didn't move and she noticed the hesitant look on his face.

'What's wrong?'

Jeb licked his lips and glanced nervously at Mitch's sleeping form. Cydney tensed and dropped the bottle.

'What is it?' she demanded.

'It's Mitch. Some crazy motherfucker shot him with an arrow. Just after we left yesterday. It's gotta be the same guy.'

Cydney didn't move, 'How bad is he hit?'

'It's not good, Cyd. He's hit in the throat. The others tell me Spice saved his life.'

'Spice? Where is she? Did she see the guy who shot him?'

Again, Jeb licked his lips and looked around as if seeking an escape route.

'Jeb, for fucks sake, where is Spice?'

'She's gone. The ranger's missing as well.'

Cydney seemed remarkably calm and it scared Jeb. She moved with slow steps to Mitch's sleeping form, knelt down, raised the damp blanket and stared down at her wounded brother.

'Did they leave together?'

'Who?'

'You idiot! Spice and the Ranger, who else did you think I was talking about?'

Jeb flushed and stood. He regained some of his courage. Cydney no longer had her big brother to back her up. She was only a slip of a girl and he wasn't going take any more of her insults or slaps.

'The Ranger was gone when I got back last night and Spice took off while we were sleeping. And there's more, that bitch Julie joined up with the mountain man so now there's three of them. By the way, don't call me an idiot. I'm sick of you treating me like shit.' He stood with legs apart and fists clenched, challenging her authority.

Cydney looked shocked. Her features changed to one of apprehension and she rose to her feet and approached the defiant biker with hesitant steps.

'I'm sorry, Jeb. I didn't mean to upset you.'

She reached up and placed one hand on his cheek looking into his eyes with a concerned expression. With the bruises and cuts, that Jeb had inflicted on her the previous evening, she looked vulnerable and hurt.

Jeb softened and smiled. He relaxed and reached for her hand. She grabbed his hand, twisted his fingers back and kneed him sadistically in his testicles. He dropped to his knees, helpless with shock and pain. She grabbed a handful of his hair, leant down and hissed in his ear.

'Next time you decide to grow a pair of balls, I'll cut them off. Now, get that fire going and fix me a coffee and something to eat.'

She punctuated her statement with a swift knee in his face and shoved him to the ground before stalking off towards the river.

Jeb moaned and held his jewels in both hands and waited for the pain to subside. His eyes watered as he lay in the fetal position praying that his balls weren't crushed beyond repair. His broken nose bled copiously onto the muddy ground but still he cradled his prized assets like fragile eggs. He'd seen many people underestimate Cydney in the past and suffer the consequences. She'd fooled people a lot smarter than him, but he never thought he'd be one of her victims. He would never make that mistake again.

Cydney washed her face by the stream. The running water distorted her reflection and highlighted the bruises she'd let Jeb inflict. Things were not going good. Her strategy to surprise the mountain man had come unraveled, Mitch was seriously hurt and three people had deserted the gang within hours. Julie had joined up with the mountain man and his little Indian girl and maybe the other two would as well. *Big deal… He's gonna need more than three sissy girls and a broken down tree-hugger to beat us!* She smiled and made her way back towards the fire and her brother.

As she walked, her head cleared and her thoughts hardened into sharp relief as if someone or something was guiding them. She found Billy-Bob's sleeping bundle and gave it a sharp kick.

'Wake up, you stoner. You got work to do!'

Billy-Bob rolled groggily from his bedroll and blinked in the early morning light. He succumbed to a violent shiver as he reached for a water bottle. It was empty and he looked around the camp with bleary eyes.

'Anyone got any water?'

'For Christ's sake go to the river and get some! Take a bath while you're there. What's the matter with everybody? I leave you guys for less than a day and everything turns to shit.'

She kicked a rock so hard that Jeb had to duck to avoid it. Before anyone could respond, Mitch stirred under the blanket and let out a moan. Cydney rushed to his side and lifted his blanket. He stared at her with bloodshot eyes. He tried to speak but could only croak.

'What happened?'

'That crazy army vet shot you with an arrow.'

'Throat hurts… Where's Spice?'

'She took off. Her and the Ranger both.'

Mitch paused for thought.

'Something wrong… I remember something funny.' He frowned as he tried to recollect details. He swallowed several times.

'Thirsty.'

Cydney turned and shouted at no one in particular.

'Get my brother some water and get that fire going. His lips are blue!'

Billy-Bob grabbed a water bottle and stepped to the stream while Jeb poked at the fire with little effect.

'I remember…' Mitch whispered, Cydney bent closer so he wouldn't have to raise his voice. 'That bitch Spice stopped me from shooting Julie. I heard her shouting something to her across the river. Someone else was there too… On the other bank.' He trailed to a stop and licked his lips. Cydney heard the breath rattle in his throat as he tried to sit up.

'I never trusted that short-assed little cow.'

'She ran off… With the Ranger?'

'Not at the same time, but they're both gone this morning.'

'She's a cop.' Mitch's voice was weak but his eyes shone and his tone was decisive.

'Jeb reckons she saved your life. She must have had medical training.'

'Doesn't matter… She's still a fucking pig.'

'Don't worry we'll find her and kill her along with that bastard who shot you. Just rest and get your strength back. I need you strong, Mitch.'

The big guy leant back on the ground and took a huge gulp of air. It wasn't often that his sister showed any empathy or compassion so he made the most of it while he could. Cydney stood and surveyed the camp. She saw a bedraggled and dispirited bunch of shivering people wrapped in sodden clothes. A light crept into Cydney's eyes and she seemed to grow visibly taller.

'Look here people. Look here now!'

Her voice reverberated around the camp with a power and clarity the Predators had never heard before. The light in her eyes turned into a fire. She waited a few seconds until everyone focused on her.

'You look a sorry bunch right now. You're wet and dirty and have been hungry for days. But, that's about to change. You're all gonna get cleaned up, build a fire, get dry and drink some hot coffee. Then we're gonna organize a hunt.' People stirred and some of them stood to listen.

'First off we're gonna hunt food. We'll find out who can shoot. Mitch will recover while we turn ourselves into a real hunting party. Then the real fun will start.'

People began to smile; Cydney's hypnotic delivery held them spellbound, and they looked at her with growing admiration.

'There's a dry cabin waiting for us and food to see us through the winter. That's our goal. There are people who'll try to keep it from us…' She looked around the camp ensuring she had their rapt attention. 'But they won't stop us. *No one will stop us!*'

Her words had an electric affect on those listening. Cydney had struck a chord with them. They'd needed someone to take charge, set goals and standards and give them some hope. The tattooed brunette had emerged at the perfect time with almost prophetic rhetoric to galvanize and inspire them. From feeling damp and miserable, they now felt inspired and invigorated.

Afterwards, no one could say who started clapping. It started with a single clap then a ripple and then everyone was on their feet cheering and stomping. The mini celebration helped them forget their wet feet and sore throats. The cheering subsided after several minutes and people began animated conversations as they split up different tasks amongst themselves.

Cydney returned to Mitch's side and slumped down beside him looking winded; he looked at her in wonder.

'Where did that come from, Sis? You were like a dictator or something. Like Hitler or Mussolini. You had me going as well. Jesus!' The words tumbled out with a cough and a wad of blood and phlegm.

Cydney ignored the blood.

'I don't know.' She seemed as surprised as Mitch. 'The words just came from nowhere like someone else was saying them.'

They sat in reflective silence. It was a rare moment for both of them. The light came back into Cydney's eyes and she jumped to her feet full of energy once again.

'Billy-Bob,' she began, she didn't shout but, once again, her voice carried to everyone in the camp, 'collect all the weapons and make sure they're in good working order. Tally up our ammo and keep most in reserve. Then evaluate everyone's shooting ability. Assign weapons to the most proficient. Those that can't shoot will share guard duty. I don't want those bastards creeping up on us until we're ready. Jeb, draw up a map of the cabin and its surroundings. If you can't find any paper, clear a space on dry ground and make a mock-up of it. Mitch and I will work out a plan of attack based on the model so be as accurate as you can. If you can't remember, then take one of the teenagers and scout the place again. That's all. Get to it.'

Mitch stared at her. Where did she learn those big words? She'd sounded like his commanding officer in the army. Loud, decisive and supremely sure of herself. He had always been a little scared of her but now he was in awe. She seemed like a different person. In fact, she seemed like several different persons. He motioned for her to come close so he could whisper to her.

'You seem to be in charge so can you get me some soup from somewhere? I'm starving and I don't think I can swallow solid food.' He looked at her like a hungry puppy.

'I can do better than that,' she said as her eyes glazed over.

Cydney reached her hands down and put them around Mitch's throat. He flinched but couldn't pull himself away. Her hands didn't tighten but he could feel a steady pressure. A tingling sensation over his upper body made him shiver and his eyes widened in fright.

'Be still,' she ordered in an unfamiliar voice. He froze.

The haggard look left Mitch's face. Redness returned to his pallid cheeks at the same time as the whites returned to his eyes. His shoulders widened and his chest expanded like a balloon filling with air. She released her grip and he took in a great gulp of air and coughed violently. No blood came out this time.

'What the hell did you do, Sis?' He looked at her with a mix of fear and wonder.

She blinked as if waking from a deep sleep. She frowned at the change in Mitch.

'Nothing. I didn't do nothing,' she shouted. Then, to Mitch's surprise, she jumped to her feet and ran out of the camp and into the safety of the surrounding forest.

Low branches tore and scratched at Cydney's face as she ran through the trees reopening the wounds that Jeb had inflicted the previous night. She ran as if the hounds of hell were hard on her heels. Tears ran down her face and mingled with the blood. Finally, a good half-mile from the camp, she tripped over a fibrous root and sprawled headlong onto the forest floor, her chest heaving as her lungs fought for breath.

No one from the camp would have identified her as the confident and authoritative figure who had delivered the rousing speech only minutes earlier. She regained control of her breathing and, with agonizing effort, managed to sit upright. She stared at her hands with eyes as big as saucers. She turned them over as if the palms would reveal hitherto unknown secrets. There was nothing special about them. The fingernails were dirty and cracked in places, the knuckles were red and swollen and she couldn't stop her fingers from twitching and her hands from trembling. She clasped her hands together and squeezed in an effort to stop them shaking. These same frail and damaged hands had just healed her brother from a near mortal wound. How was that possible?

Cydney remembered giving the speech but not the words she had used. She remembered the overall message and the galvanizing affect her words had on the listeners. Mitch had likened her to Hitler and her mind pictured the images she had seen on YouTube of the Nuremburg Rallies. Hitler had told the beleaguered German people exactly what they wanted to hear at exactly the right time. Cydney had done the same with the ragtag group assembled in the clearing. She let out a bitter truncated laugh that sounded more like a dog's bark. A dozen wet and hungry fugitives and refugees were hardly in the same league as the masses that the Fuhrer had mesmerized at Nuremberg.

She had always thought that Hitler had channeled some evil force that he used to control the masses and deliver his speeches. Now she realized that the opposite was true; the evil force had been in control all the time. She knew this because it was happening to her and she was powerless to stop it.

Unlike Peter's experience, it wasn't a vision or revelation. It wasn't a sharing of knowledge that led to her making informed decisions. It was totally dominant and manipulative. The same characteristics that Cydney had used to dominate her brother were being revisited on her a thousand-fold. She didn't feel refreshed, invigorated, renewed or inspired; she just felt used. She hadn't felt a benign spirit working through her to heal her brother out of kindness. The evil one healed her brother to help it realize its goals, which had something to do with the mountain man, his cabin and the strange native girl.

A sly look came across Cydney's features as she realized that maybe she could use this new insight to her advantage. She stood on shaky legs and listened for the sounds of running water. This time of year it was a constant background noise on the mountain as the summer thaw melted the snowcaps and formed many streams and tributaries. She located the direction and made her way to the nearest rivulet. She knelt at the bank of the shallow, slow-running tributary and looked at her reflection in the sparkling water. Her face was a mess of cuts, bruises and blood mingled with dirt. Hardly the face of an inspiring leader. She bent to the water and cupped it in her hands. She raised the water to her face and whispered a prayer to an unseen malignant force.

'Make me strong and powerful to carry out your wishes,' she breathed and immersed her face in the water.

She felt her face wriggle and contort in her palms like a snake coiled in a bag and she shuddered with disgust at the image it formed in her mind. At the same time, she felt an insidious invasion of her very being as the snake took over a part of her soul. With a gasp, she pulled her hands from her face and heard the slight splash as the remaining drops of water from her hands re-entered the stream. She waited for the ripples on the surface to return to normal and stared at her reflection. The cuts and blood splatters had vanished and the swelling was gone. Her skin shone in the water's surface and she looked younger. But, somehow, the water didn't reflect her eyes and empty sockets stared back at her; a sudden jolt of abject terror drove her back on her haunches.

She'd paid a terrible price for using the healing power and it was non-refundable. She'd asked the spirit to heal her face and by doing so had opened herself completely and the evil one had taken full advantage. She'd come to think of the evil as a serpent and she felt it writhing and hissing in her mind probing her thoughts and divining her desires and fears. It allowed her awareness but was in complete control of her actions and words.

She looked at her hands and found they were steady with no swelling and even her fingernails seemed clean. So why did she feel so dirty? She stood and walked back to the camp on autopilot.

Chapter Fifteen

Peter was deep in thought as, together with Suzie, he fixed some stew for the newest recruits. Outside, on the porch, Julie fixed Spice's ravaged face and fussed over her with no sign of her earlier animosity. Tim leaned against the rail, cradling a shotgun and scanning the tree line.

Back inside the cabin, Suzie stood close to Peter as they worked, their shoulders occasionally touching.

'A penny for your thoughts, Peter,' the young native girl said.

He looked up and realized that she'd been watching him for some time. A ghost of a smile played on her lips and her eyes held a mischievous look. He smiled but said nothing. He was not much for small talk.

'I guess if your thoughts were on this morning at the river then they'd cost a lot more than a penny,' she said.

He looked up startled, and she laughed at his discomfort. He squirmed with embarrassment, as she giggled at his reddened cheeks.

'Oh, Peter. You should see your face. You're so easy to wind up. I'm sorry, but I couldn't resist. Look, it's OK. After all you're both over twenty-one.'

He made a lunge for her but she skipped out of the way.

Peter risked a glance out of the window to see if Julie had overheard Suzie teasing him. There was no sign that she had.

'You can keep teasing me and running for now but soon your belly will too big and I'll catch you. You won't tease me then!'

'Oh, Peter, lighten up. I'm only having some fun. Seriously, you looked troubled. What's on your mind?'

'I'm just mulling over tactics. We have extra bodies now so I have more options.'

'That's good, right?'

Peter nodded but stayed silent. Suzie wouldn't let go.

'So, if that's good, why do you look so worried?'

'Well, two things are bothering me. Firstly, people are finding my cabin too easily. I mean, nobody ever stumbled across it by accident in all the years I lived here. Now, suddenly, everybody and his dog know how to find me.'

Suzie looked sideways at Peter, 'Well, if it's any consolation it was your dog that showed me the way. I would never have found it on my own.'

'Yeah, I know that. She's got a lot to answer for.'

Suzie punched him on the arm, 'You brought Julie here and the Ranger always knew the location. So, that just leaves the two bikers. Why don't you speak to Tim as he's the only one that definitely knew where you were. Didn't you say that he told them about you?'

'Yes. But I don't think he would give them the exact location and directions. That was his only bargaining chip. His insurance to stay alive, if you will.'

'Don't sweat it. Just ask him and clear it up.'

Suzie waited for the mountain man to continue but was disappointed once again.

'You can be really exasperating at times, Peter. I guess all those years living alone robbed you of social skills. What's the second thing that's bothering you?'

'That's the one that bothers me the most. It's about these damned spirits. Twice now they've led me astray.'

'Are you sure, Peter? Or did you interpret the messages incorrectly?'

Peter looked at her, frowned but said nothing.

'After all, you are new to all this,' she said, tactfully.

Peter opened his mouth to respond but thought better of it. He'd assumed that when the spirits showed him Mitch killing the woman and her little girl that he was the leader of the group and responsible for the orange glow. It was a natural assumption to make given the vision they'd shown him. But, it was a false assumption. Was that his fault? Maybe, maybe not. It didn't matter now. It was the dream that bothered him the most in any case. He took Suzie by her arm.

'I had a dream before I took off after them. You remember that?'

'Yes,' she replied. She couldn't resist a little smile. She'd known he'd tell her the details if she waited long enough.

'In the dream, a warrior told me to always be the hunter and never the hunted. So, I went down the mountain to hunt them and it nearly ended in disaster. I left you exposed and vulnerable. It was a mistake, but what other way could I interpret the message?'

'Peter, we don't always read things right the first time around. I have a confession to make. Do you remember I told you that the Spirit Bear appeared to protect me from you?'

'Yes, of course. I thought you were nuts.'

'I was. The more I think about it, the more I know I was wrong.'

'Well, maybe next time you'll let me shoot it!'

'No, you don't understand. The bear came to protect *you* not me.'

Peter stared at the young girl as if seeing her for the first time.

'It's the mountain, Peter. I was looking at it all wrong. The spirits lured you to the mountain years ago to prepare you for this very moment. My brother was never the mystical warrior who the shaman foretold would protect me. That was a young girl's delusion fueled by admiration for her older brother. It was always going to be you. The spirits chose you from the beginning.'

'You don't know that, Suzie.'

'Yes I do. You have an old soul; you've lived before on the Sacred Mountain and deep down you know it. The sacred place my brother spoke of is this clearing and your creek. You chose to make your home in the ancient land of our people and it was no coincidence.'

Peter sat at looked inward for answers. He knew she spoke the truth. He'd felt that he'd been waiting for the girl.

'I held a shotgun pointed at you and the bear appeared. It came to see that no harm came to you, Peter. Don't you see?'

'I don't know… It certainly behaved strangely,' he admitted.

'It wouldn't have harmed me but it needed to distract me and protect you from harm.'

Peter added more water to the pot while he listened to the girl.

'Peter, look and see who the spirits have gathered around me for protection. You told me that you couldn't be in four places at once to defend the cabin; now you can. You have three people to help you. Do you think it's all coincidence?'

'OK, so what are you saying? How does that help me with interpreting my dream?'

'Think back on your dream. Play it back in your head until you understand. Remember, you may not have interpreted it correctly the first time.'

Peter rinsed his hands in the bowl he used in lieu of a sink and wiped his hands on a clean cloth.

'Let me go to the river and think for a while,' he said, 'I need some time to reflect.'

She nodded and watched as he ducked out the cabin door. She turned to the pot on the stove, used a spoon to taste the contents and screwed up her face. She would have to teach Peter how to season his food better.

Peter walked past those on the veranda without saying a word. He strode to the stream with Mishka following close behind. It took him a few minutes to settle himself on the bank and relax to the sound of the running water. He could hear faint laughter from Julie as she ministered to Spice back on the veranda, but it was not an intrusive sound.

Birds sang high in the trees and a slight breeze disturbed the dry leaves on the riverbank making them dance to the music of the forest. He heard a wolf howling in the distance. That didn't concern him much as they stayed far to the north during the summer months, when the bears came out of hibernation, and always gave his cabin a wide berth in any case. He'd always thought that Miska's scent made them avoid the area but now he had other theories. Maybe they too sensed the sacred nature of the place. It seemed to Peter that animals were in tune with what Suzie called the 'flow of life' and that seemed to include the spirit world.

Peter sat and closed his eyes much as he'd seen Suzie do when she meditated. His arms rested on his knees and he imagined he was playing with the elk's tooth in his hand turning it over as he'd done in the dream. His mind cleared and he imagined himself sinking into the ground and bonding with the Earth.

He heard Running Bear's voice in his head as clearly as if he sat next to him.

'Always seek to be the hunter and never the hunted,' it said.

'Yes, but I went hunting and screwed up. I left Suzie exposed,' Peter said.

'The hunter may make many mistakes but the hunted only one.'

'But what do I do now?'

A conversation from the dream came back to Peter:

'When are we going to hunt real game?'

'We are hunting.'

'We are waiting.'

'A scouting party is stalking a herd of Waapiti. Together with the dogs, they will drive them back through that narrow gully to where we wait.'

It was an epiphany, Peter's eyes opened wide and he gasped in realization.

They should herd the Predators up the mountain into the clearing, which would become their killing zone. Maybe Peter, the Ranger and Mishka could do the herding and the girls could pick them off from the safety of the cabin? Were they good enough shots? He felt that Spice and Julie might be, but did it matter? They would be sitting ducks. Did the Predators know that their numbers had grown? He suspected that Cydney would, as she also had guidance from the spirit world.

The strategy had holes and needed refining but at least it

was a plan. Peter felt hope invade his mind. He might yet get to spend more time in paradise with Julie. One thing still nagged at the edge of his mind. Should he tell Tim and Spice about the spirits and the unseen forces at work? Peter and Suzie confided in Julie only after she'd overheard them deep in conversation about their influence. Would it unsettle the two government-trained officials and weaken their focus? He decided to return to the cabin and seek Suzie's counsel.

Mishka ran to Peter with a stick clamped in her jaws and cavorted in front of him. Despite the heaviness weighing on his mind, he grinned, wrestled the wood from the dog's mouth and played an impromptu game of catch all the way back to the cabin. *Damn dog is the only thing that keeps me sane,* he thought.

Peter found his four companions sitting around the veranda eating stew and chatting as if they were on vacation. He marveled at the innocence of the scene. He'd been wrestling with emotions and problems down by the creek while his friends chilled and ate their fill. Julie looked up with a smile of welcome.

'Grab some stew, Peter. Here use my bowl, I'm finished, and there aren't any others.' She handed him her empty bowl and their eyes met. Peter had a sudden feeling of intimacy with the blond girl as if they were sharing a forbidden secret. He flushed but no one seemed to notice.

'Spice was just telling the story of how she escaped from the camp and met up with Tim. They were really lucky to find each other.'

'It wasn't luck or coincidence,' Suzie said quietly, her voice trailing off. She looked at Peter and he knew what was coming next.

'Let me fill my bowl before you say any more,' he said to

the young woman. She nodded and he ducked into the cabin.

So, he needn't ask Suzie's advice any more. She was about to enlighten the newcomers and it promised to be a revealing conversation.

Suzie held court from the relative comfort of Peter's only chair. The rest made themselves as comfortable as possible around the porch. Peter sat on the rail and balanced the bowl of food in his lap. Mishka waited at his feet hoping her master would spill a morsel on the ground. Suzie faced the two newcomers and directed her comments to them.

'Well, now that we're all here, let me start by formally welcoming you to Peter's sanctuary. It's nice to meet you both,' she began. They nodded in acknowledgement but didn't interrupt. 'You both told your stories earlier and spoke of luck, coincidence, fortunate circumstances and good timing. Did you ever stop and think how outrageous your luck was?'

Tim glanced at Spice and frowned, he turned back to face Suzie, 'Well, Everything did seem to fall into place very neatly, especially getting my gun back so easily.'

Suzie smiled.

'Let's take the events separately before we look at the big picture,' she said. 'Firstly, Tim escapes, with Peter's encouragement, and is left lost and weaponless on the mountain. All he wants is to retrieve his gun, regain some sense of purpose and join Peter in his defense of the cabin. Then Spice slips away from the camp, bringing Tim's gun, and manages to retrieve a shotgun in the pitch-black night in pouring rain. Then in the vastness of this wilderness, you both find your way to exactly the same shelter. What are the odds of that? Seriously, Tim, how did you feel when you saw that Spice had your gun?'

'Like I'd won the lottery.'

'Yes, and you know the odds on that. What would you say if I told you that unseen forces had a hand in bringing you to this place and point in time?'

'If you mean fate, I might agree with you,' Spice spoke for the first time.

'More than just fate brought you here. There are forces at work here that modern man doesn't recognize or acknowledge. I need you to open your minds and listen to what I'm about to tell you.'

Spice held her hand up, her cheeks flushed, her mouth opened but no words came. The others waited patiently; finally, she spoke.

'When the rain started and I found the shotgun, I was in a panic. I was almost blinded by the rain and my backpack was stashed somewhere under a bush and I had no idea where,' she paused and her eyes glazed over as if seeing the incident in her mind's eye. 'I prayed. I haven't done that for many years but I did then. I never really thought about it until now; but, shortly after I prayed, I found the backpack and the next thing I know I'm waking up next to Tim. It was a miracle.'

'That's good, Spice. You feel that your prayers were answered?'

'Yes.'

'By whom?'

'Well, Jesus. Or God.'

'You believe in God, Spice?'

'I should, my father was a lay preacher,' Spice said. 'I know it was a miracle finding my backpack and Tim like that.'

Suzie looked deep into Spice's eyes and chose her next words with care, 'Jesus said, "My Father's house has many rooms". Do you remember that verse?'

'Yes, John 14:2. I know it well but what's its relevance here?'

'It's simple really. He just meant there are many paths to enlightenment. You chose your route based on your upbringing and your people's culture and religion. I did the same, so my journey has taken a different path, but we both ended up here at the same moment in time with the same goals. So, please keep an open mind for me and listen to what I have to say. Can you do that for me?'

As she finished, she glanced back and forth between the girl and the Ranger.

Spice felt for Tim's hand and gripped it tightly, 'We both have a belly full of your food so the least we can do is listen to what you have to say,' she said. The Ranger nodded in agreement.

Suzie took a deep breath and started.

'I'm with child and in danger from elements on the mountain that seek to kill me or at least terminate the birth. After the murder of my brother, I found myself on this mountain facing the evil ones alone. I prayed to the spirits of my ancestors, just as you did to your God,' she nodded at Spice, 'and they answered by surrounding me with people trained to protect, heal and serve. They sent me a soldier, a nurse, a federal agent and a guardian of the forest. The President couldn't ask for better protection. That didn't happen by accident or fate. The spirits brought you here and the spirits will guide your actions throughout the conflict to come. Now, whether you choose to call them by another name or not is of no real significance. We are facing a battle against evil and we must use whatever spiritual beliefs we have to help us.'

It was a powerful speech and the air crackled with the emotion of her words. They all sat immobile and it reminded

Peter of the encounter with the bear. The forest froze as time stood still and the mountain worked its magic on them. The federal agent and the guardian of the forest still held hands and Julie took Spice's free hand in her own. Peter suddenly knew what to do - taking Suzie's hand, he encouraged them to form a circle linked by hands. It was eerily similar to the previous night when there had only been three of them but now there were five.

Peter closed his eyes, opened his mind and invited the spirits in. It was no longer a struggle for him to communicate at will. A series of images flashed through his mind: Mitch killing the little girl, Cydney taunting crazy old Ben as she fired an arrow at him, Spice praying then miraculously stumbling across her backpack in the pouring rain and screaming with relief, the Spirit Bear sleeping peacefully on the forest floor conserving its energy for the conflict to come. The images faded and reality crept back as Peter opened his eyes. He looked around and saw his companions blinking as if waking from a trance.

Nobody spoke for several minutes and Peter was not sure what the others had seen. Had they seen the same images or had the spirits sent them a different message? He only knew, by the look in their eyes, that the spirits had visited them and had left a profound impression.

Nothing anyone said could have any relevance at that moment so Peter stood and entered the cabin to prepare a pot of tea for them all. The others began to clean the utensils outside on the porch using a bowl of rainwater drawn from Peter's barrel. No one thought to walk to the stream. They remained close in companionable silence, each lost in their own thoughts and reflections on the evening's revelations.

Chapter Sixteen

Peter and Tim slept on the porch while Spice camped down by the stove and Suzie and Julie once again shared the cramped bed. Peter lay awake for a long time mulling over his plan, perfecting and modifying it as he lay on the wooden decking. His plan would stretch their skills to the limit but it seemed the most logical way to go. Tim slept deeply as his body made up for the rigors of the previous few days. As Peter nodded off to sleep in the small hours, Tim's worried mind snatched his body from its slumbers to keep him awake worrying until almost daybreak when, once again, his exhaustion overcame him and he slept. He wasn't the only one who lost sleep during the night.

Peter rose early and stuck to his usual routine as the others caught up on their sleep. He left them undisturbed, as they might not have the luxury of sleep in the coming days. After bathing in the stream, he spent thirty minutes practicing with the bow. It was a beautifully balanced weapon and once again, Peter marveled at Ben's skill and craftsmanship. The old man had had many years to perfect his technique and the result was a joy to use. Peter found that he had a natural feel for it and the lessons learned in his dream as Charging Bull came flooding back to him.

After stashing the bow, Peter raided his supplies and made a vegetable broth, which together with some dried fish, served as an early lunch for the late risers. As the morning wore on, the others woke one by one and took turns in the stream to clean up before settling down to eat. Julie found time to give Peter a morning hug without the others seeing, which pleased the mountain man more than he was willing to admit.

Over lunch, Peter quizzed Spice about the Predators.

'You lived with the Predators for two years - tell me about them. Is there anything you know that can help us bring them down?'

'Well, they usually rely on numbers and intimidation; they obviously don't have the numbers any more. But, within each chapter was an echelon of the hardest and toughest members, the stone-cold killers. They called this elite group "The Sons of Disobedience". Some chapters only had one or two members who qualified. At the Sturgis Rally, all the Sons of Disobedience congregated for the first time and elected Mitch as their President. Mitch formed them into a nomad chapter within the Predators. Any chapter that has disciplinary problems within its ranks can call them for help. They are the worst of the worst. They'll travel anywhere in the country at short notice to dish out discipline to bikers who cause problems for their local Presidents and enforcers. Jeb and Billy-Bob are both members of the "Sons" and Cydney seems to have some sort of power within the faction.'

'So, what did they have to do to get into the group?'

'Like I said, they're cold-blooded killers. As a nomad chapter, they would even be prepared to kill other Predators if necessary. If you can imagine a gang that would scare even the Hells Angels then you'll have an idea how bad these people are.'

'You chose some real nice folks to hang with. So, back to my original question, do they have any weaknesses that we could exploit?'

'Well they can be wild and undisciplined at times. Billy-Bob, their so-called master-at-arms, is a real stoner but he's fearless, loyal and would give his life for Mitch. So would Jeb.'

'Well, hopefully we'll help them make that sacrifice,' said Peter. 'What about the girl?'

'She and Mitch are always trying to outdo each other. Each one tries to be more reckless, daring or ruthless than the other. It's a never-ending power struggle between them. You could call it the ultimate sibling rivalry. I think that's why Mitch climbed so high within the Club; she pushes him all the time.'

'Well, he's in no condition to outdo her now. I think we can almost discount him at this stage.'

'Never discount that son-of-a-bitch,' said Julie in a hoarse voice.

Peter looked up startled. He had almost forgotten the presence of the others. The information that Spice revealed was chilling and disconcerting. He needed to lighten the mood.

'Who comes up with these names? "Sons of Disobedience" sounds like it was made up by a Hollywood scriptwriter.'

'Actually, it's a biblical reference. It was the name given to the off-spring of the Angels who disobeyed God and fell from heaven.' Tim quietly said.

'Well, we'll just have to cast them down into hell where they belong,' Peter said with utter conviction.

'There's one thing you should keep in mind, Peter,' said Spice.

'What's that?'

'Things started to really unravel quickly while we were at the

Sturgis Rally. The government declared martial law, a dawn to dusk curfew and gas rationing. There were thousands of bikers at the rally including around three hundred Predators. The club decided to stick together and head away from the cities, which were under the control of the army and the National Guard. A fight broke out amongst all the rival clubs; the police withdrew and let us kill each other. It was a slaughterhouse. The state troopers and militia waited for the survivors to emerge and picked us off. I stayed close to the Sons of Disobedience 'cos I figured if any group would survive it would be them. Mitch managed to lead a small group of us through all that and that's how we ended up here on this mountain. Peter, don't underestimate them. They're survivors and vicious killers who've fought government agencies and rival gangs most of their adult lives.'

'We're all survivors, Spice. We're all here against the odds. This is my territory and we'll fight under my rules of engagement. The Predators' luck is about to run out.'

The group fell silent as they finished their food. Peter realized that the group was fearful of facing such a terrifying enemy.

After lunch, Peter sat in the chair and held court while the others arranged themselves haphazardly around the porch and listened. Mishka, sensing that to hang around would be boring, disappeared into the tree line on a secret canine mission that was sure to end in time for supper. Overhead, high clouds took turns in hiding the sun and the air grew colder as the day progressed. The group's mood darkened as the temperature dropped and Peter faced somber and serious faces.

He'd seen hardened soldiers harbor doubts before an engagement and recognized the symptoms. The previous evening's honeymoon was definitely over. They'd all had a night to reflect on the seriousness of their situation and the dangers they faced and Spice's assessment of their foe had furthered subdued them. Peter looked at the glum faces and decided they needed an inspirational speech by a charismatic and dynamic leader. *It's a damn pity they only have me,* he thought. Still, they looked to him for leadership and he needed them at their best.

'You guys know anything about military tactics or doctrine?' he began.

They all shook their heads. Spice held her hand up as if she was in school and Peter nodded at her, 'I was trained in siege tactics by the ATF. But they were the same bunch who screwed up at Waco so I don't know if that helps.'

There was a moment's silence, then they all chuckled at Spice's attempt to lighten the mood. Tim pushed her playfully and Peter realized that things would be OK. They were a resilient bunch, who would rise to the occasion, he was sure of it.

'Well, let's hope that none of them were trained the same way,' Peter said. 'If we're not careful we'll end up being under siege ourselves but I don't think it will come to that.'

'So, Peter, what's your plan?' asked Julie.

'I'll come to that in a minute. Before that, I want to point out a few things that might give you guys some confidence in the days ahead.'

'I could use some confidence,' said Tim, 'but an AK47 might be more useful. I don't s'pose you have any stored away?'

Peter smiled and continued, 'Firstly, we have the high ground, which gives us an advantage before we start. Secondly, we have a strong defensive position: the cabin. They have to launch an attack uphill against an entrenched enemy with clear sightlines. In military terms, they need to outnumber us by a ratio of at least five to one if they rely on a frontal assault. They have half that number. They have twelve bodies left after you two came over,' he nodded towards Tim and Spice, 'eleven in reality because Mitch will never fully recover from his wounds - if he survives at all.'

'What are their alternatives to a frontal assault?' asked Tim.

'Keep us pinned down in the cabin with a couple of well placed snipers while they probe for weaknesses using forays of small groups and hoping we run out of water, food or ammunition.'

'That's the siege situation you spoke of,' said Julie.

'Yes, but that won't happen.'

'Why?'

'Well, for a start I don't think they have the rifles and secondly we won't let them.'

'What about fire? Couldn't they just burn the cabin and flush us out?' Julie put into words what others were dreading.

'They want our supplies and our shelter for the winter. They won't risk destroying it all with fire. They're too lazy to fend for themselves so they want to take it from us not destroy it.'

'Good point, Peter. I never looked at it like that. So how are we gonna stop them from laying siege to us?'

'I'm coming to that but there's one more thing I want to talk about. They're not an invading force of trained soldiers but mostly scared civilians held together by fear and intimidation.'

'You make it sound easy,' said Julie, 'but we're not trained soldiers either.'

'What do you know about Special Forces?'

'Only what I've seen on the movies. Like Rambo you mean?'

Peter snorted, 'No, I mean the real deal. Small teams of

four people undertake most Special Forces ops. They each have a special skill, which may be in weapons, medicine, explosives or languages depending on the mission. Does that sound familiar?' Peter looked around at their faces for a flicker of understanding.

Suzie was the first to catch on, 'Oh, come on, Peter, you're surely not comparing us to Special Forces?'

'Why not? We're the closest thing to it on this mountain. Spice and I are both trained in marksmanship, Julie has medical training and a background in hunting and Tim's an expert on the terrain and weather patterns in the area. Sounds remarkably like a special ops team to me. You said yourself that the President couldn't have better protection'

'I can shoot too,' Tim said.

'Where does that leave me?' asked Suzie, 'What's my contribution to the team?'

'Our job is to protect you and your job is to stay out of the line of fire,' Peter said in a firm voice.

'Come on, Peter, you can't ask everyone to risk their lives for me. It's different for you. We came to an understanding before any of the others showed up. Now things have changed and we're not alone anymore.'

Tim Martin spoke before Peter could respond.

'Hold on there, Suzie. We invited ourselves to your party so we follow the house rules. I wanted to help Peter and if his plan includes protecting you that's fine by me. Are you others on board with me on this?'

'Absolutely,' said Spice.

'No question,' said Julie, reaching for Suzie's hand. 'I have a feeling that if it wasn't for you we wouldn't all be sitting here together in any case.'

Peter wondered what the spirits had shown them while they sat holding hands in the circle the previous night. Whatever it was, they all seemed to be of one accord and that suited him just fine.

'OK, so let's get down to my plan.'

'Thank goodness,' said Julie. 'Please don't keep us in suspense any longer!'

'Yes, he does go on doesn't he?' Spice said with a grin.

'Never known anybody talk so much,' said Tim.

Suzie started to giggle then laugh and the others followed suit until even Peter broke down and minutes passed as the group released their nervous tension by laughing uproariously.

The laughter finally subsided and Peter knew he had to draw a line to end the jocularity and focus their attention on the serious matter at hand.

'OK, guys, that's enough. We're gonna take a break, gather ourselves and then I'll brief you on the plan. Ten minutes, people. Be ready.' With that, he detached himself from the group, ducked inside the cabin and put a pot of water on the stove.

His words and actions struck home. The four of them became quiet and serious but the somber uncertainty had vanished and been replaced by a grim determination.

* * * *

Cydney looked around the campsite and smiled to herself. It was organized and tidy, a marked contrast to previous days. There was a definite demarcation line between the Predators and their followers. The camp was set up so that the Predators were bivouacked furthest from the river so that no one had reason to walk through their sleeping area. They'd dug a fire pit in the middle of the camp and sleeping areas were arranged in a rough circle around it. The biggest tent belonged to Cydney and Mitch but everyone had some form of shelter from the rain even if it was only a loose canopy over a groundsheet.

Cydney delegated tasks to various people based on their talents and one woman kept a constant eye on the fire and had coffee brewing twenty-four hours a day. Cydney knew that the supply wouldn't last long but needed morale to stay high until they captured the cabin. She ducked back into the tent and found Mitch cleaning dirt from under his nails with the pointed tip of a switchblade.

'The camp's taking shape now. It doesn't look like a garbage tip anymore.'

He just grunted and continued to concentrate on his nails.

'I had a weird dream last night,' she said. Mitch glanced up startled and nicked his thumb with the blade.

'Shit,' he said and dropped the knife sucking his thumb like a little boy with a paper cut.

She ignored him and continued as if talking to herself, 'In the dream, that little squaw woman was ordering the soldier boy about. He was running round after her like a little puppy dog. There's something about her. I can't put my finger on it but she's important to him. I just know it.'

'Yeah, well maybe we can use that. I had a weird dream too but it's hard to explain and sounds stupid.'

'Try me and see,' she said.

'I dreamt that the little shit with the bow and arrow could fly and he was flying over our camp and spying on us.'

They looked at one another, Mitch waited for the laugh of derision but it didn't come. Cydney shivered as she remembered her panicked flight down the mountain from the cabin. She recalled the feeling of terror as she felt the bastard flying above her like an avenging angel of death. Then she felt the serpent uncoiling in her head and her stomach lurched. She brought herself under control and looked squarely at her hulking brother.

'Stay in the tent, Mitch. Don't go out at all especially during the night. I want him to think you are dead or dying. You can be our ace in the hole, our secret weapon.'

'It was only a dream, Sis.'

'No it wasn't. Stay in the tent. Do you hear me?' She stared at him with an intensity in her eyes that shriveled his testicles up into his body for protection.

'I hear you, Sis,' he whispered and sucked again on his little finger although the bleeding had stopped.

Cydney felt the snake writhing under the surface and had a sudden flash of knowledge. She knew something evil was at work; some dark force manipulated them for its own ends. The gang wanted the shelter and food but the snake wanted something else. The native girl! The snake wanted the girl eliminated - but why? Cydney didn't experience a tingling sensation or the sense of falling, like Peter; but instead, the serpent seemed to tighten its coils inside her head and she felt a pressure that was almost unbearable. A baby! The girl carried a baby that the snake loathed and feared.

Suddenly a scream broke her train of thought and made them both jump. As Cydney moved to the tent's entrance to see the cause, a shot rang out.

'What the hell?' Cydney pulled her weapon and ducked out through the tent flap. Despite his sister's earlier warning, Mitch followed close behind.

∗ ∗ ∗ ∗

Around mid afternoon, a new arrival found his way to the Predators' camp. He'd been following a tributary upstream when he'd smelt freshly brewed coffee and made for it like a moth to a flame. Maurice was a true urbanite who felt at a loss more than half a mile from a Starbucks. When the city had started to get a little too wild, he'd accepted his uncle Jasper's long-standing invitation to visit him in his hunting cabin out in the boondocks. He'd made the annual trek with his father since he was a kid and was not unfamiliar with the art of the woodsman. But, it was the sort of thing he associated with a vacation and never intended to make it a lifestyle choice.

Life in the city had become unbearable as gangs took over the city by force, looting the stores and rampaging on the streets like Romans sacking Carthage. Maurice had fled north in his SUV, found his uncle's cabin burnt to charcoal and continued driving until he realized he was lost and out of gas to boot. Like those before him, he'd taken to the forest for food and refuge from those fighting like desperate animals for the last scraps of food, water and fuel. Little did he know what he was walking into.

Maurice was a designer woodsman with all the latest equipment and clothing complete with a hand-held global positioning device. That was useless to him now, and he was grateful for the sporadic tutelage his uncle had given him over the years. He had run out of dried rations the previous day and was hungry and tired. Most of all he was tired of the solitude and craved company, conversation and coffee, the three C's that ensured places like Starbucks thrived in the modern world. The three C's overcame the important C of caution and he strolled into the Predators' camp like a lamb to the slaughter.

It seemed he'd stumbled upon an oasis of civilization in the middle of the untamed wilderness. The camp appeared deserted until he noticed a woman tending to a bubbling pan of delicious smelling coffee suspended over an open fire. She had her back to him and was deep in thought when he announced himself.

'I say, that coffee smells fabulous. Could you spare me a cup?'

The woman tensed, turned her head, saw the stranger and screamed. Afterwards, she couldn't say why she'd screamed. After all, he didn't look threatening – especially to someone who'd lived in the shadow of the Predators for any length of time. He reacted by yanking his rifle from his shoulder and pointing it at the frightened woman. Billy-Bob emerged from his tent with gun in hand, assessed the situation and promptly shot poor Maurice in the head from five yards; a feat he'd have trouble ever repeating.

Pandemonium followed as Jeb, Mitch and Cydney burst from their tents shouting and brandishing their guns. The others peeked out from their tent flaps but remained inside their canvas havens.

'I got him! I got the bastard! He wasn't so tough - just one shot straight between the eyes. Ha, no more mountain man, no more army vet, I got him.' Billy-Bob danced around the fire as if he'd scored a touchdown on Super Bowl Sunday.

The other members of the Predators looked on in bemusement as their master-at-arms cavorted like a character from 'One Flew over the Cuckoo's Nest'. Cydney approached the dead stranger, used her foot to roll the corpse over and examined it closely. She saw a fresh-faced young man with soft fuzz on his chin and neat manicured hands.

'You stupid idiot!' she shouted at Billy-Bob who froze in mid prance as if he'd been shot with a stun-gun.

'Why am I surrounded by morons?' asked Cydney to no one in particular.

Jeb spoke and made matters worse.

'Who is it?' he asked.

Cydney raised her eyes to the heavens.

'Not another one! Who is it? How the fuck do I know? There were over eight billion people on the planet before this shit started and you ask me who he is - you're a bigger fool than Billy-Bob. I can tell you who he isn't; he isn't the guy who shot Mitch with the arrow or knocked you out cold. He isn't a mountain man that's for sure. Whoever he is, he's dead now thanks to our resident idiot-at-arms.'

Mitch walked over to the body, lifted it like a rag-doll and tossed it to one side. He bent and picked up the rifle the body had concealed.

'Well lookie here, Sis! We won the lottery! This here is a top of the range hunting rifle with a telescopic sight. Billy-Bob, stop standing there like a virgin in a brothel and search his backpack. See how much ammunition he's got for this baby. Jeb, set up some targets, I can't wait to try it out.'

Cydney calmed in an instant. This turn of events could swing the entire situation in their favor. She decided that she'd forgo the pleasure of castrating Billy-Bob for the time being. The army vet, in his cabin, was a dead man walking and he didn't even know it.

Chapter Seventeen

Peter and his companions sat drinking instant coffee that Spice had produced from her pack. The sudden crack of a pistol shot reverberated up the mountain from the direction of the Predators' camp. From somewhere in the tree line, Mishka responded with a single bark. They listened but no shots followed.

'With a bit of luck, Cydney lost her temper and shot one of the gang,' said Julie. 'One less for us to worry about.'

'Wouldn't that be nice!' said Spice.

'OK, enough wishful thinking. What do any of you know about snipers?' asked Peter, ending their coffee break abruptly.

'Not much.'

'Snipers work in teams of two, a shooter and a spotter. The terms are self-explanatory. Julie will be the spotter, using my binoculars, while Spice will be the shooter. We have two rifles and Spice will choose the one she's most comfortable with. I'll have to calibrate the sight on the new one we picked up off the bikers. So, you two will stay in the cabin and pick off anyone that so much as sticks their nose into view. If either of you need to take a break, for whatever reason, then Suzie will take over as spotter and Julie can be the shooter if necessary. Any questions?'

'I've used binoculars before,' said Julie, 'and I have to keep lowering them to get a true perspective of what area I'm looking at. How will I be able to let Spice know where to shoot?'

'Good point. I'll lay out a series of markers along the treeline at regular intervals. I'll put some stakes in the ground with different colored material on them like little flags. You can use those for reference points.'

'OK…' Julie sounded dubious.

'Where are you going to get the colored material from, Peter?' Tim asked, 'I don't see anything lying around in your cabin.'

Peter's face reddened, 'Well I was going to ask the ladies. I know that Julie has some bright underwear…'

Julie slapped him and the others laughed.

'Why don't you let Julie have a rifle too and let me spot for both of them?' asked Suzie.

'Because Tim will be using the other rifle.'

'And where will I be?' asked Tim.

'You'll be out on the mountain with me, herding the targets into the line of fire.'

'Just the two of us to control nearly a dozen people?' Tim sounded dubious.

'One sheep dog can herd dozens of sheep, which reminds me, Mishka will be helping.'

'OK, sounds feasible so far as it goes. But, if we have one rifle and Tim has the other what are you gonna use?' asked Spice.

'Old Ben's bow.'

The occupants of the porch fell silent, Peter could sense their doubt and didn't blame them one bit. He wasn't one hundred per cent convinced himself. But, it was better than hauling the heavy shotgun around as its effective range was much less than the bow. He needed to convince them and the best way was to show them. He stood, ducked into the cabin and emerged seconds later with the bow and a quiver of arrows.

'Pick a target for me, Tim,' he instructed.

Tim looked around the clearing focusing on the tree line where potential enemies could take cover. He spotted a tree whose girth approximated that of an average human, was several feet into the forest and was partially obscured by branches and leaves from intervening trees.

'That tree with the silver bark. There's a large knot about head height… See how close you can get to that. It would be a snap to hit it with a rifle shot.' Tim's tone revealed the doubts he felt as to Peter's chances of hitting the target he'd set.

Peter didn't hesitate, the quicker and easier he made the shot the more confidence it would instill in his friends. Tim had set him a difficult, but not impossible, target and Peter gave thanks that he'd practiced that morning. He focused on the knot in the tree and without taking his eyes from the target, selected an arrow from the pouch, notched it to the bowstring, opened his shoulders and let fly with a smooth and unhurried motion. He'd casually turned away by the time the arrow found its intended target.

'Damn, Peter. I'd still have been lining up the rifle. How did you do that?' Tim was dumbfounded. The others looked at him, astonished at his previously unknown prowess. It reminded him of the dream and brought memories and feelings rushing back making his head spin. He sat in the chair to hide his dizziness.

'That's great, Peter. What's more, it's a silent way to take out an enemy. They'll never know where it came from.'

'The perfect weapon for the guerilla tactics we'll use,' said Peter.

Spice held her hand up to get their attention; it seemed to be a habit she couldn't shake, 'Will one rifle be enough from the cabin? I mean, it'd be better if we had a volley of fire, wouldn't it?'

'We'll have the perfect scenario,' Peter answered. 'Between the three of us we'll have a triangular field of fire. There'll be nowhere for them to hide.'

He could see the animation in the faces around him and something more; he could see hope in their eyes. They now believed they had a chance to live through the pending attack. He wasn't a charismatic orator but his actions with the bow had spoken louder than any words.

A gunshot sounded from down the mountain and the party swiveled their heads in unison to see where the shot had originated; Tim grabbed for a rifle as birds took to the skies and Mishka came running into the clearing barking loudly. A second shot followed, then a third. Peter realized he'd been wrong about one thing because at least one of the shots had come from a high-powered rifle.

'What the hell?' Tim shouldered his weapon and searched the tree line in case the shots were a diversion.

'Relax,' said Peter as calm as he could be. 'There's no one in the trees, Tim. Mishka would have alerted us ages ago.'

'What are they doing?'

'My guess is they're practicing. Seeing who can shoot and who can't. Which tells me they may not have enough weapons for everyone. I just hope they waste a lot of rounds because they can't have brought too much up the mountain.'

Peter looked sheepish.

'They have a whole backpack full of ammunition, I'm afraid.'

Peter looked at him and then at the others. He could see that the continuing gunshots were having a detrimental psychological effect on them. All his good work could be undone by the gunfire coming from the enemy's camp.

'Two can play that game. Spice, come with me and I'll break out the ammunition so you can give your first sharpshooting lesson. I have a year's supply tucked away so we can practice till the cows come home.' He saw the grins break out on their faces and knew he had them back again, but their confidence was fragile and he'd have to constantly re-assure them. He'd have to figure out a way to hurry the action along before the stress got to them again. In the meantime, remembering his lessons from the dream, and allowing for his limited supply, he'd have to spend some time digging the arrow from deep in the tree.

* * * *

Later that evening, Peter sat on the riverbank with Tim for company. The girls were doing whatever it is girls do when men go off to have cigars and brandy. But, they had neither smokes nor liquor at hand as they sat by the gurgling stream and watched the sun sink towards the trees. Mishka lay with her head on her paws some distance away and dozed. The occasional twitch of her ears and flick of her tail told Peter that she was dreaming. *That's one lucky dog - not a care in the world...* he thought.

'This is my favorite time of day,' he said. 'It's so peaceful. It's like watching a child drift off to sleep after a tiring day.' He stared into the distance as if reminiscing.

'I never knew you had poetry in your soul, Peter.'

Peter returned his gaze to reality and focused on Tim, 'How did the two bikers find the cabin so easily, Tim?'

The sudden change in the topic of conversation took Tim by surprise and he didn't answer for several seconds. Peter waited.

'I had a military-grade hand-held GPS that still held a charge. I guess the army will keep the satellite, and the receiving stations, functioning long after everything else has stopped working.'

'Yeah, the satellites are powered by solar energy and will still be orbiting centuries from now when the human race will be just so much dust and ashes. We even managed to pollute space. Ain't we something?'

'Well, I stored your co-ordinates on the GPS the last time I was here. It didn't take them long to figure it out. Pity, two more days and the battery would have been dead. Sorry, Peter.'

'It doesn't matter; they'd have found me anyway.'

Tim looked sideways at his friend but didn't pursue the issue. He picked up a small pebble and tossed it into the stream; it disappeared without disturbing the surface.

'I've been meaning to ask you about your cabin, Peter.'

'What do you want to know?'

'You built it so quickly that I was shocked. I saw you haul some stuff up the mountain like the plastic guttering and stuff but how did you get the stove up here?'

'Same way that I found the location,' Peter said, 'I have a friend who was a chopper pilot in Guam. He owed me a favor.'

'A damned helicopter? Oh, Christ! I'd never have guessed in a million years. You and your self-sufficiency, using a helicopter of all things!'

'Hell, I got it for free. Mama told me never look a gift horse in the mouth. Besides, that was a long time ago now.'

'Are you telling me, if you had to do it again, you wouldn't use a helicopter anymore?' Tim sounded dubious.

Peter laughed and evaded the question, 'I couldn't even if I wanted to, Tim. No fuel left, remember?'

Both men lapsed into silence after that. Peter's words, although spoken in jest, had a sobering effect on them both. The world would never be the same again. Peter had survived in the wilderness for years without a thought for the rest of the world. He lived apart and separate from all the problems of the earth. He didn't use their technology and he didn't miss it in the slightest. But, now the world's problems were on his doorstep and wiping their dirty feet on his welcome mat. Refugees from a dying civilization had invaded his space and threatened his existence.

For Tim it was even worse. At least Peter was on familiar ground and defending his home. Tim had no real home anymore. None of them did. Their whole world had turned upside down. A week ago, he'd been a respected figure in a quiet rural town living in a 'civilized society'. Now he was fighting for his life as part of a tribal culture in the wilderness. Someone had turned the clock back two thousand years and forgotten to tell him.

Mishka barked in her sleep and twisted as if to bite an attacker.

'Even Mishka's having nightmares now,' Peter said quietly.

Tim picked up another pebble and it suffered the same fate as its predecessor.

'Have you ever drawn up maps of the area? I need to get a clearer picture in my mind about the topography if I'm going to be any help to you. I'm guessing we'll be attacking them from different directions, trying to get them to go where we want, when we want. So we won't be together.'

Peter looked at him and smiled, 'I can do better than that. Remember the chopper? I have some sweet aerial photos of the area. I took plenty while I was searching for the ideal location to live. Let's go back to the cabin and you can check them out before the light goes for the night.'

A shot rang out from down the mountain. They hadn't heard one for a while and it came as a surprise.

'That sounded like a rifle,' said Tim.

'It was.'

A grim look passed between them as they stood to return to the cabin.

* * * *

Later that night, the five of them sat around the porch sharing mugs of hot tea. Mishka lay a short distance away and chewed noisily on a bone. Peter broke their companionable silence.

'So, tell me guys, what the hell happened down there in the real world? What did the politicians do to screw things up so badly?'

'Which conspiracy theory do you want, Peter?' asked Tim.

'What do you mean?'

'Well, most of us know what happened but none of us really knows the how or why of it,' said Spice.

'Well, start with what you *do* know. It's gotta be more than I do,' said Peter.

Julie started, 'There was a series of attacks, accidents and natural disasters that led to a sudden shortage of oil. It all happened almost overnight. There was some stuff on the internet about it being planned by a group called the New World Order, but there was a news blackout when the power went down and I didn't hear any more but street talk after that.'

'The government imposed a curfew and martial law, Peter. Things got really bad,' Spice added.

'Oh yes, they also formed some sort of Union with Canada and Mexico and spoke about a new currency. But, most TV stations went off the air and you couldn't really get a good grasp on what had happened,' added Tim.

The group lapsed into silence as Peter digested this new information. He'd always felt that society was not what it seemed on the surface. The people voted every four years to elect an administration and a President to run things but he always thought that was just an illusion of choice. He always felt that it didn't matter who the populace voted for, because the President didn't really run things. The people who controlled the money ran the world. A shadowy group who controlled the oil, food and water supply and owned the media. When they decided that they didn't need the people anymore, they would make their move. Peter had opted out for those very reasons. It didn't seem to matter because there was nowhere to hide. Not even on the mountain.

He finished his tea, stood, walked a few feet to his vegetable patch and tipped the dregs onto the soil. He would have to rely on Suzie's knowledge of wild flora to supply them with greens for the time being. Their growing numbers would quickly exhaust his small patch. He chuckled to himself at the irony of it all. He was experiencing his own private population explosion and power struggle on the mountain. Susie's sacred mountain was now a microcosm of the whole world including an armed struggle for limited resources. This would be a severe test of her belief in the natural flow of things.

Julie appeared at his side; he took her hand in his, looked into her eyes and smiled. There were certain advantages to having company in the wilderness and Peter and Julie snuck away from the cabin to realize them. Mishka's ears pricked up and she watched them go but made no attempt to follow.

If the others noticed the couple's clandestine foray into the darkness, they never mentioned it. They sat and slowly sipped the last of their tea.

'We'd better get some sleep,' said Tim. 'We don't know when this thing's gonna take off and then we won't be sleeping 'til it's over.'

Suzie stood, 'Spice, you can share the bed with me for tonight and Tim can camp down by the stove. The two lovebirds can have the porch when they get back from their stroll.'

The three of them smiled.

'Shouldn't we take turns keeping a lookout?' asked Tim.

'I think Mishka will give us advance warning if they try to sneak up on us during the night. We can leave her on the porch. Peter puts all his faith in her when he sleeps,' replied Suzie.

'I guess,' Tim said uncertainly. But, when the two girls went inside, he stayed on the porch and kept Mishka company while waiting for the couple to return.

Chapter Eighteen

'So, you know what you gotta do?' Cydney asked.

'Yeah, my target's the cabin. I focus on the damned Indian girl.' Mitch threw his coffee dregs into a corner of the tent, 'Listen, Sis, let me go for the bastard who shot me with the fucking arrow. I owe that son-of-a-bitch. Besides I don't know what she looks like.'

'Don't try that one, you know everybody else and she's the only Indian girl on the mountain, Einstein. I told you the girl is the key. Grab her and he'll fold, I know it. Somehow, she's important to him.'

'How do you know she'll stay in the cabin?'

'Don't ask me to explain how I know, I just do, OK? She's pregnant and she'll stay in the cabin, trust me on that.'

'OK, OK. I'll do it. When do we go? Everyone knows their part and we can't keep practicing. We'll use all our ammunition.' Mitch hated waiting and spoiled for a fight.

'I'll let you know. I'm waiting for the right time.'

'Oh yeah? So how will you know when that is?'

'Don't worry about that. I'll know when the time comes.'

Cydney's dominance over her brother was total. The serpent had given her an extra edge that proved too much for Mitch. He no longer had any say in the decision making. It had been that that way since she laid her hands on his injured neck and healed him. Mitch resented the fact and whined but didn't disobey.

'I hope it comes soon 'cos I'm fed up with this bitter coffee. That damn woman keeps boiling the same old dregs every day.'

Cydney knew they'd run out of fresh coffee but in the big scheme of things it mattered little. She didn't bother replying. Mitch tried again.

'I had to drag Billy-Bob off one of the kids earlier. I thought he was gonna kill him. All this waiting is no good for anyone's damn temper, Sis.'

Cydney's face turned into an ugly mask with staring red eyes.

'We'll go when I say and not before,' she bellowed. Her voice sounded like fingers scratching a chalkboard and Mitch felt his bowels loosen a little.

Cydney snatched at the tent-flap, stooped and was gone. Mitch let out a deep breath. She scared him when she spoke with that voice. He felt his skin crawl as if insects crawled all over him. He shuddered and pulled his jerkin closed to ward off the evil feeling.

Cydney stormed around the camp kicking rocks and staring at its occupants daring them to say something. They all kept their eyes averted. She regained her composure and the serpent retreated to lay coiled in the dark depths of her soul.

Mitch was right about one thing; they needed to attack soon before people started to desert the gang. She'd sensed disillusionment amongst the followers in recent days. The affects of her rallying speech had soon worn off. The stale coffee and restricted diet melted their morale quicker than snow in the desert. She'd not seen the teenager Billy-Bob had fought with for several hours. She had a feeling he'd gone. She hoped for a signal soon.

* * * *

Another tense day passed and Peter and Tim sat on the porch as the sun turned a brilliant orange to signal the day's end. A breeze caressed the trees, causing the leaves to emit a rattling round of applause at the evening sky. They'd spent the day reconnoitering the ground that Tim would cover when the Predators made their move. Now, tired and replete from their evening meal, they sat and chilled while the girls relaxed in the cabin and fussed with the stove.

'It's really beautiful and peaceful, Peter. I can see why you chose to live up here.'

Peter didn't answer. He moved in his chair and reached down to stroke Mishka, who lay contentedly at his feet.

'Have you worked out a plan yet?' asked Tim.

'What do you mean?'

'Well, we don't know when they're going to attack or how you would anticipate or provoke one. We're at a disadvantage if you want to funnel them up the gully. I mean we can't just stay out on the mountain indefinitely and wait for them to make their move.'

'I know. It's been puzzling me.'

The cabin door swung open and Suzie came onto the porch holding a small, intricately stitched, leather pouch. She handed it to Peter without a word.

'What's this for?' Peter frowned as he turned the worn and ancient pouch over in his hands.

'When the Shaman told me a mystic warrior would come

to protect me, he gave me this for him. He said I would know the right time and the warrior would know what it was. I feel now is the right time to give it to you.'

Tim looked puzzled, *Mystic Warrior? Peter?*

'It's beautifully made,' the mountain man said, in a quiet voice.

'Yes, it's been handed down from father to son, mother to daughter for centuries. Its origins are shrouded in mystery but it's at least five hundred years old.'

Peter's eyes widened. Generations of Suzie's people had cherished this artifact, handled it with reverence and she had simply given it to him.

He looked at the girl with eyes that asked a thousand questions.

'It's yours, Peter. The people held it in trust for you.'

Peter loosened the cut leather drawstring and opened the pouch wide enough for his hand. He reached into the bag and pulled out a crude necklace. Time stopped for Peter. He stared at the elk's tooth and his mind flashed back to his dream. He didn't move or speak. Mishka, realizing petting time was over, rose to her feet, stretched and jumped off the porch to disappear into the tree line. Still Peter didn't move.

Tim and Suzie exchanged looks and the Ranger shrugged. He had no idea what was taking place.

'Do you know what it is, Peter?' asked Suzie.

Peter roused himself, looked up at the girl and broke his silence.

'Yes. A hunting chief called Running Bear gave it to me when I made my first kill. I shot the biggest elk he had ever seen and he gave me this tooth as a trophy. He also gave me the name Charging Bull.'

Suzie fell back against the wall of the cabin as her legs gave way under her. Tim jumped up to support her but she waved him away.

'*You* are Charging Bull?' she whispered the question already knowing the answer.

'I dreamed I was. Sometimes I think I am. It's all so confusing.'

'It makes sense to me,' said Suzie. 'Now I know you *are* the right one.' She stared at Peter and her eyes shone with admiration and wonder.

'Why are you looking at me like that? It makes me feel uncomfortable. It's just me, good old Peter.'

'You're more than just Peter. You know you are. You're the reincarnation of Charging Bull.'

'How is that possible?'

'I don't pretend to know that, Peter. But, you are and you must accept it.'

'Who was Charging Bull? Why's he so important to you?'

'He's a legend amongst our people. The elk slaying is a children's bedtime story. The elders say he could outrun a mountain lion and wrestle a bear and was the wisest and bravest of all warriors. He had many sons and we turned from a small tribe into a nation because of him. We call him the father of the people. Legend says he will return in a time of great danger and save the people once again.'

Tim laughed, 'Hey, buddy, time to be a hero. Now I know I'm on the winning side.'

'It's nothing to laugh about,' said Peter, but he smiled at Tim's enthusiasm.

Peter held up the necklace and they all fell silent. The ancient tooth had worn smooth and turned a dark brown color but he knew it just by its weight and feel. He lifted it up over his head and let it fall around his neck.

He felt the familiar tingling and sideways lurch as if he were falling. Suddenly he was alone on the porch, storm clouds raced overhead and electricity filled the air. Thunder and lightning assaulted his senses simultaneously. A shot rang out and he saw a shadowy figure lurking in the tree line. Another shot and he felt a splinter of wood from the cabin embed itself in his cheek. He dove to the floor as a third shot whistled close to his ear.

'Peter!'

Tim grabbed at Peter, not realizing what was happening. It broke the spell and the mountain man came back to reality in less than a heartbeat. He reached for his cheek to remove the splinter but it wasn't there anymore.

'Leave him, Tim. He's OK. He's having a vision,' Suzie said.

Peter looked up at Tim with a sheepish expression and blinked at the last rays of the setting sun. The storm clouds had gone along with the vision. He climbed to his feet and sat in his chair with a thump.

'You scared the crap outta me,' accused Tim.

Suzie ignored him, 'What did they show you, Peter?'

'The Predators are going to attack during a storm. They'll use the weather for cover.'

'That makes sense.'

'It doesn't make sense to me, Peter.' Tim wasn't convinced.

'Tim, you don't have to believe, but the spirits showed me the attack. The sky was dark as night but it was daytime. There's gonna be an electrical storm, not much rain, and they'll attack then. By the way, we were right - they do have a high powered rifle.'

'It would have been nice if we were wrong about that.'

'Peter,' gasped Suzie, 'look at your pendant!'

Peter tucked in his chin and stared down at the elk's tooth. It shone as white and pristine as the day Running Bear knocked it from the beast's mouth with his stone tomahawk and warmth emanated from it causing a tingling in his chest.

Tim reached out to touch it but stopped his hand in mid-air.

'I'll be damned,' he whispered. 'I guess I believe you now.'

Peter stared at Tim with an intensity that unsettled the forest ranger.

'What's the matter, Peter?' he asked.

'I made some mistakes, Tim. I don't want to repeat them and I don't want you falling into the same trap.'

'What are you talking about?'

Peter glanced at Suzie, 'You may not like the things I'm about to say, Suzie. But, they must be said.'

'Go ahead, try me.'

Peter nodded and turned to face Tim, 'You must be willing to kill without mercy in this conflict, Tim. It's kill or be killed. I missed an opportunity to take out Cydney and her friend when they came for Suzie. That was a mistake. We can't afford to hold back from now on. All our lives are at stake.'

Peter waited to see the effect his words would have on his companions.

'I think you should get Spice involved in this conversation, Peter. After all, you have asked her to be the sniper in the team,' Tim suggested.

'I have no worries about Spice. The US government trained her and nobody trains killers better.'

'That's not fair,' said Tim, he sounded upset. 'Spice isn't a killer.'

Suzie reached out and held Peter's arm, 'I understand what you're saying, Peter, and I realize that desperate times call for desperate measures and that sometimes lives must be sacrificed for the greater good but, please don't lose yourself in this hatred and violence. Don't turn something on that you can't switch off.'

The three off them sat in silence. The cabin door opened and Spice emerged onto the deck.

'I heard my name - what have I missed?'

Before Peter could answer, Tim spoke up.

'Come with me to the creek, Spice. There are some things that I need to speak to you about.' He looked at Peter and received an approving nod in return. Spice saw the exchange and put her hands on her hips.

'What are you two cooking up? I think you just want to get me alone by the stream in the dark, Ranger Martin,' she smiled impishly.

Tim's cheeks turned almost purple and Spice laughed mischievously, 'Oh, come on Tim, I'm just teasing!' She took his hand. 'Come on then, let's hear what you have to say.'

The two of them walked hand in hand towards the creek. When they were out of earshot, Suzie turned to Peter.

'He cares about her very much,' said Suzie.

'I guess,' was Peter's laconic reply.

'Oh, you men. No romance in your soul.'

'There'll be time for romance when all this is over, if we live that long.'

'Tell that to Julie.'

Peter reddened but said nothing. A few seconds passed and, avoiding Suzie's eye, he rose and entered the cabin to look for Julie. Suzie smiled as she heard him bolt the door. She guessed he did have some romance in his soul after all.

* * * *

Mitch was dead to the world and Cyd had to shake him violently to arouse him.

'C'mon, wake up you lazy dog!'

She pinched him on the inside of his upper arm as she'd done as a kid. He sat up with a growl, fists clenched ready to strike. His eyes focused on his sister and his temper cooled in a second.

'For Christ's sake, Cyd, that hurt! I hate it when you do that shit,' he said, petulance in his tone.

'Never mind that, big boy. It's time to go.'

'What time is it?'

'What does the hour matter? You been itching for action and now it's here you wanna know the time. Get up.' She forced a scalding cup of coffee into one of his meaty hands.

Mitch sat up, took a tentative sip and spat the bitter black substance onto the tent floor.

'Holy crap! That stuff could strip paint.'

'Never mind that. Do you have everything ready?'

'Yes, I've been ready for the last two days.'

Mitch climbed to his feet dressed in the same clothes he'd been wearing for days, checked the pistol in his waistband and shouldered a small backpack.

'OK, I'm ready.'

'Remember to take the route we've planned and keep out of sight. Wait for Jeb to get into position with the rifle before you make your move.'

'Yes, I know. We've been over it a dozen times. They'll never know I'm there, Sis.'

'You'd better hope the wind is in the right direction or they'll smell you coming from a mile away. You stink.'

Mitch scowled, 'So, when you gonna move? How long will I have to be up there?'

'We'll move out before midday. Don't worry just stay close and you'll see the signs.'

Mitch ducked out of the tent with Cydney close behind. The camp was quiet as its occupants slept through his departure. Cydney grabbed his arm and made eye contact to make sure her next words sank in.

'Remember, focus on the Indian girl. Don't worry about the others, just her. You got that?'

'Yeah, yeah, don't keep on. I got it.'

'Don't let me down, Mitch.'

Mitch nodded, hitched the backpack, turned and took off up the mountain. His sister sighed, shook her head and turned back to the tent. Mitch was a loose cannon but he was her ace in the hole. She was convinced the mountain man thought he was dead or dying and that could work to her advantage.

Mitch bent forward as he negotiated a steep incline and pushed on up the mountain taking a long route designed to take him above and behind the cabin. He felt cold and sensed an evil presence in the night. He was unaware of the dark, malevolent spirit that shielded him from prying eyes as he ascended the mountain to his destiny.

Chapter Nineteen

Peter rose early, left Julie sleeping in his bed, unlatched the door and felt a fleeting moment of guilt as he found the others huddled on the porch, asleep. He'd dozed off after making love to Julie and it seemed his other guests had decided to sleep outside rather than disturb the two lovebirds. He tiptoed off the porch and made his way to the stream without disturbing his considerate friends.

As he floated on the surface of the gently moving stream, he allowed himself to fall under the guidance of the spirits to check on the Predators. He soared high above the ground and soon hovered over their camp. He saw the orange glow from the big tent and knew that Cydney still slept. Her glow seemed stronger than ever and it disguised all other auras in the camp. He flew higher and saw two faint glows working their way down the mountain in a hurry. He smiled to himself as he realized that people continued to desert the Predators' gang.

He rose even further and saw two bundles huddled close together for warmth. They slept lower down the mountain and Peter had never seen them before. He saw, from their auras, that one was just a youngster. He hoped they would stay away from the coming conflict. He could not bear to see another child die.

He looked to the north but didn't see Mitch working his way up the mountain. The evil spirits were using all their power to camouflage the big biker's aura from his searching gaze.

Peter's essence returned to his floating body and the water felt warm and comforting to him. He finished his morning ritual and walked back to the cabin in dry shorts. He met Tim and Suzie on the porch drinking coffee.

'Did you save some for me?'

'I thought you drank the herbal stuff in the morning, Peter?' Suzie teased.

'Well since Spice brought the coffee, I thought I'd treat myself before you lot drank it all.'

'Help yourself from the pot if you can find a cup,' said Tim.

Peter ducked inside and soon returned with a steaming mug.

'Is Julie awake yet?' asked Suzie.

'Yeah, she and Spice are fighting over my only mirror,' Peter didn't wait for a response before dropping his bombshell, 'I think the Predators will attack soon, maybe today.'

'What makes you think that? The sky is clear and you said they'd attack during bad weather.'

'Two more deserted them during the night. If I were Cydney I'd make my move before I lost more people.'

'That's good news, Peter. Two less to worry about,' said Suzie.

Tim kept silent. He hadn't come to terms with Peter's strange forays into the spirit world and chose to ignore them when he could.

Spice and Julie emerged from the cabin, Julie gave Peter a quick peck on the cheek and the two girls trotted towards the river. Mishka emerged from the tree line and followed them like a four-legged bodyguard.

Peter turned to Tim, 'We'll keep an eye on the weather. Be ready to move at short notice. I really feel that it will go down today. You know what to do?'

'Yes, pick off any targets and move in as they get closer to the cabin.'

'Yes, we'll tighten the triangle of fire the closer they get. Be careful not to shoot me though,' Peter smiled to lighten the mood.

'What about the rifle they have?'

'I've been thinking about that. I've cleared most bushes from the tree line but there's one spot that's ideal for a sharpshooter to get a perfect bead on the cabin. It's a depression in the ground with rock for cover - a natural sniper's nest. If they know their stuff, they'll find it. We'll wait for Spice to come back from the river and I'll point it out to both of you. That should be our focal point as they get closer. It's the area where danger will come from and it's also where we can end it. If we take out the person with the rifle we'll have the advantage.'

'That sounds like a good plan. What about Mishka?'

'I'll take her with me and set her to chase them towards me. She's done it before with small game and once with a young goat. She'll catch on. She's a smart dog.'

Tim looked doubtful, 'Goats and rabbits don't carry guns.'

Peter looked towards the stream as if checking for the big dog, 'I know, Tim, but I can't lock her in the cabin. She'd tear the place apart to get out once she heard the shooting. I'll just have to trust that it's not her time and the spirits protect her.'

That silenced Tim as he felt uncomfortable talking about the subject. Suzie caught Peter's eye and they exchanged a smile.

'So, a good breakfast is the order of the day, I think,' she said, saving Tim from further discomfort.

'Yes, a good military doctrine,' said Peter. 'Eat when you can.'

Tim was on familiar ground now, 'My turn to fix the food, guys. I got a feeling it's gonna be rabbit.' He disappeared into the cabin and they could soon hear him rattling about in the kitchen area.

Suzie finished her coffee and saw the other girls returning from the stream. She stood, went to the cabin door and turned to face Peter.

'I'll take over the cooking and send Tim to you. Spice is almost here. Take them and show them that sniper's hideout while it's in your mind,' she said.

'Good idea. I'll get them to help me lay out the markers as well.'

Suzie commandeered the stove and ushered Tim out of the cabin. He joined Peter and the two girls and they all scouted the tree line to familiarize themselves with the indentation protected by the immovable rock that would most likely make the best sniper's nest.

Afterwards, Peter and Tim fashioned several stakes and hammered them into the ground with the butt end of Peter's large axe. They positioned them equidistant from each other along the edge of the tree line.

'They look pretty well spaced,' said Tim as they cleaned up afterwards.

'Yes, we did a good job,' said Peter. 'Why don't you ask Spice if she has any brightly colored underwear we can use as flags?'

Tim's face turned the color of a ripe beetroot, 'Why me?'

Peter laughed at his friend's discomfort. As they entered the cabin, Suzie saved any further blushes by handing them a bundle of multicolored shredded material.

'Here you go guys. The girls and I already tore up some lingerie to stop you from having too much fun. I won't tell you which one of us had the red underwear.'

Peter laughed, as he knew the answer to that already. The banter lightened the mood and they spent the rest of the morning joking and teasing each other as if they didn't have a care in the world. Tim and Peter tied the remnants of the women's underwear to the stakes, washed up and ate an early lunch together with the emancipated ladies.

After lunch, Peter retired to the cool interior of the cabin to sharpen his knife on an old grinding stone he kept under the bed. Tim kept an eye on the weather from the porch while the women cleaned up down by the stream. A sudden flash caught Tim's attention and he saw the dark cloud for the first time. He opened the cabin door and looked inside for Peter.

'You should come see this,' said Tim from the doorway. The dark look in his eyes warned Peter that he wouldn't like it.

Peter stopped grinding his knife on the old stone, stood and followed Tim from the cabin. Bright sunlight dazzled Peter's vision and it took him a few seconds of blinking to adjust his eyes. Then he saw it. A dense black cloud hovered low over the forest. It was too low to cast a shadow. It roiled and churned with an evil life force that sent a stab of fear into Peter's heart.

Tim turned to Peter and his lips quivered as he spoke, 'I think this is the storm you saw in your vision.'

It was more than a storm. No rain accompanied the agitated cloud and no rumblings of thunder disturbed the forest. Outside of the cloud, bright sunshine filled the sky but no light pierced the black veil.

'It's directly over the Predators' camp. How long has it been building, Tim?'

'It appeared from nowhere. I caught a silent flash of lightning from the corner of my eye, looked up and it was there. It's eerie, man.'

Peter stepped down from the deck and sat in the lotus position. He closed his eyes and invited the spirits to guide him. He needed them more than ever. They responded immediately. His essence floated high above the clearing and he willed himself over the cloud. He stared as hard as he could into the coal-black darkness. He saw nothing. The dense swirling cloud hid everything from view. A column of black vapor reached up towards him like an evil finger. He moved away from it but it followed him and became thicker as if trying to form a hand to grab him. He returned to his earthly form, shook his head, stretched and stood to face Tim.

'What is it, Peter?'

'It's nothing I've ever experienced before. It's not a natural weather phenomenon, that's for sure.'

'Whatever it is, it's dark and evil looking.'

Peter knew exactly what caused the evil black cloud. The dark spirits shielded the Predators from his seeing eye. The two of them stood bathed in bright sunlight in stark contrast to the evil darkness only just down the mountain.

'Peter, I think it's moving closer!' Tim's croaky voice revealed the fear he felt.

Peter picked up a cup from the porch rail, filled it from the water barrel and handed it to Tim, 'It's deceptive because it's swirling so much, but we don't have much time. They'll be on the move soon. We have to warn the girls and get in position. Are you ready, Tim?'

Tim gulped the water, 'Yes, I'm ready.' The drink had taken the dryness from his throat and he sounded sure of himself.

Peter gave Tim a reassuring pat on his shoulder and ducked into the cabin to collect the bow while Tim checked his rifle. The girls had seen the cloud and they gathered on the porch as the two men prepared themselves for the final showdown in grim silence. Mishka appeared from the tree line and sat in the clearing as if awaiting instructions.

The five reluctant heroes formed a circle and held hands. Peter looked at each one in turn.

'You all know your roles and you all know what's at stake. Do not hesitate to shoot if you see a target. Forget all your taboos and social inhibitions. It's kill or be killed. When it's over, those of us left alive can pray to our various gods for forgiveness and redemption. Are you ready?'

'Hell, yes!' said Tim.

Spice spoke in a quiet voice, 'May I say a prayer before we fight? We may not all be here to pray when it's over.'

Suzie responded first, 'Yes, please do.'

Spice bowed her head and the rest followed suit.

'Lord, please give us strength as we wrestle not against flesh and blood, but against principalities, against powers, against the rulers of the darkness of this world, against spiritual wickedness in high places. Amen.'

They all responded with a fervent 'Amen'.

'That was beautiful, Spice,' said Tim.

'My father's favorite quote, Ephisians, 6:12.'

'It's really apt; I can see the dark forces coming up the mountain in that cloud.'

Peter couldn't stop himself, 'Tim, don't forget our enemy is flesh and blood and hiding in that cloud. They will bleed and they will die. Just shoot straight and true.'

'I hear you, Peter.'

As they split up, Julie took Peter in her arms and pulled him close, 'Don't die on me now, big guy. I couldn't live without you.'

'Yes you could, but let's hope you won't have to.' Peter pulled his head back and looked into her eyes, 'It's time for the good guys to stand up and be counted. When this is over, we'll spend some alone time by the river.' He smiled and her heart melted.

'You promise?' she whispered.

'Absolutely.'

Peter extricated himself from Julie's embrace, checked the arrows in his pouch and stepped down from the porch. He clicked his fingers and Mishka ran to him with her tail aloft and eyes alert. He looked sideways at Tim and they exchanged a nod.

'Let's do this,' Tim said in a firm voice.

They walked from the camp in different directions with Mishka following on Peter's heels. Each knew the route to take and neither hesitated. They soon disappeared beyond the trees leaving the girls alone on the porch.

A few minutes passed as each woman realized the enormity of the coming conflict. Spice broke the silence and took charge.

'OK, ladies, let's take up our positions. Suzie, is there enough fresh water inside? It could be a very long day.'

The girls turned and filed into the small cabin, bolting the door behind them.

* * * *

Darkness descended over the campsite as if a giant hand had flicked an invisible switch. Cydney knew it was time. She stood in the centre of the camp and collected herself for the final push. The serpent uncoiled itself, reached into her mind and assumed control. Her pulse quickened as she put up a brief mental struggle. It was no use and she surrendered to the irresistible force. The evil essence filled her soul and her eyes took on a malevolent red glow. A cold dampness filled the area and goose bumps broke out on Cydney's exposed skin but she didn't notice. She picked up an empty pot and wooden spoon that lay by the fire pit, and banged them together like a dinner gong.

'It's time. C'mon people, get it together.' Her words echoed around the darkened clearing with the clarity of a ring announcer at a prizefight.

Jeb and Billy-Bob joined her by the campfire. Jeb held the hunting rifle they had acquired from Maurice and his companion relied on a pump-action twelve gauge. They stared at the dense black fog that surrounded them.

'What is this shit?' Billy-Bob asked.

'It's our shield. We'll use its cover to move up the mountain,' Cydney replied.

'What is it? Where did it come from?'

'What do you care? It's here and it's what I've been waiting for. Just be grateful, dummy up and do what I tell you.'

Billy-Bob looked at Cydney's eyes, took a deep breath and nodded.

'We lost two people during the night,' Cydney informed them.

'Shit!'

'It doesn't matter. The mountain man and his little friends won't see us under the cover of this cloud. We'll use the others as our perimeter and we'll stay in the centre. There's enough of them left to draw the fire away from us. By the time they're dead we should be in the right place. The idea is to get you into the firing position at the same time that Mitch attacks from the rear,' Cydney said to Jeb.

The bearded biker nodded.

'Remember, the Indian girl is the key. You've seen her Jeb. If everything gets fucked up then she becomes your priority. Do you understand?'

'Yeah. We should have wasted her when we had the chance.'

Cydney's manic red eyes bored into Jeb and he dropped his gaze and shuffled his feet.

'Get those plebs organized. Tell them to stay to the edge of the cloud and move uphill. If they hesitate, threaten to kill them.'

The two men moved off to cajole their charges and Cydney checked that her pistol contained a full clip. A vicious curved hunting knife hung from a sheath on her belt. She hitched her jeans, faced north and began to hike up the mountain in the wake of her minions. The evil swirling cloud parted to show her the trail as she strode sure-footedly towards her destiny.

* * * *

Tim noticed the slow progress of the cloud and waited for a target to present itself. He heard Mishka bark and realized that the big dog was harrying and herding at the heels of their enemy, driving them closer to where he and the others waited.

His heart fluttered and his stomach burned with nervous tension. He wasn't sure if he could shoot someone in cold blood. What if it was a teenager or one of the women that came into his sights? He knew he wouldn't hesitate to shoot one of the Predators, but could he bring himself to kill a regular person? Some of them were innocent captives as he had been.

Peter had told them that people had deserted the gang just like he and Spice had managed to do. He rationalized that any 'innocents' left with the gang were there by choice. He couldn't convince himself. He saw movement in the cloud, shouldered his weapon, took a deep breath and fired. He heard a cry and knew that his aim had been good. He felt no remorse. He had fired at a shadow that could have been anything or anybody. He could do this. He squinted into the evil morass seeking another shadowy target.

* * * *

Spice aimed the rifle at the depression that Peter had pointed out as the ideal sniper position. Julie scanned the tree line with the binoculars. Neither of them spotted anything. Julie lowered the glasses, rubbed her eyes and turned to Spice.

'This is more difficult than I thought, even with the markers that Peter placed.'

'Just sweep slowly and tell me to shoot left or right of the last marker you saw.'

'What happens if the cloud sweeps in so close that I can't see them?'

'Don't worry about that just yet,' said Spice while worrying about it herself.

Julie raised the binoculars and returned to the tedious study of the tree line. The girls lapsed into silence. The atmosphere in the small cabin crackled with tension and each girl secretly wished for the action to start. At least it would give them something to release their pent up stress. The cloud moved closer at an agonizing pace seeming to stand still for seconds at a time. They heard Mishka bark and then the sound of a single rifle shot.

A sudden flurry signaled the passage of a flock of birds over the cabin. Then several rabbits and a small deer ran from the tree line across the clearing and disappeared behind the cabin.

'Jesus, even the animals and birds are fleeing from that damn cloud. It's evil.'

Silence ruled the forest. Nature hid from the wickedness and not even a breath of air disturbed the leaves. Bright sunlight bathed the clearing and turned the air hazy, making Julie's task even harder. The cloud began to send curling fingers around the trees lining the clearing as the enemy crept closer.

'C'mon, show yourselves,' Spice said under her breath. The waiting wore away at her nerves.

Julie drew in a sharp breath, 'Left of the green marker!'

Spice swiveled her rifle and fired two shots in quick succession. Julie saw a disturbance in the thick fog and leaves flutter into the sunlight.

'You hit something!' she blurted.

'Yeah, I hope it wasn't just a bush.'

The echoes of the rifle shots echoed faintly down the mountain and the girls lapsed into silence once again.

* * * *

Mishka loved this game. She chased slow, clumsy humans up

the trail and nipped at their heels from time to time. The poor light didn't put her off but the occasional flash of lightning caused her heart to miss a beat.

A new whiff of danger reached her nostrils and raised her hackles. As the scent grew stronger and she heard the first howl - a trickle of urine escaped her. A pack of wolves was pursuing her. Cold terror gripped her and instinct took over; she broke off her own pursuit and led the pack in a different direction, away from her master. She let out a faint, involuntary whine.

The wolves stayed far to the north during the summer months, leaving the bears to rule the mountain, and only ventured into the area when the bears hibernated for the winter. What dark power drew them to the mountain now? During the winter, Mishka and her master rarely ventured far from their cabin and never without each other. Wolves seldom encroached near the cabin or the creek and one shot from Peter's rifle sent them packing. Yet now a wolf pack with scent in their nostrils and bloodlust in their hearts was hunting her relentlessly and she had no idea how to escape.

She chose a scrambling, circuitous route designed to slow and confuse the chasing pack. Her knowledge of the environment gave her a slight edge, as she knew every twist and turn. Still they gained on her as surely as the peloton riding down a solitary leader in the Tour de France. She led them up the mountain, seeking higher ground to make her final stand. She ran towards the light but the dark mist containing the wolves bore down on her with a relentless inevitability.

She broke clear of the tree line, ran up and around a rocky outcrop, and stood with her sides heaving and her tongue hanging out as she waited for the closing pack; she could run no further. She looked down, as the alpha male broke free of the trees with the pack close on its heels. An evil darkness descended over the outcrop and Mishka saw the wolves' eyes glowing in the dim light. To get to her they would have to climb up the same way, come around behind her and attack her one at a time.

Quiet and menacing, the pack circled below the outcrop confident in their strength and numbers. Mishka's bulk, a disadvantage in the chase would now give her an edge against the leaner wolves. They had stamina and numbers on their side. They would harry and worry at her until her strength ran out and close in for the kill. She'd chosen a spot where they couldn't get behind her or attack her from the sides.

The first two wolves ran up the side of the outcrop and the big dog turned to face them. The rest of the pack waited below hoping Mishka would be forced off the high rock and fall into their midst.

Mishka growled but, ignoring the warning, the two wolves inched closer taking turns to feign an attack. The dog attacked first with a sudden vicious lunge, which caught the lead wolf by surprise. Mishka's jaws clamped down behind the wolf's lowered head and snapped its neck with one great bite. Seizing its chance, the second wolf tore at Mishka's thigh and retreated before the dog could retaliate. She yelped and the rest of the pack ascended the trail for the kill. Mishka stumbled on three legs as she prepared to face the next assault. Her lame hindquarters left her at the mercy of the pack. A defiant growl escaped her throat; she would fight to her dying breath.

* * * *

Peter squinted into the darkness concealing the Predators. He'd tried using his 'Gift' but nothing could penetrate the evil protective shroud. The evil spirits concealed their minions from his inquisitive gaze and Peter had no choice but to move in dangerously close.

Keeping an arrow notched in his bow and crouching to keep his silhouette small, he strained to see shadows in the darkness. He hadn't heard Mishka bark for some time and worried about her. The cloud of darkness crept up the hill towards his cabin and Peter's frustration built. He caught a movement and let fly an arrow in the same breath. He heard a crunch of breaking twigs as something fell to the ground and he knew he had hit his target.

He heard a rifle shot from the opposite side of the gully and prayed that Tim's aim was as successful as his.

The Ranger fired for a second time at a fleeting shadow. He'd taken out two targets, that he was sure of. He felt no remorse as his quarry seemed inhuman and nebulous. It reminded him of video games he'd played as a teenager.

* * * *

Mitch stooped low as he neared the rear of the cabin. The high ground yielded little cover and he didn't want to reveal his presence just yet. The dark cloud fascinated him. He had recognized it as the signal that his sister had been waiting for and knew that Jeb would soon be in position. He heard frequent gunshots but had no way to gauge the ebb and flow of the battle. He'd set off the previous night with a compass and a course that had been carefully scouted and mapped by Jeb and one of the teenage boys in his entourage. His winding route had kept him well away from any possibility of detection by the mountain man.

The plan had been to gain entry to the cabin from the rear but, as Mitch approached, he realized that he would have to improvise. Peter had built his cabin so that it backed onto a steep incline and the roof at the rear was mere feet above the ground with no windows or doors. Mitch crept stealthily to the roof, bent almost double, and dropped to his knees for the final approach.

He crawled up onto the roof and found it covered with drying skins and fish. He navigated his way an inch at a time up the slope, trying not to disturb the drying food or make any noise. He peeked over the top and saw the clearing for the first time. It seemed deserted. Two shots rang out from almost underneath his prostrate body and he tensed in shock. From the sounds, he estimated the position of the window the shots came from. He would have to make a sudden and violent entrance into the cabin through either the window or the door.

Mitch weighed his options and realized that he would have to rely on lady luck whatever choice he made. He looked for the small rock jutting from the ground that marked the sniper's nest that Jeb would make for. He located it and noticed a wooden stake with a red marker immediately in front of it. His military training enabled him to identify its purpose. He quickly spotted the other markers and swore under his breath. The damned mountain man was good. He'd prepared a killing ground in front of the cabin and Mitch would have to be fast and lucky to execute his end of the plan.

He waited until the dark cloud was almost on top of the red flag and made his move. He slipped silently back down the rear of the roof and edged his way around the side of the cabin, hugging the rough wooden wall. He peered out from the corner of the cabin and saw the red marker. He waited for the slightest sign to indicate that Jeb was ready. It would soon be over now.

Chapter Twenty

Peter's frustration grew and he pulled the bow over his shoulder resting the shaft down his back leaving both hands free. He pulled the razor-sharp Bowie knife from its sheath, crouched low and made his way towards the ominous dark cloud. He entered the fog and could barely see three feet in any direction. The elk's tooth began to glow on his chest and the tingling sensation flooded his senses.

He used his hearing and sense of smell to make up for his lack of vision. His nose picked up the pungent odor of stale sweat and marijuana and he heard twigs breaking as one of the bikers came closer. He stood on the balls of his feet and waited to pounce. A small breeze pushed the dark cloud aside for a brief moment and he saw Billy-Bob creeping along clutching a shotgun and straining to see through the cloud towards the cabin.

Peter took three silent steps behind Billy-Bob, reached up with his left hand to pull his head back and, with a savage slash, slit his throat from ear to ear. He held on to the biker as his body thrashed and bled out and then simply let the corpse fall to the ground. Peter ignored the blood covering his torso as he cast around for another target. The elk's tooth glowed like a miniature sun as Peter's form disappeared into the dark fog.

* * * *

Tim glimpsed Jeb but failed to get a shot off before the dark fog wrapped him in a shroud of invisibility once again. He'd seen the rifle clutched in the biker's hands and knew that Jeb would make for the sniper's nest that Peter had shown him. Tim had to stop the biker before he got a shot off.

The Ranger took a deep breath, crossed himself and walked towards the swirling dark morass.

* * * *

Jeb strained to see ahead and recognize any landmarks. He had a good sense of direction but the fog had him befuddled. He heard shots and shouts all around him and knew that people had died. The fog seemed to lose density as a light breeze disturbed the forest floor. Fate gave him a helping hand and he fell into the small depression that was to be his sniper's nest. He cursed as he realized how close he'd come to cracking his head on the rock that would provide his cover. Before him, the fog cleared and he had a clear view to the cabin. He stuck his head up to look for Mitch and saw him crouched near the side of the cabin. A shot rang out and a bullet grazed the rock inches from his head sending a shower of shale and dust into his face. He ducked back down like a tortoise retreating into its shell. That had been too close.

* * * *

Cydney knew that the fog was thinning. The battle between the spirits raged in the elements and the wind and sun would gradually disperse the protective cloud. It didn't matter. Jeb and Mitch were in place and she was ready to fulfill the demands of the serpent. Her eyes shone and her lips pulled back to form a depraved and ugly grin.

* * * *

Spice knew she had missed. She cursed under her breath. She might not get another chance as good as that. Julie reached out one hand and squeezed her shoulder reassuringly while she used the other to keep her binoculars focused.

'Don't worry. You'll get him next time,' she said.

'He won't make that mistake again,' Spice replied.

They settled down to wait for the next target.

* * * *

Jeb lined the rifle up, making sure to expose as little of himself as possible. He had the advantage of the telescopic sight and could see the window clearly through the round lens. He saw Spice's rifle barrel protruding from the window and glimpsed movement in the shadows behind. He lined up on the barrel and adjusted his aim to centre on the faint silhouette behind it. He squeezed the trigger until the rifle bucked against his shoulder. He heard a muffled scream and the barrel dropped from view inside the cabin. He saw Mitch spring from his hiding place and run across the porch towards the cabin door. He let out a whoop of delight. The plan had worked and they had won.

* * * *

Mitch moved as soon as he heard Spice scream. He jumped onto the porch and in four strides found himself at the cabin door. One great kick from his size fourteen boots blasted the door from the frame and Mitch leaped through the doorway.

Julie stood in front of him with her mouth open in shock. Before she could move, Mitch lashed out one meaty fist and dropped her to the floor.

'I'll deal with you later, bitch,' he said.

He stepped over her inert form and saw Spice crumpled on the floor with blood seeping from her shoulder and a pallid complexion. She seemed unconscious. Mitch grinned and looked for the main prize.

The little Indian girl sat calmly on the bed with her hands clasped in her lap. She made no eye contact with Mitch and said nothing.

'So, you're what all the fuss is about. Don't look like much to me.'

She didn't reply. Mitch shrugged, snatched her from the bed and dragged her towards the cabin door. He easily held her with one arm as he pulled the Luger from his waistband with the other. The girl didn't struggle and seemed resigned to whatever fate had in store for her.

Mitch held her in front of him like a shield as he walked her out of the cabin. His right hand held the Luger at her temple.

'Let's see your mountain man come rescue you now, bitch,' he said to Suzie. She remained silent.

* * * *

The fog thinned and gave Tim a clear view of the clearing. He howled as he saw Jeb's shot go through the window and hit

Spice. He was too late. He ran to the sniper's nest and took Jeb by surprise. He landed on Jeb's back with both knees and winded the big biker. He leaned down, wrestled the rifle from Jeb's grasp and looked up in time to see Mitch burst into the cabin. *Damn*, he'd have to deal with Jeb first.

Tim put the barrel of his rifle to the back of Jeb's head and prepared to fire. He stopped himself. This wasn't like a video game anymore. This was up close and personal. He could feel the man squirming with life underneath him. He tried to remember what Peter had said about kill or be killed. He caught a movement from the corner of his eye and saw Mitch emerge from the cabin holding Suzie at gunpoint.

It was the distraction that Jeb needed. He reached down the side of his boot, removed the knife he kept secreted there and thrust upwards into Tim's thigh with the point of the sharp blade. He grinned as he heard the Ranger scream in shock.

Tim felt a sharp pain in his leg and his heart began to race. He looked down and saw blood spurting from his leg with each beat of his heart. Warm blood shot out several feet and Tim knew that he would be dead in minutes. He'd seen a logging accident when he was a teenager and knew that his femoral artery was severed. He had minutes left. Why hadn't he listened to Peter? He felt cold and light-headed. Jeb squirmed and he fought to keep his balance. The rifle grew heavy in his hands as color faded from his cheeks and his life force ebbed away.

* * * *

Peter broke through the fading mist and saw Mitch with a gun to Suzie's head. He heard Tim scream in agony and knew that they had lost. He removed the bow from his shoulder and notched an arrow but he couldn't get a clear shot. He would have to kill the biker on the first try or Mitch would pull the trigger and kill the girl.

How the hell had he survived the arrow to the throat? Not only had he survived but he also seemed to be fighting fit. Peter had never felt so helpless. Where were the damned spirits now? He looked down at the elk's tooth and it glowed and pulsed furiously with a tingling energy that bolstered Peter's nerve.

'Mitch, die you bastard!'

Peter had a feeling of déjà vu when Julie's voice rang out from the cabin as she fired Spice's rifle point blank at Mitch from behind. This time her aim was true and the top of the biker's head exploded in a cloud of red mist. He dropped to the ground like a felled tree and sent Suzie sprawling in the dust. Finally, Mitch was dead. Peter lowered his bow, took a deep breath and weighed up his options. Tim became his concern now. He'd heard the Ranger scream out in pain and he might need help.

Before he could move, an anguished scream curdled his blood and froze him to the spot. Cydney burst from the last vestiges of the black mist and ran towards the cabin firing her pistol repeatedly at the cabin window. Shot after shot peppered the window and its frame as she sought revenge for her brother's death. Peter's muscles refused to obey and he stood helpless as Cydney emptied the gun.

Then it was over, and the frenzied girl threw the empty gun to the ground where it kicked up a tiny cloud of dust. Without breaking stride, Cydney pulled the wicked curved blade from its sheath on her belt. Her eyes shone with an evil red glow and her focus shifted to the fallen Suzie. She changed direction towards the pregnant Indian girl, the serpent in full control.

* * * *

The fog had lifted somewhat but that wouldn't help Mishka now. Two wolves lay dead on the bluff and one would never walk again, but Mishka was finished. The Alpha male moved in for the kill. Mishka faced him defiantly but she had nothing left. The dying dog let out a plaintive howl that echoed over the mountain and the big wolf hesitated briefly but soon resumed the attack with his pack behind him.

Sudden bright sunlight covered the bluff and startled the wolves. Once again, the Alpha male hesitated and lifted its head to sniff the air. It sensed danger.

The Spirit Bear attacked without warning scattering several wolves on its first charge through the pack. It turned and charged again. It was enough to send the already depleted pack into flight mode. The bear stood on its hind legs and let out a roar that shook the ground. The wolves disappeared into the tree line as if they were never there.

The bear dropped to all fours, glanced briefly at Mishka, turned and loped off in the direction of Peter's cabin. The big dog struggled to her feet and followed as best she could.

* * * *

Peter saw everything in slow motion. The fog had almost entirely dissipated and his perspective was good. Cydney ran towards the prostrate Suzie with the dagger in her hand and murder in her heart. He saw the Spirit Bear break into the clearing from the far side in pursuit of the skinny tattooed girl. The bear would never catch the girl. It was up to Peter now.

He dropped to one knee to steady his aim, pulled an arrow

from his pouch, notched the bow and pulled it back to its limit. He had plenty of time and aimed carefully at the centre of Cydney's chest.

Just as Peter released the arrow, the evil spirits made their last move in the game. A crow flew across Peter's line of sight, spoiling his aim and sending the arrow into the girl's shoulder. Cydney twisted but carried on running, her features contorted in hate and concentration.

Peter cursed and weighed up the situation. He still saw everything unfolding in slow motion. The bear would not make it and he didn't have time to get off another arrow. It was over. Suzie and her baby would die and he was powerless to stop it.

Peter knelt on the sacred ground as if glued to the earth. He felt the elk's tooth burning into his flesh with a searing pain that made his eyes water. He had never felt so desolate and helpless and let out a scream of anguish and frustration.

A shot rang out, echoing Peter's scream. Cydney's head jerked back and she tumbled lifeless to the ground, feet from the prostate form of Suzie. Peter's eyes widened in surprise as the Great Spirit Bear came to a slithering halt over the fallen Indian girl and stood guard over her, its huge chest heaving for breath.

Peter's military training took over and he immediately turned his attention to Tim's predicament. He rose from his kneeling position like a sprinter from the starting blocks and raced across the clearing towards his fallen comrade.

Tim fought dizziness and tried to maintain his balance astride Jeb's back but to little effect. Jeb retrieved his rifle, struggled into position and let off a series of shots towards Suzie. The shots rained into the huge form of the Spirit Bear but the animal absorbed them without flinching. The clearing fell silent as Jeb ran out of ammunition and Peter fell upon him like an avenging angel. One quick, efficient slash of the mountain man's knife and it was all over.

Peter dropped his knife and grabbed Tim before the Ranger fell to the ground. A voice rang out from the direction of the cabin.

'Tim!'

Peter looked up and saw the pained looked on Spice's face as she and Julie emerged from the cabin. The blonde girl supported Spice as they struggled from the porch towards the men. Suzie sat up and surveyed the scene with glazed eyes as if emerging from a deep sleep. Tim clutched at Peter's arm.

'I'm sorry, Peter,' he whispered.

The mountain man looked down at the Ranger's ashen features. He saw death in the man's face and his eyes filled with tears.

'Hush, Tim,' he said his voice hoarse with emotion.

'I didn't listen.' The Ranger's voice was so low that Peter strained to hear.

Spice almost fell to the ground beside Tim, 'Oh my God, Tim!'

Tim's eyes flickered towards the auburn haired girl and a serene look came over his features.

'I'm sorry, Tiffany. I should have killed him without thinking. I'm sorry.' He mouthed the last word but no sound escaped his blue lips.

Peter relinquished his grip on Tim as the girl's arms enfolded the dying man. Spice stifled a sob and whispered into Tim's ear.

'Tim, you're such a gentle soul... I understand why you

didn't...' She took a deep breath as she fought back the sobs that threatened to wrack her body. 'Nobody has called me Tiffany for so long. It sounds so beautiful when you say it. Thank you, Tim.'

She stiffened and those watching heard the death rattle from the blood soaked form of their fallen friend.

Spice didn't let go but held on to Tim so tightly that it seemed like they were one. Suzie arrived at the scene and took Julie's hand as they both watched in solemn silence.

Peter's senses alerted him to movement from the tree line and he span on his haunches. Who had fired the shot that killed Cydney? He had a sudden insight and realized the identity of the two forms whose aura he had seen further down the mountain.

'Come out, John,' he yelled at the trees.

The others looked up in surprise at his words. The storekeeper stepped out from behind a knurled old tree pointing his rifle at the tiny knot of survivors with his son clutching at his waist.

Peter relaxed for the first time that day, 'Good to see you, John. You can put your gun down now, it's over.'

'Step aside, Peter.' John said in a hard and brittle voice unrecognizable from the whining tone Peter remembered on his last encounter with the shaken father.

'What are you doing, John?' Peter stood and faced the man.

'Step aside, Peter. I killed the bitch who shot my wife but there's one more of the gang to deal with.' John's eyes focused on Spice with an intensity that Peter recognized all too well.

'John, you don't understand. Spice is one of us. She was never a member of that gang. Put your gun down.'

Spice rose from the fallen figure of Tim, stepped out from behind Peter and faced towards John with an empty look in her eyes as if she would welcome the escape that the anticipated bullet would give her.

John's eye's narrowed and he flexed his trigger finger ready to shoot. The elk's tooth on Peter's chest flashed with heat; he saw a look of puzzlement and confusion spread over John's features and his resolve weaken in less than a heartbeat. Time stood still for seconds that seemed like minutes and then John slowly lowered the rifle.

Peter let out his breath and heard a distant whining. *Mishka!* He span and saw his canine companion lying some distance away, only the faint twitching of her tail betraying signs of life. Once again, he found himself sprinting to a fallen comrade.

Mishka lay immobile, her chest barely moving, her eyes closed. Peter saw her eyelids flicker as if she were dreaming and he laid his trembling hands on her back. The dog's breathing was so shallow that Peter could barely detect it.

The mountain man felt numb. The emotional roller coaster of the previous ten minutes had left him drained and this latest turn of events proved too much. His brain registered the lacerations and welts that covered his stricken dog and he realized that death had its grip firmly on Mishka and once again, the helpless feeling assaulted him. He bowed his head and cursed whatever god or spirits had brought his beloved dog to this painful end.

The magical pendant hanging at his chest glowed with a familiar burning sensation and Peter felt his hands tingle. A surge of pure energy coursed through his veins as he experienced the spirits working through him to heal the ravaged body of the injured dog.

Mishka stirred beneath Peter's hands as the life force poured back into its body. The shocked man saw wounds close and swelling subside as the animal's eyes opened wide and its body filled with strength and vitality. The dog wriggled free of Peter's hands, stood on trembling legs and licked his face, tail wagging furiously. Peter fell back and sat on the ground too shocked even to hug or subdue the dog's enthusiasm.

Suzie stood above them and saw the Elk's tooth on Peter's chest fade from pure white to yellow to brown in the space of a few seconds.

'The spirits rewarded you, Peter,' she said.

'What happened?'

'The ancient ones healed Mishka through you.'

Peter's eyes hardened, 'That's great but why didn't they heal Tim when I held him? Why did they let him die and save my dog instead?' He grabbed Mishka by the scruff of her neck and tugged hard, the big dog fell still and sat on her haunches breathing heavily.

'Sometimes the spirits exact a heavy price, Peter. Look around you. Look at those who died here today and those who lived. Would you have settled for just losing one of us this morning?'

'No… maybe… I don't know… but why Tim? Why not me?'

'I don't know the answer to that, Peter. I don't know that I ever will. I don't know why the spirits took my brother when they did. I just know that we have to go on. There is no other choice.'

Peter let go of his dog and the animal ran to where Julie knelt over the prostrate form of Spice.

'Oh damn,' said Peter, 'I forgot about Spice.'

The two of them hurried to the fallen girl and found Julie cleaning the flesh wound in Spice's shoulder. The Spirit

Bear had disappeared as mysteriously as it had appeared and no one seemed to notice.

'Will she be alright?' asked Suzie.

"I think so,' replied the blonde nurse. 'The bullet passed right through – and I have the penicillin and morphine and can stitch it quite easily. She's just in shock right now. We need to get her inside and keep her warm and comfortable.'

John and his son Michael stood off to one side. Peter looked up and saw them as if for the first time.

'John help me get Spice inside then I'll show you where I buried my emergency cache. There's a tent in there that we'll need to pitch before nightfall. My cabin can't accommodate us all.'

'What about the dead, Peter?'

The mountain man looked around the clearing and took a deep breath.

'The most effective way would be cremation. We'll make a funeral pyre and use the last of my kerosene. We must move quickly. If the bodies start to decompose, they'll attract all sorts of scavengers. We know there are wolves close now.'

Peter's military background helped him cope with the emotional turmoil and he turned to the practical matter of survival.

'What about, Tim?' Suzie asked.

'We'll give him a proper burial. I'll find a sheltered spot down by the stream. It's the least we can do.'

They carried out the grim tasks that Peter had outlined until nightfall and never spoke about them again.

Epilogue

Suzie sat on the porch-chair rocking back and forth as the infant boy suckled at her breast. His tiny hand grasped her smock with a vise-like grip and she gazed down into his eyes with maternal love. Mishka sat at her feet as if daring anything or anyone to harm the child. Peter smiled as he approached from the stream carrying a brace of wriggling fish.

'That damn dog hasn't moved more than ten feet from Joshua since he was born. I think she loves him as much as you do,' he said to Suzie.

Mishka wagged her tail at the sound of her name but didn't move from her post. Suzie used her free hand to tidy a strand of her stray hair from the baby's face, looked up at Peter and smiled.

'Don't tell me you're jealous of a little baby, Peter. You'll have to get used to it – Julie's beginning to show.'

'Yes, I know. Somehow, I hope we have a little girl.'

The implications were not lost on Suzie. Unless they moved off the mountain to find others, her son could be the last of his line.

'Why do you think the spirits placed so much importance on little Joshua?' asked Peter.

'His father was a pureblood native of our tribe as I am.

I think Joshua is the only surviving full-blooded male. If he hadn't been born our people would die out.'

'I thought you said we were all brothers and sisters no matter our birth?'

'We are, Peter. But it takes a pure bloodline to birth a new nation. We're at a new beginning and Joshua's sons and daughters will be the forerunners of a brave new culture that I hope will learn from the mistakes we made.'

'So, you are saying that this little bundle here is the future and the past?'

'I guess I am.'

'Then I think he should have this.'

Peter removed the necklace from around his neck and held it out to Suzie. The discolored brown elk's tooth spun on its leather string; the girl hesitated to accept it.

'Go on, Suzie, take it. It no longer works for me - its magic is gone, the spirits have left. I haven't felt their presence since we defeated the Predators. It should be passed down through the tribal members again.'

'Peter, the spirits haven't left. They're in the rocks, the trees, and the ground you stand on. They're in the wind and the heat of the sun. They're everywhere around us. They're just letting us get on with the business of being human, hoping we've learned from our past mistakes.'

'Will they ever come back?'

'They will if they're needed. For the moment they're entrusting the earth to us once again. We must live as brother and sister and share the planet in peace and protect it and all its creatures.'

Peter smiled, 'You sound like one of those conservationists from Greenpeace.'

'Don't mock, Peter. I know you believe it as well. The way

of the people's in your heart. That's why the spirits chose you.'

The cabin door opened and Julie came onto the porch carrying a cup of steaming vegetable broth, which she placed on the porch rail for Suzie. She hopped down, ran to Peter and gave him a hug with one arm as she took the fish from him.

'These are huge fish, Peter. Well done my brave hunter,' she teased him.

'Yes the stream was generous today,' said Peter with a grin as he poked his tongue at Suzie.

Suzie laughed, 'You're learning, Peter.'

Mishka's ears stood to attention and Peter looked around to see Spice emerge from the tree line. She carried a rifle in one hand and a large rabbit, by its hind legs, in the other.

'I see the traps were generous today too,' Peter quipped.

Spice joined them and saw the fish dangling from Julie's hand.

'I guess we're gonna eat like royalty tonight,' she said. 'That broth smells good, is there any left?'

'That's for Suzie, she needs it to nourish her milk,' said Julie in a tone that brooked no argument.

Spice shrugged good-naturedly, 'I passed John's cabin on the way, he's never gonna finish unless you help him Peter. His son tries but he's not strong enough yet.'

'It's massive, I think he must be expecting guests,' said Peter.

'Not everyone lives like a hermit, Peter.'

'What do you mean?'

Julie raised her eyes to the sky, 'How do you think we're all gonna carry on living with this tiny cabin and the tents you threw up? We got lucky with a mild winter but the next one could be worse.'

Peter reddened. Suzie reached out her hand for the necklace

that Peter still held, 'Peter, you can be so naïve sometimes. I can't believe you never cottoned on. John is building that cabin for all of us. There'll soon be two babies, three women and two men in this community and John's boy as well. We can't all fit in your cabin or did you expect me to live in the tent next winter with Joshua and Spice?'

Peter had no reply. Instead, he handed Suzie the necklace as if to make up for his lack of foresight. Julie rescued him from further ridicule.

'It's OK, Peter. You've been living by yourself for so long that it'll take time for you to adjust. This isn't temporary. We're here to stay.'

Spice held up her hand, as was her custom, 'I have something to tell you guys.'

'You're leaving us,' said Suzie. 'I've been expecting it for some time.'

'Yes. I spent a lot of time down by Tim's grave these last few days and I've made up my mind.'

Peter stared at the young woman, 'Where will you go? What about your shoulder?'

'My shoulder's fine, Peter. Thanks to Julie. I will look for other pockets of people. I might find some bigger groups with more men to go around.'

She looked down at the ground and shuffled her feet in embarrassment.

'But you're part of us now.'

'No, Peter. It's OK for you; you have Julie and a baby on the way. Suzie has Joshua and John has his son to raise. What about me? I have no one. I must go back down the mountain and see what's left of the outside world. I need to do this - please don't try to talk me out of it.'

Julie answered for them all, 'It's OK - we understand.'

Peter snorted. He didn't understand at all. As he so often did, he turned to Suzie for counsel, 'What do you have to say about it?'

'Peter, this is a female issue. I don't expect you to understand all of it. You men are great providers but the women are the nurturers and the glue that holds the people together. We're starting again and Spice needs to follow her instincts to preserve the species. If we left it to the men, you'd kill each other in wars and battles until no one survived. She needs to find a good man to provide for the child she wants. It's nature, Peter. You can't fight it, so let her go with our blessing.'

'But, it's dangerous out there. There could be lots of groups like the Predators.'

'There could be a lot more groups like us, Peter. My guess is that struggles like ours have been going on all over the world. I'm not saying that good wins out over evil all the time but there are more good people than bad, so Spice has a right to go and find them.'

'So, rabbit or fish for supper, Peter?' asked Julie. The mountain man realized he'd lost the fight and sighed deeply.

'Fish – they say it's good for the brain and God knows I need some help in that department. I can't keep up with you women.'

Joshua finally pulled away from the nipple and Suzie lifted him to her shoulder where he let out a satisfied burp. She held him in her lap and supported his back with one hand as she placed the necklace over his tiny head with the other. The tooth settled near his knees, as the thong needed cutting down to size.

'Look at the elk's tooth, Peter,' said Suzie, her voice cracked.

They all looked. It shone luminescent white, seeming to reflect light in all directions at once. Spice made the sign of the cross as she'd done as a child. Peter resisted a sudden urge to fall to his knees.

'It belongs to him. It's found its rightful owner at last. I only borrowed it for a short time.'

They all stared in wonder at the shining tooth until finally the luminescence faded and left the relic an ivory white. Minutes passed as fascination held them spellbound. The sound of axe hitting wood, echoing from John's cabin site, snapped Peter out of his personal spell.

He turned to Spice, 'I'm still not happy with you leaving. You may not even find anybody out there. They could all be dead. Disease, famine, wars or anything could have wiped out millions. It's like biblical prophecy coming true. We haven't seen a plane or met anybody new since the conflict. I've picked up no signal on my shortwave radio. We could be the only pocket of people for thousands of miles.'

Behind them, Julie gasped, 'Peter look, look up in the sky!'

They turned and gazed to where Julie pointed.

Two hot-air balloons drifted across the afternoon sky at a sedate and majestic pace. Even at that distance, they could see several figures in the wicker baskets that hung below the colorful canopies.

John's son, Michael, came rushing into the clearing waving his arms and shouting, 'Hey! Hey!' He stopped. 'Do you see them? What are they? I love the colors. Look at that yellow one with the red heart on it and the other one with the two hands painted on the side. What are they, Uncle Peter?'

Peter gazed up at the heavens and realized that Spice was right, there were others out there and they were searching as well. Maybe there was a chance to rebuild the world and make it better. It was time to say goodbye to the age of technology and start over. Maybe this time humankind could live as brother and sister and be in harmony with nature. Michael's persistence dragged him back to Earth.

'Uncle Peter, what are they?'

Peter turned and looked at the wide-eyed young boy, 'They are our hope, Michael. They are our hope for a better future.'

The Beginning…

About the Author

Born in the suburbs of London in 1955, Ray was an avid reader from a very young age. As a young boy, he read the abridged classics, after lights out under his blankets, using a flashlight his grandfather gave him. He Journeyed to the Centre of the Earth, Travelled Around the World in Eighty Days and rocketed from the Earth to the Moon inspired by the writings of Jules Verne and H.G Wells – all from the safety of his bed. It was this, and the fact that he lived under a flight path from Heathrow Airport, that kindled his later passions for writing and traveling.

His favorite subject at school was creative writing and his ambition was to become a journalist and an author. He loved boxing, and as a young teenager, he trained at the Hayes Boxing Club, in London, where he rubbed shoulders with some of the better amateur boxers in the country. He left school at sixteen, anxious to see the world, and started his working life as a trainee accountant. As soon as he turned eighteen, he quit his job and began to travel around Europe. Over the next two years, he took odd jobs in the winter in the UK and traveled on the continent in the summer months using a combination of hitchhiking, cycling and trains. He enjoyed many diverse and wonderful experiences from the Running of the Bulls in

Pamplona to watching the sunset over Athens from the mystical ruins of the Acropolis.

In the winter of his twentieth year, Ray took another 'temporary' winter job as a trainee croupier in a London Casino. It turned into his career for the next forty years - so much for his dreams of journalism and writing, which ended up on the back burner. Ray continued to travel the world, living in Australia and visiting the Philippines and the Far East.

Ray settled in the Bahamas in 1990 and worked for over twenty years in the Atlantis Casino on Paradise Island. He travelled throughout the Caribbean where many of the scenes in his first book, The Hatcher File, are set. Ray parted ways with the casino in 2012 and turned to his original passion of writing – finally chasing his childhood dream of becoming an author.

He had several short stories and articles published in local Bahamian magazines and newspapers before releasing his first novel in 2012. For three months in early 2015, he resided in Bimini where the legacy of Hemingway inspired his first collection of short stories. In September 2015, he published his second novel, 'The Mountain', at the same time he re-launched a revised and updated version of 'The Hatcher File' and published the collection of short stories under the title of 'In the Footsteps of Hemingway'.

Ray is a keep fit enthusiast and keen cyclist. Although a British citizen, he is now a permanent resident of the Bahamas and represented his adopted country at a squash tournament in Jamaica in 2004 at the age of forty-nine. He now spends his time between his children and grand children in Nassau and his parents in London (and yes, they still live under a flight path from Heathrow!).

www.ingramcontent.com/pod-product-compliance
Lightning Source LLC
Chambersburg PA
CBHW071144180726
48291CB00007B/2326